ASCENSION

David Lloyd

To Terry
Best Wishes

Pen Press Publishers Ltd

Printed in Great Britain by Cpod, Trowbridge, Wiltshire
Pen Press Publishers Ltd
25 Eastern Place
Brighton
BN2 1GJ

ISBN 978-1-905621-90-3

Cover design Jacqueline Abromeit

Dedication

For Chemin... without whom...

Acknowledgement

The author would like to thank the following people for their support, help and encouragement over the past six years: Chemin Alam-Lloyd, Barbara and Mahboob Alam, Carolyn Dutton, Athena Churchill, Paul Muller, James Puchowski, Lynn Ashman and all at Pen Press.

About the Author

David Lloyd first started writing in 2001 and worked in the I.C.T. industry for more than twenty years before leaving to pursue other interests. *Ascension*, his first novel is the opening part of a trilogy that is due for completion within the next two years. He lives in Bristol, England with his wife Chemin and daughter Nadia.

Visit: *www.davidlloydauthor.com* for more information.

Prologue: September 1977

The distant sound of a motor engine distracted the solitary figure of the youth casting stones into the river from the wooden jetty at its edge. His rhythm had been exact; each oval pebble striking the water at precise intervals causing a pattern of circular eddies on its still surface. The intrusion was probably the team of men he had already seen a couple of times that week, and so ignoring their approach around the bend of the river he looked away and continued to cast his stones. From across the water a motor dinghy headed directly towards him. The ripples in the water became distorted in the wake of the vessel's approach and on board were three frogmen, their faces concealed by diving masks, one steering the boat and another two looking in his direction.

They had been observing him for several days; at home, at high school, when he would walk into town, when he had made his frequent trips to the river. Subject 37 would be obtained here; it was the place least likely to be populated. They had been spotted by a number of individuals during the past few days; spotted carrying out geographical research that was no more genuine than the fake equipment stored onboard their vessel. If anyone appeared on the walkway now, no one would suspect anything. Aside from a friend who had left minutes earlier and what had looked like another loitering in the parking lot at the top of the walkway, subject 37 was alone now; the time was right.

The dingy was brought gently to rest by the side of the jetty and the two frogmen climbed out of the boat. They stood facing the youth and he recognised them immediately. Perhaps they wanted some information from him. He had wondered what they were doing in Ashbury Falls; now would be his opportunity to find out. Their equipment looked intriguing; unopened yellow boxes with no markings on them. Perhaps they were conducting experiments of some sort.

He became uneasy when the driver suddenly nodded to his colleagues. If they had wanted to ask him something they surely would have removed their masks by now and there would have been no need to exit the boat. They advanced towards him, their faces still covered and when he began to retreat to the walkway they began to give chase. He dropped the pebbles instantly and sprinted up the walkway as far as his limp would allow him, not daring to look behind him. When he reached the first corner of the walkway he tripped. Suddenly what he had seen in a horror movie as a child was becoming a nightmarish reality. Reptilian-like aliens had surfaced from an isolated lagoon and had dragged screaming teenagers back into the water to be stored and used later for food. Whether this was going to be his fate or that there might be a perfectly sound explanation didn't matter – he had to get out of there. He clambered to his feet and was about to call out for help when he felt a sharp pain in his hip causing him to stumble again.

He fell hard, landing on the wooden planks. Before he could think to get to his feet he felt a hand touch the training shoe on his right foot which then turned to a firm grip around his ankle. A second hand grabbed his other ankle and within seconds he felt himself being dragged back down towards the jetty. Unable to turn, his body sprawled on its front and with his arms outstretched in front of him, the planks of the walkway pummelled his chest and stomach causing one bruising sensation after another. In desperation he reached out to try to grab hold of the railings to the side of him but missed by a fraction. When he realised that he was now only feet from the base of the walkway he felt a foot press heavily against his back.

2

'What do you want?' he called out, fear raging in his eyes as he lay face down unable to move.

The frogmen stood over him for a few moments breathing heavily in their masks. Then one of them grabbed him by the collar, pulled him to his feet and handcuffed his arms behind his back. The other stood in front, his face obscured by the shiny surface of his mask. With the exception of the dinghy's engine droning in the background nothing could be heard accept the sound of his own heart pounding within him. He felt a sharp pain in his arm and looked down to see that his other captor had stabbed him with a needle and syringe and was injecting him with a clear amber fluid. He cried out loudly as they dragged him to the boat but was silenced momentarily when he felt a sudden blow to his face.

As they were about to climb in he managed to summon enough strength to force one of the frogmen to plunge sideways into the water with him. He kicked violently at his attacker under the water as the two struggled to reach the surface. He applied another kick as their heads emerged, this time at the frogman's mask causing the covering to crack. The other frogman grabbed his collar from behind and knelt in the dinghy, forcing him under the surface of the water again and held him there whilst his colleague recovered from the trauma to his head and pulled himself over the edge of the dinghy, clambering onto its soft undulating base.

In the water subject 37 struggled desperately, unable to free himself from the iron-like grip holding him under. Air bubbles burst forth from his nose and mouth and rose like hundreds of miniature balloons released from a high pressure tube, and as he was about to swallow a copious amount of water which would have begun the agony of the drowning process he was suddenly lifted to the edge of the boat. He gasped for air, choked and spurted what seemed to him like a torrent of liquid from his throat and mouth into the water just below his chin. Seconds later he found himself submerged again without time to breathe in sufficiently to hold his breath for any decent length of time. This time they held him under for longer – much longer. As he felt himself starting to pass out they pulled him up out of the water again but this time up into the boat. Almost immediately he began to feel drowsy and lost the strength to resist them any further. The effects of the injected drug, coupled with the trauma of almost being drowned were achieving their purpose.

'No…' he began to mutter repeatedly in his stupor as the faces of the three frogmen above him began to fade to black. Within seconds his world turned to darkness.

His unconscious body was rolled over by two of the frogmen until it lay against the front of the dinghy. As they positioned it to follow the curvature of the boat's pointed front, their injured colleague nursed his aching neck and cheekbone, cursing subject 37 whilst realising he would have done exactly the same had their situations been reversed. They pulled a large waterproof covering over the body and placed their boxes of fake equipment onto its edges to ensure it would not flap open and reveal something suspicious looking during what would be a fast getaway up the river.

The driver positioned himself again at the rear of the boat and when his colleagues had settled he engaged the engine in reverse. The dinghy began to pull away from the jetty as the frogmen surveyed the banks of the river, confident that their endeavours had been a success. The driver turned the boat around and then with full throttle drove the dinghy at speed back up the river. The turbulence caused small waves to splash against the jetty's pilings but as the dinghy disappeared from view around the bend in the river, its waters gently returned to a state of still peacefulness and the atmosphere to the serenity that had drawn subject 37 to it in the first instance.

The sound of footsteps echoed in the silence as another teenager made his way to the foot of the walkway. He looked around him and then stepped out onto the jetty. He was expecting to find someone but clearly they had already gone, probably deciding instead to take a walk back into town along the footpath that bordered the riverbank. As he returned to the edge of the walkway he looked down and noticed a number of oval pebbles spread haphazardly over the wooden planks at its edge. It looked as though someone had dropped them. He knelt down and grabbed a handful. Still unconvinced that he was alone he scanned the area around him and then regarded the pebbles. Finally he released his grip allowing them to drop slowly from his hand.

1

September 1997

Carla Dempster lay unconscious on the stockroom floor of Dempster's hardware store, her motionless body sprawled awkwardly across the narrow passageway between the metal racking either side of her. Her fall from the ladder had been sudden and heavy. As she fell it toppled and grazed the side of her forehead before landing on her left arm and resting itself against the side of her face. The box of nails that she had been trying to place back on the shelves had split, showering both her and the floor with its sharp needle-like contents. Not more than a couple of feet away stood the lone figure of Ritchie Templeman staring down at her, unable to decide what he should do next. Pacing slowly backwards and colliding with the racking he believed his only option was to get out of the store as quickly as possible. He turned and sprinted towards the entrance, almost pulling the door off its hinges as he swung it open to make his speedy exit. Carla's husband Jack was returning after running errands and shouted to him from across the street. Ritchie, surprised, glanced over. His eyes meet Jack's briefly as he reached his car and without delay he got in, started the engine and pulled hastily out from the curb, almost running over Jack's feet as he accelerated away.

Jack hurried into the store noticing that the bell was no longer working and attributed it to Ritchie's hasty exit. He called out to his wife but there was no response. Believing that the cash register had been opened he promptly walked around the back of the counter, opened it expecting to see it emptied of bills, but discovered that nothing had been taken.

'Carla!' he called again as he started to empty in bags of nickels and dimes that he had obtained from the bank.

'What was she doing leaving the store while I was out?' he said in an undertone as he started to look for his inventory book.

'Storeroom!' he remembered; he had left it in there earlier.

Upon entering he noticed that the light was on and began to feel uneasy as he again called out to his wife. As he approached the end of one of the gangways he saw the large red book for which he was searching perched on the end of one of the racks just a few feet away. It was almost ready to topple over the edge. It was only as he took it from the shelving and looked down that he noticed a pair of feet sticking out into the gangway from the adjacent racking, and to his horror he realised that they belonged to Carla. He rushed over to her, moved the ladder away and quickly checked to see if she was breathing. To his relief he noticed her chest was moving and so carefully brushing the nails away from her face and body he checked for obvious signs of injury. Her face was marked with tiny scratches – the nails he thought. His first aid skills were a little rusty; luckily for him he didn't need them when he saw his wife's head turn slowly as she began to come around.

'What happened?' she said in a shallow, disoriented voice.

'You've had a fall, remember?' he replied trying to reassure her. 'Are you in pain?'

'My arm.'

'Can you stand up?'

'Give me a second and I'll try.'

She slowly sat up, took a deep breath and then grabbed hold of Jack to lift herself up, stumbling as she tried to get to her feet. Jack caught and steadied her, supporting her weight as he walked her slowly to the door. He led her to the small kitchen in the corner of the store that contained a sink, some cupboards and a hot water boiler. He sat her down and waited until she was comfortable before opening one of the cupboards and took out the first aid kit to clean up the gash on her forehead.

'I'm calling the Sheriff's office,' he said as he dabbed the wound.

'Why, Jack? It was just a fall.'

'Ritchie Templeman was in here; he must have pushed you. You must remember.'

'I was up the ladder trying to put a box of nails back on the shelves and then everything went black.'

'This might sting a little,' he said, applying some ointment to the wound.

She flinched and then felt a sharp pain in her left shoulder. It had taken the full impact of the fall.

'If our daughter ever sees him again...' he said becoming angry.

'Calm down, Jack.'

'I'll get a damn court order if I have to!' he added handing Carla two painkillers and a glass of water. 'She's still at school for goodness sake!'

'I don't think that will be necessary.'

'He's retaliated. He's got sour from what I said to him the other day.'

'You shouldn't have interfered, Jack.'

'The hell I shouldn't. I'm calling Sheriff Conway.'

'I think I'd better go home. Can you manage here?' asked Carla.

'You can't drive like this, I'll take you home.'

'No it's OK, I'll be fine.'

'No, Carla, I'll take you home.'

'Really, Jack, I'll be fine. Just give me five minutes and then I'll get going.'

'I need to make that call,' said Jack yielding to her insistence. He headed back into the store, red mist in his eyes.

'Just get out of here will you!' yelled Joaney Dempster, fuming at her two-timing excuse for a boyfriend. 'I don't want you coming around anymore. It's over, got it!'

Her boss at Wax Rack, a small store in the Ashbury Falls mall where she worked after school hastened to get Ritchie Templeman to leave promptly. There were customers browsing and he didn't want a scene. She had spared her father the need to lecture her that evening. He would be happy now – she had not been doing well at school of late, and Ritchie's departure from her life would she thought, benefit her mother who was in her view 'having problems'. She had been dating Ritchie for the past three months but at twenty-five he was too old for her and he had messed with her one too many times. Seeing him kissing some other girl in his Ford Convertible the previous evening had been the final straw.

Ritchie stormed from the mall's entrance. His long collar-length hair draped either side of an unshaven face that was reeling with anger and humiliation. When he eventually reached his car, he got in and promptly drove out of the parking lot onto Cambridge Road that led from the highway back into town. Driving as though on autopilot and all the while thinking about Joaney, he was giving little consideration to the road ahead and allowing his concentration to wane. This would never happen whilst he was behind the wheel of what was probably the only thing in his life that he loved and cherished. Today was different. As he passed through the red light on the junction of Cambridge and Denman Road he was dramatically awakened when he almost collided with a Nissan Primera that was crossing the junction. The Nissan braked suddenly and Ritchie had to swerve violently to avoid it, almost colliding head on with yet another vehicle that was approaching on the opposite side of the road. Somehow he managed to regain control and get back on the right hand side of the road before promptly accelerating off. His heart was almost beating out of his chest. He knew he had been that close to having his body mangled in a blood-drenched carnage, or strewn across the road behind him. He had missed the oncoming vehicle by inches and knew it as he let out a blasphemous cry whilst tightly holding the steering wheel with a grip of steel. The driver of the Nissan pulled over, got out, took off his sunglasses and watched in disbelief as Ritchie's Ford Convertible disappeared from view down Cambridge Road.

Carla was gazing out of the window of the Pied Piper diner when the driver of the Nissan pulled up into the parking lot – she had not returned home as she had said she would. Instead she had visited a friend at work. She watched as the man in his late thirties, five foot ten with brown hair and dressed in stonewashed denims got out of the car and walked into the diner. She noticed the car displayed a Virginia licence plate and assumed that it might be a rental vehicle. The man approached the counter, sat on one of the bar stools and looked around for a few moments before he caught the owner's attention.

'What can I get you?' asked Carla's friend Jenna Kirshaw.

'Black decaf,' he replied. 'I'll take one of those subs too.'

Carla recognised immediately that he did not have a Virginian accent. It sounded native to Illinois.

'From Chicago?' she asked.

'How did you guess?' he replied noticing the Band-Aid on her forehead. 'Nasty cut you've got there,' he added pointing to it.

'It's nothing,' she replied. 'I have relatives in Chicago so I recognise the dialect.'

'Here on business?' asked Jenna.

'Kind of,' he replied. 'I'll be over in that seat by the window.'

Less than ten minutes after Ritchie Templeman had returned home there was a knock at the front door. He was sat in his

11

room getting over the shock of the near miss with the Nissan so his mother answered it. To her surprise Deputy Rolands from the Sheriff's office was standing at the foot of the porch and looking at the house.

'Yes, Officer, can I help you?'

'I'd like to speak with Richard Templeman. He does still live at this address?'

'Why yes – he's in his room. What's this all about?'

'I just need to talk to him, Ma'am.'

'OK I'll just get him. Is anything wrong, Officer?'

Rolands didn't reply.

A minute later he came to the door and was taken aback by Rolands' presence.

'Is there a problem, Officer?' he asked nervously. This was obviously to do with the incident on Cambridge Road he thought.

'Can you confirm your whereabouts this afternoon at around 3 pm?' asked Rolands.

'I was in town. I had the afternoon off. Why do you ask?'

'Did you visit Dempster's Hardware Store?'

'For a short while.'

'Why?'

'I wanted to speak with Mrs Dempster. I needed to find out where her daughter was.'

'And did you speak to her?'

'No she wasn't there.'

'Are you sure about that?'

'The store was empty.'

'Problem is, Ritchie; Jack Dempster claims his wife was pushed off a ladder in the storeroom – a nasty fall by all accounts. He said he saw you running from the store as he was returning. Then he found his wife on the floor. So what happened, Ritchie?'

'I don't know, I didn't see her,' he replied as the nerves set in.

'So you just stopped by and she was already in the storeroom, right?'

'I guess so, like I said nobody answered when I called out.'

'You'd better not be lying to me, Ritchie.'

There was painful silence as Rolands stared at Ritchie, unconvinced of his account but powerless to prove otherwise. Ritchie felt his body start to tremble. He was a bad liar at the best of times and who would believe that he had stumbled on her by accident?

'I hear that they are not at all keen on you seeing their daughter, am I right?'

'We broke up today.'

'Nice coincidence. Folks tell me that this isn't the first time you've had a run-in with the Dempsters. Perhaps you just thought you'd pay a visit to the store and when you discovered her husband was out you decided to set things straight. Do you get my drift? Except you didn't count on him returning did you?'

'I don't know what you're talking about and I don't have to stand here...'

'I'll be watching you, Ritchie, watching to see if you step out of line. People in this town don't take kindly to you do they?'

'Why should I care?'

'Because there are some who would just love to see you gone, Ritchie. Get my drift now? I suggest you keep away from Joaney Dempster and her parents. Are you clear on that, Ritchie?'

Ritchie looked on in defiance, his expression smug, that is until Rolands grabbed him by the chin and squashed his face in a tight grip.

'Are we clear, Ritchie?' he asked again, glaring into his eyes.

Ritchie nodded as best he could.

'Good. That's better,' said Rolands slowly letting go.

Ritchie rubbed his chin as the officer turned and walked back to his patrol car. He glanced over his shoulder for one final eye contact with Ritchie before getting in and driving off.

The driver of the Nissan was examining the far wall of the diner. There were all sorts of memorabilia and photographs that provided an interesting insight into its owner's life. Gradually you could see the tapestry of events unfold with every picture and souvenir telling its own unique story. His eyes then became fixed on a photograph of a man shaking hands with Elvis.

'It's not a fake,' Jenna said leaning over his shoulder.

'Really? You read my mind.'

'That's my father with him,' she added, 'taken in sixty-seven in New York when he was a press agent for RCA.'

'Was he a big fan?'

'No, not really, but I guess he seized the opportunity for a priceless memory. Do you need anything else?

'No thanks,' he replied handing her a ten-dollar bill. 'Keep the change.'

As he headed for the entrance he noticed Carla sat a few tables away drinking a latte and staring into space.

'Is your head OK?' he asked her, drawing attention again to the cut.

'It'll be fine. Are you staying in town?' she asked.

'Yes, for a while.'

'Got anywhere in mind?'

'I don't know. Perhaps you can recommend somewhere.'

'Sure, I'd be glad to. What kind of place are you looking for?'

'Somewhere that's quiet and out of the way.'

'There are a couple of motels about a mile or so from here, but if you want a nice comfortable New England hotel, you should try the Farrington. It's just on the western edge of town. Come here and I'll show you on the map.'

Carla led him to a map on the wall just by the entrance to the restrooms.

'Turn right out of here and left at the junction onto Harbor, follow it out for about two miles, go over the river and it's first on your right. I'm Carla Dempster by the way.'

'Mike Fabien,' he replied. 'I have to shoot. Thanks for your help.'

'You're welcome,' she replied as he turned and went to leave.

'What do you do?' she asked.

'I'm a writer.'

Her eyes followed him as he left the diner and got into his car.

'Are you OK?' asked Jenna from behind her.

'Yes... I guess so,' replied Carla in a vacant tone, her eyes still fixed on the car that was leaving the parking lot.

Mike Fabien turned out of the parking lot onto State Street and slowly moved to the junction of Harbor. As the lights turned green, he cautiously moved forward and turned left into the road, watching for any stray Ford Convertibles that might be around the corner. During his drive through the tree-lined neighbourhood through which Harbor road cut, only about three other cars passed him. It was late afternoon and the sun's reflection shimmered on the river as he drove across the wooden bridge, and there approaching him on the right was a sign for the Farrington Hotel. He turned the car into the entrance and drove up an incline to the parking lot. The hotel was raised up from the road with a sloped lawn to the front. It was a large white house with circular turrets, Victorian style features and was surrounded by trees. He parked the car around the back of the house in the larger of the two parking lots and noticed that additional accommodation had been built to the rear. Beyond that all he could see was woodland, but he noticed the sun's reflection on the water through the trees, enough to see that the river flowed around the back of the hotel. As he entered reception a woman in her early thirties greeted him.

'Can I help you, sir?' she asked.

'Yes, I'd like a double room for three weeks.'

'We have a room overlooking the front with en suite. The rate's two fifty a week. Would you like to see it?'

'OK.'

She led him upstairs to room 3 and opened the door. It looked welcoming and comfortable. He didn't sleep well in hotels but this would have to do.

'The rate includes breakfast, seven-thirty to ten.'

'This will be fine – I'll take it.'

'If you'd like to settle in and then come down to the desk, I can take a swipe of your credit card.'

'I'll be right there, thank you.'

'If you need anything just call,' she added before leaving.

He dumped his jacket and a case containing his laptop on the bed before switching the TV on. Flitting through the channels, frustration soon set in.

'Springsteen was right; fifty-seven channels and nothing on,' he thought before deciding to retrieve his luggage and give his credit card to the girl on the desk.

2

As the morning sun filtered through the window of his darkened office, Reuben Stein was sat in his reclined chair tapping its leather arms with the fingers of his right hand. He had had to pull the blinds so that they were almost closed, just leaving enough of a gap to let in some light that cast stripes across his cluttered desk. He had been thinking for a while to reorganise the office layout so that he wouldn't have to sit in gloomy twilight until the afternoon when the sun moved to the back of the building that his office occupied. It was only then that he could open the blinds and get the full benefit of the daylight. But that would take unnecessary time and energy during what was becoming the critical part of a deal that he had taken months to prepare for. Spread over his desk were copious amounts of paperwork next to his laptop; plans, reports, correspondence from lawyers and others, all of which created a mass of information that could easily have driven him to madness. In his current frame of mind he was almost at the point of picking the whole lot up and throwing it haphazardly into the air.

Rita his secretary entered to inform him that Woody Smithfield from the Logan Chakowah development project was on the phone.

'Not now, Rita!' he said perturbed and shaking.

'I'll tell him you'll call back later then?' she replied promptly having seen him in this state before.

'Yes, yes, do that,' he replied abruptly.

As Rita left he got up and walked to the window, pressing his palms against the pane. He looked down at the street below, his eyes moving in rolling motions. When his head suddenly jerked violently he stepped away from the window, walked back over to his desk, picked up his briefcase and headed for the door. As he opened it, he saw Rita sat at her desk looking busy.

'I'm going out, Rita. I don't know when I'll be back, please take messages, I'm leaving my mobile off,' he said passing her on the way out.

He rushed down the stairs and entered the claustrophobic lobby where the front door opened onto the street. Pulling it ajar, he went outside failing to notice that in the process of doing so he had nearly knocked over an elderly man who had been quietly strolling along the sidewalk.

'Reuben!' the man called out, but he didn't answer; he hadn't even seen him.

'What is it with that boy?' a shaken Hank Jebson asked himself as he stood in bewilderment watching Reuben pace hurriedly down the street to his car.

Within seconds of starting the ignition, Reuben pulled out onto the street and drove off; giving no consideration to the vehicle whose driver had to brake suddenly as he swerved out. He turned left and headed south down State Street towards the river, his eyes fixed on the road and his mind on the place to which he was driving. After travelling about half a mile he came to the bridge that spanned the river, and going straight over he took the next left into a large parking area surrounded by conifers. He pulled up into a space, cut the engine and sat there clutching the steering wheel until deciding to open the window. He was having one of his turns.

Sitting there for a while, looking at the trees through the windshield of the car, he gazed at the opening leading to the wooden walkway that descended to the jetty by the riverside. The last time he had been here was on a similar day to this one in 1977. He had avoided going anywhere near it since.

His head began to jerk in small sideways motions. Without realising he began to tap the soft cushioning of his steering wheel with his fingertips as he gazed towards the opening. Perspiration surfaced through the pores of his skin as the tapping became louder and his head movements more severe. Swinging the door of his car open, he leaped out and after closing it he put the keys in the lock, fumbling as he did so, his hands trembling to the point that he decided in the end to leave it open. He put the keys in his pocket and took a steady walk towards the opening he feared so much. When he reached the walkway he stood still and gazed at the wooden planks that slowly began to descend before him. He was alone. The memories returned like a train from a darkened tunnel, almost paralysing his body and preventing it from taking that first fearful step. Slowly he began to walk until his pace increased. Then he began to run; so fast that he collided with one of the wooden beams as it turned at ninety degrees to form the descent of the walkway. A painful bruising sensation flared up within his ribs but it did not hinder his descent and he continued on until he reached the foot of the walkway. As he ran out onto the jetty, he tripped and almost fell, somehow managing to get his footing at the last moment. All that surrounded him was the still of the water and an eerie silence as the sweat from his face misted his glasses. He took them off. As he gazed into the water he felt his knees give way causing him to slump down onto the hard wooden planks. It was then that he began to weep, clutching his head with his hands like a traumatised child, and calling out loudly for a long lost friend as his vision became blurred with the tears.

After a while he noticed a figure coming towards him.

'Ronnie?' he said quietly.

It wasn't his friend; the figure was too short. Instead a young boy, eight, maybe nine years of age was stood there looking at him.

'What are you staring at, kid?' he said as he sobbed.

The boy said nothing as he watched Reuben slowly get to his feet and stare back at him with reddened eyes. He ran off swiftly to join his friend who was throwing stones into the water at the other end of the jetty. The sound of the stones hitting the water made him shake and in the distance he could hear the two boys laughing before they disappeared along the bank of the river, leaving him alone on the jetty, staring at the shimmering water.

Mike Fabien closed the door of his room and hurried down the stairs to reception en route to the dinning room in anticipation of breakfast, but discovered that it had been cleared and that there was nobody around. He looked at the clock and saw that the time was approaching 10.30 am and at that point he realised that the girl had told him that breakfast wasn't served after ten. He was late, the realisation of which amplified the empty feeling in his stomach and his desire for a large cup of decaffeinated coffee. He had decided to visit the Pied Piper again later that morning and would probably grab a brunch there instead if needed.

It was a beautiful September morning and the air had a real freshness about it, making the decision to take a walk around the grounds of the hotel before heading into town an easy one. As he passed around the edge of the lawn, he saw a man doing some maintenance on one of the window frames.

'Big job?' he asked.

'No, just a rotten window ledge. Be fixed in no time.'

As he surveyed the building he noticed how well it had been maintained and that it was an outstanding piece of period architecture. The large oaks behind provided a picturesque backdrop that gave it a haunting beauty, looking similar to ones in photographs that he had seen in magazines in the past.

On his return he walked back into the dining room to see if any of the staff were there, and moments later he heard a voice from behind him.

'Good morning, can I help you?'

He turned around to see that the girl who had checked him in the evening before had appeared in the room. She was wearing a blue polo neck sweater, neatly tucked into a pair of faded Levi's, and a pair of cowboy boots. He noticed too that her belt had an eagle design with studs around the strap.

'I missed breakfast. Is there any chance I could get a cup of decaf and some bagels?' he asked.

'I don't usually do this for guests,' she replied. 'But OK, just this once.'

He watched her tall slim figure disappear into the kitchen as he sat down at a table by the window and began to contemplate the day ahead. As he ran through the planned schedule in his mind he realised that he had forgotten the notebook he needed for the research he had come to Ashbury Falls to undertake. He had left it on the side of the bed ready to bring down with him. He thought about fetching it but decided to wait until it was time to leave. He did not want to miss his last chance for breakfast and waited for the girl to return. A couple of minutes later he turned and noticed her walking towards him with a mug of coffee in one hand and a plate of bagels in the other.

'May I?' she asked.

'Be my guest,' he replied, gesturing for her to sit down on the chair opposite.

Her dark shoulder length hair contrasted perfectly with her light coloured skin and blue eyes as she smiled briefly and introduced herself.

'Jamie Farrington.'

'Mike Fabien,' he replied shaking her hand. 'So this is your place then.'

'Don't worry, I won't throw you out for violating breakfast protocol,' she replied. 'My parents used to run this hotel when I was a little girl, and I used to help them whilst I was at high school. They left it to me and I've been running it ever since.'

'You must enjoy your work,' said Mike.

'I did think of selling up a few years back and moving to Boston for a change of scenery, but I never did. I guess I'm too attached to the place.'

'You've put a lot of time and effort into this hotel, it shows.'

'So what brings you to Ashbury Falls, Mike?'

'I'm here to do some research for a new book.'

'Really? We don't usually get writers coming to visit. I hope you enjoy your stay. The place is kind of quaint.'

He regarded her as attractive and a woman who cared deeply about the way she looked. Not even the scarlet nail polish on her immaculate fingers had any chips in it, and he noticed that there were no rings on them.

'Thanks for breakfast.'

'You're welcome,' she replied and got up to leave. 'I have some chores to do so I'll leave you to enjoy.'

'Maybe we can talk again later,' said Mike.

'Have a good day now,' she replied and then returned to her duties.

3

It was lunchtime; the Pied Piper was getting full and in the far corner sat Ritchie Templeman as the final minutes of his lunch break ticked away. He worked at the tyre store not far from the diner and had had enough of the tiresome, droning fitting sound of the machines that he would operate day in day out. Resigning himself to the fact that it was time to head back he rose unenthusiastically from his chair and headed for the counter to pay the cheque, wondering what he would do that evening now that he had no girl to date. Jenna took his cash, gave him a couple of dollars change and as he was about to leave, called him back.

'What were you doing in the stockroom of Dempsters yesterday, Ritchie?'

'What's it to you?' he replied.

'Jack Dempster reckons you pushed his wife off a ladder. Did you?'

'What, have you just been recruited to the Sheriff's office or something?'

'Well?'

'It's none of your business,' he replied and swung around to head for the entrance. At that moment he collided with a man who was in the process of entering. They stopped and looked at one other momentarily as though they had either met before or some kind of confrontation was about to erupt.

'Pardon me,' said Ritchie coldly, as he manoeuvred his way around the man and headed for the door.

'Hello again,' said Jenna noticing the face she had met the day before.

'Who was that?' he replied.

'Oh, just Ritchie Templeman. He's a loser but he hasn't realised it yet. Did you settle in at the Farrington OK?'

'Yes it's great. Give me another cup of black decaf will you,' he asked as his eyes scanned the diner.

'So you got to meet Jamie then.'

'Nice girl.'

'Interesting I would say,' she replied. 'Carla tells me you're a writer.'

'Yes.'

'And do you have a name?'

'Mike Fabien.'

'If you're interested, she was engaged once but he dumped her all of a sudden and it messed her up. I think they met in Boston whilst she was in college. Sometime after she started dating some biker guy, very different as you can imagine. Used to pick her up and take her out of town to some biker joint. Must have been about seven years ago. She even started to look like a biker chick as I recall. Always came across as insecure, do you know what I mean?'

'She keeps a great hotel,' said Mike.

'Ask her out on a date, I'm sure she's full of secrets. You writers love that sort of thing don't you?'

'Maybe you've got secrets, Jenna.'

Before she could reply the door of the diner opened again and the frail figure of Hank Jebson walked in.

'Coffee, a Swiss cheese sandwich and pickles,' he ordered as he sat down in his usual place.

'One of your regulars?' asked Mike turning his head as Hank went to his table.

'That's Hank Jebson, my most valued customer,' she replied. '...Coming up, Hank.'

'Does he talk to strangers?' asked Mike enquiringly.

'He'll talk to anyone, but try not to probe if that's what you writers do.'

'Why not?'

'Just don't, OK.'

Mike waited a while for Jenna to bring Hank his lunch. Then he cautiously walked over to the table at which he was sat.

'Do you mind if I join you?' he asked.

'Sure, have a seat. I don't know you do I?'

'No.'

'The name's Hank Jebson.'

They shook hands.

'Mike Fabien.'

'OK, one decaf,' said Jenna as she placed a large mug on the table in front of Mike.

'Decaf! Get this young man some real coffee!' Hank jested. 'You're not from around here are you?'

'No I'm just visiting.'

'So where are you staying and what are you doing here?' asked Hank directly.

'I'm staying at the Farrington and I'm here to do some research for a book.'

'You're a writer then. I suppose you're snooping around getting the low-down on folk's lives, am I right?'

'Kind of,' replied Mike nervously.

'Well, good luck to you, son. This town could use a man like you to get the skeletons out of the cupboards.'

'So tell me about yourself, Hank.'

'How long have you got?'

'I have to be somewhere in twenty minutes,' replied Mike reassuringly as Hank took a bite of his sandwich.

'I've lived here forever, seen folks come and go, happy days and sad ones, all the different colours of life.'

'You've seen some changes then?'

'Yes, I've seen changes all right, mainly the way the town has grown over the years. There were just a few streets here when I was a boy, State, Howard, Menton, and the others that make up downtown. This used to be a house owned by the Menton family, they named the street after them, been here for generations, owned a lot of the land around the area which they gradually sold off to developers. The family eventually moved to Pennsylvania back in the late sixties and then the new east and west housing estates were built on the land. Folks have moved in but it's not like it used to be.'

'That's progress for you, Hank,' Mike commented.

'Not in my eyes.'

'Why, have things changed, Hank?'

'Maybe I'm just getting old and can't get used to things now. Seems like the pace of life is so much faster these days and in the end everything just comes down to numbers. Things were different back in my day. I will tell you something though; I noticed things got kind of strange back in the seventies, mainly in the youngsters, strange temperaments and the like. The town's been quiet since then but I don't think things have been quite the same, something's amiss, you know?'

Mike nodded cautiously.

'Have you met Carla Dempster yet? She's a friend of Jenna.'

'Yes, we met briefly in here yesterday, why?'

'She's suffered from depression since her late teens. Jack, her husband has stood by her all these years, patience of a judge, like a son to me that boy.'

'She seemed OK to me,' replied Mike.

'There are other things I could tell you about her but that wouldn't be fair now would it.'

'I may be a writer, Hank, but I'm not falling for that line.'

'Fooling, who's fooling?' replied Hank in a less than joking manner.

'You're serious?'

'And take Reuben Stein as another example. Damned near knocked me over earlier. I've never seen a boy so uptight.'

'Who is he?' asked Mike.

'A local property developer. His father drove him hard so it's no wonder he turned out the way he is. Now look where his father's ethos has got him.'

'What's happened?'

'He's invested a lot of money in a housing development to the south of town. It promised a big yield in three years for all the investors, but things are not going well.'

'Why, Hank?'

'It's a deal to build luxury homes on a secluded estate. Trees, a lake all that kind of thing. A place that the rich can afford to buy their piece of paradise.'

'What's the problem?'

'It's in danger of collapsing. There has been a lot of local protest because of its beauty. How the deal had ever been agreed is a mystery to us all, but I'll bet some heavy money was involved somewhere down the line. Now its legality is being challenged. Charles Moreland is his name – he's done some research.'

'Into what?'

'The land's history. It seems the protestors have discovered that the area was once thought to have been an Indian burial ground. With Moreland's backing, the validity of the sale of the land for development is being contested by the lawyers and Moreland has had plenty of resources to hire the best on behalf of the protestors and the few remaining Indian descendants who lived in the vicinity and neighbouring counties.'

'What's in it for this Moreland guy?' asked Mike.

'Beats me – he's rolling in it anyway, but good luck to them all I say. Tearing up beautiful land like that to build more houses. What the hell does this town need more houses for?'

Hank began to cough. Mike like the other customers noticed that he had also started to raise his voice.

'Can't argue with you on that, Hank,' called a voice from another table.

'What, are you some kind of reporter, son?' called another directing their attention to Mike.

'Leave him alone,' replied Hank. 'Can't anyone have a private conversation around here?'

'That'll do, gentlemen!' said Jenna, 'this is a diner not a debating house. But for what it's worth I'm with you on that one.'

The excitement died down. Hank coughed again, his face looking strained.

'Don't worry about me, I've got on too many soap boxes in my time.'

'You should have been in the house of representatives,' said Jenna jokingly.

'Don't talk to me about politicians, never heard an honest word from any of them.'

'Tell me about your family, Hank.'

'My family?'

'Yes.'

Hank had suddenly gone quiet. There was a long pause before he spoke again.

'Well it's only me now. My wife and son have been long gone.'

'I'm sorry to hear that,' said Mike.

'Mention the name Hank Jebson, and one of the first things folk talk about is my son. They all feel sorry for me, but I don't need that – I've had to deal with it for a long time now.'

'I'm sorry, I didn't mean to pry.'

'It's OK; I'm used to strangers asking me about it anyway. The place was crawling with reporters around the time. Maybe I'll tell you about it sometime.'

'Sure. I should be going now,' replied Mike looking at his watch.

'Nobody around here believes me, Mr Fabien.'

'Believes what, Hank?'

'Carla, Reuben, my son, the others.'

'What others?'

'Never mind, son, the past is the past,' said Hank clearly bringing the conversation to an end. To Mike it felt as if Hank had laid some sort of bait.

'Take care, Hank,' said Mike. He shook hands and then got up to leave.

'I live at 1154 Cambridge. You must have driven down it to get into town,' added Hank.

'Yes I remember,' Mike replied and then turned to Jenna. She had been listening to the conversation.

'Don't pay any attention to Hank. He's a sweet old man with a broken heart but a vivid imagination,' she said quietly.

'How's your friend Carla?' asked Mike before gulping down the remains of his coffee.

'If only you knew,' she replied.

'Does she work here with you?'

'No. She and her husband Jack own the hardware store on Howard.'

'Give her my regards will you, and here's for the coffee.'

'No charge. Call in again hey?'

'Yes I'll do that. See you now.'

With that Mike left the diner, got into his car and drove off.

Hank remained in his seat finishing his lunch and just quietly listening to the chatter that surrounded him. Soon he would get up to go for a stroll around town to exercise his tired aching muscles and fill his mind with visions of life in the modern age.

'He'll be back,' Hank thought to himself, and then he got up to leave.

Carla could not face the thought of going into work that day, indeed she had been hoping for some time that Jack could be persuaded to sell the store and they could move on to something else. She had decided that Jack could manage by himself and that she might read a book, paint or do anything as long as she didn't have to go to the store. By now however it was well into the afternoon and she had done nothing, she had not even given any thought to dinner and the fact that Joaney and Jack would be home in a couple of hours hadn't even crossed her mind.

As she lay on the sofa, the agony of the miscarriage she had had two years after Joaney had been born began to torment her again. As she caressed her lower torso over the place where her womb had once been, the pain of knowing that she could have no more children had again been haunting her every waking hour in recent weeks. It made her feel as empty as the place that her hands now covered. The depression had returned and thinking of Jack, it was all too apparent to her that he wasn't coping with it this time for she knew she had become like a Jekyll and Hyde character and hated herself for it. It was when she looked at the clock and noticed that the time was 15.37 she realised that she had been lying there most of the day, and that something was ringing in the background.

The day had started well. She kissed Jack goodbye after breakfast and then sat in the garden. It was going to be another gorgeous day; the fresh air and the sunshine made her feel relaxed and she was in a reasonable mood. She made herself some tea and went back into the garden to prepare herself for the day ahead. Then it was time to get on with some housework. She needed to go upstairs to get the laundry from her bedroom at the front of the house, which overlooked a long driveway that curled around the edge of their well-kept lawn. As she picked the laundry out of the basket, she glanced out of the window and happened to see a car pull up on the drive of their neighbours, Dick and Francis Hudson. Out of the car came a couple with their two children, a girl about eleven and a boy probably a couple of years younger. The children ran up to Dick and Francis and embraced them; the couple greeted them with kisses and handshakes.

Carla's head jerked suddenly. At first she didn't recognise the visitors who seemed to be looking closely at the Hudson's house. They had had some work done to the roof recently, perhaps that was what they were looking at. Her eyes became fixed on the woman and then on her partner. It was Jack. Had he come home early, she thought? Nothing could have prepared her when she suddenly looked back at the woman and saw her own face; her and Jack standing on the driveway conversing with Dick and Francis, Joaney there too and their son Jess. That would have been his name she remembered. They remained a while just talking, the children running around on the lawn.

'Joaney, Jess, come on let's go see what Dick and Francis have got for you,' Jack called out as the woman stared at her from the lawn with a bitter look before disappearing to join the others. As the laundry dropped from her hand to the floor in a sprawling heap, tears had begun to roll down her face.

She ran out of the bedroom and down the stairs into the lounge, trying to remember where her medication was. Opening drawer after drawer in an attempt to find the bottle of pills she suddenly felt the room begin to move from side to side, the walls swaying gently at first and then twisting slightly. The sounds around became distorted and she could hear what she thought was a ringing sound which she tried to block out by covering her ears. Then as her legs buckled beneath her and she felt the floor swallow her up, her forehead met the corner of the sofa. The impact reopened the graze wound from her fall at the store and caused her to black out.

'Answer the phone, Carla, come on,' said Jack impatiently before giving up and putting the receiver down. He had been trying to contact her all day – he needed some important figures from a file in the drawer of his study.

With that he closed the store and headed for home, driving through the sunny streets wondering if Carla was OK.

She had told him that she was going to be home today so why wasn't she answering the phone? The journey home seemed to drag on but as he finally turned into Pine Drive he saw their house situated at the far end and vented a sigh of relief. As he approached the house he saw Carla's car parked at the top of the drive and parked behind her. Opening the front door he could hear sounds in the kitchen and promptly entered to find Carla cooking dinner.

'Hi, Jack,' she said, 'did you have a good day?'

'OK,' he answered in a cautious tone. 'Have you been out today, Carla?'

'Out?' she replied, 'No, Jack, you know I said I'd be home all day.'

'I tried to call you a number of times.'

'There were no calls.'

'Carla, I called you,' he said raising his voice slightly.

'Must be a fault on the line,' she replied.

Jack picked up the phone and called the operator.

'Hi, can you tell me if there have been any problems with this line today?'

There was a pause.

'OK, thank you, sorry to trouble you.'

He turned and looked at Carla.

'No faults, Carla.'

It was then that he finally realised that blood had saturated the Band-Aid he had used to seal the wound on her forehead. He said nothing at first. He remembered that he needed to call his accountant. He could get the figures he needed himself now.

'I just need to go upstairs for a few minutes, OK?'

'Sure,' she replied as she continued with dinner.

Five minutes later Jack came downstairs and entered the lounge. The drawers were opened and the place was a mess, things were all over the floor. Carla was a very tidy person and it was often that he had to be reminded to put things away. Something was wrong. Had intruders attacked her? It didn't seem that way, as there was no evidence of a break-in. He quickly tided things away and went back into the kitchen. Carla was staring into space as she stirred the contents of the saucepan in an autonomous motion.

'Carla, what's going on?'

'Sorry, Honey, miles away.'

'What happened here today?'

'Nothing, why?'

'I'm concerned about you,' he replied, his words light.

'Concerned about me are you?' she replied harshly. 'Concerned about me? I'm going through hell and you're just concerned about me?'

'What happened, Carla?' he asked again, raising his voice.'

'Why would anything have happened today? It's just a normal day, we get up, we go to the store except I didn't go today, I didn't want to, I hope I never see that damned store again!'

'OK, Carla, calm down.'

'And then we come home and I get dinner and I lay the table for the three of us. Yes three of us! THREE!

'No, Carla, please don't go there.'

'There should have been FOUR of us! I want my baby!' she screamed.

Carla broke down in tears and Jack grabbed hold of her quickly before she could spill the contents of the saucepan over her. She clung to him and cried like he had never heard her cry before.

'Please, Jack, please give me my baby!' she repeated softly over and over as she wept bitterly.

'It's OK, Honey,' he said as he hugged her tightly. 'We'll get help, we'll get the best this time.'

At that moment Joaney entered the kitchen.

'Hello, another boring day, what's for dinner?' she said as she waltzed in. 'Have you seen my...'

Then she paused, realising what was happening. It stopped her in her track as though walking into a transparent wall. Joaney looked on in shock as she saw her mother weeping profusely in her father's arms.

'Get over it, Mother!' she shouted. 'I'm here, you've got me, remember, Joaney, your daughter, the one who didn't die, the only one you're ever going to have!'

'That's enough!' said Jack sternly. Joaney walked out slamming the kitchen door as she left.

'She'll be OK,' said Jack. He was more concerned with Carla. 'You'd better lie down for a while. Go rest on the sofa. I'll finish dinner.'

Jack left Carla in the lounge while he went into the kitchen, turned off the saucepan and put the meatloaf she had been making into the oven. He then headed upstairs to his office again and picked up the phone.

'Jenna, it's Jack. Carla's bad, can you come over... thank you, thank you so much.'

After he had made the call he went back downstairs and saw Carla lying on the sofa.

'Are you OK now?'

'I think so.'

'Jenna's coming over.'

'Good.'

'I'll sort dinner later.'

'Jack, you'll never own that chain of hardware stores so give it up, for all our sakes.'

He didn't answer as he retreated to his study again. Her glazed look confirmed what he already knew. Flashbacks of the time they almost separated, the hysterectomy and the attempted suicide made relentless assaults on him. Nothing would change; events he had buried deep in the chasm of his memory were going to resurface. All the signs were there, and now the blackouts had returned.

4

Geography was something that Mike Fabien had enjoyed studying at high school. He would always look at his father's national geographic magazines to find something of interest to research and during vacation time he would explore to see things for real. Today he had spent the afternoon by the river and traced its route through town. He had strolled down the wooden walkway that led from State Street to the jetty and wandered along the footpath that trailed the river from one side of town to the other. It had been a beautiful day and the scenic walk had been not only relaxing but had provided interesting material for his research. There had been a few rowing boats tied to the jetty and the occasional motorboat had disturbed the silence that had almost permeated his afternoon. He had walked a good half a mile to the east of town and discovered another walkway not as steep as the one downtown. It came out onto a quiet road called Eastfeldt where there were hardly any houses, just the woods on both sides.

After taking a long shower he left his room and headed down to reception. No staff were present so he headed for the dining room. It was early evening and some of the guests were already sat for dinner. He saw Jamie sitting at one of the tables in the corner with some paperwork in front of her, a pen in one hand and a cigarette in the other. She was wearing the same clothes he had seen her in that morning and from the size of the paperwork that engrossed her he figured she must have had a busy day and may not have any plans for later. She hadn't noticed him.

'Hi,' he said.

She jumped, looked up in surprise and when she saw him, she quickly extinguished the remains of her cigarette.

'I'm sorry, did I disturb you?' he asked.

'No it's OK, I was just finishing actually. Did you have a good day?'

'Yes.'

'Excuse me for a moment,' she said as she hurriedly picked up the paperwork and walked into the office behind the front desk.

As she did so a middle-aged woman entered the hotel and went around to the other side of the desk and checked the guest list. Jamie returned from the office with more paperwork and put it on the shelves.

'Do you know of any places that serve a good steak?' asked Mike.

'Yes there's Howie's Barn about five miles north of town. Why not check it out,' she replied and then pulled a flyer with a map from one of the racks.

Mike studied the map on the back page for a few moments, noticing out of the corner of his eye that Stella had disappeared into the office. He then followed Jamie into the dining room. She was tidying things, trying to look busy and avoided eye contact with him.

'Excuse me,' he said awkwardly. 'I'm not sure how to get there,' he said pointing to the map.

'Let me have it, I'll show you.'

'Have you eaten yet?'

'No, why?' she replied.

'Would you like to join me for dinner?'

'Well I've got to finish some paperwork tonight,' she replied.

'I thought you told me you'd finished.'

'Yes I had but… look I don't date guests, I'm sorry.'

'Sure,' he replied and then turned to leave. As he passed the front desk Jamie's colleague appeared from the office and so he enquired as to whether room service was available for breakfast. She informed him that if he filled out a form they would see to it. He leant on the reception desk and started to fill it out, occasionally turning his head to observe Jamie. She looked unsettled and was loitering around the dining staff who clearly needed no assistance from their boss. He handed the form to the receptionist and noticed that Jamie was now looking at him. He smiled at her and then turned to go. As he approached the hotel entrance she came into reception and called to him.

'Is the offer still on?' she asked.

'I'll drive,' he replied.

'Give me a moment, I'll get my jacket.'

Mike sat down and began reading one of the magazines on the table. The receptionist watched him for a while and then asked him if he was enjoying his stay.

'Very much, thank you,' he replied as Jamie returned.

'OK then, Stella, I'll leave you to tend the fort,' she said. 'Ready?' she asked Mike as she put on a small leather bomber jacket and walked towards the entrance.

It was just getting dark as they walked out into the fresh evening air. The hotel illuminations had just come on and brought out the beauty of its haunting architecture. They got into Mike's car and headed down the sloped driveway onto the road.

'Take a left at the second set of lights and keep going for a while,' said Jamie breaking the silence.

'Busy day?' asked Mike.

'Yes, most days are.'

'Do you take a day off?'

'Sometimes.'

'I took a nice walk by the river today.'

'It is pretty down there.'

Mike's nervousness was beginning to show. He had divorced in 1991 and had only dated a couple of women since – he wasn't used to doing this.

'Is it far?' asked Mike as he turned into a dark deserted road.

'No just a couple of miles.'

'Did you ever see that episode of the twilight zone, where this guy takes a girl out on a date? They drive down this dark lonely road and then suddenly she turns into—'

'A giant flesh eating salamander?' she interrupted.

'It was something like that wasn't it?'

'Don't worry I'll get you back safely.'

'That's good.'

'I only change every third week.'

Howie's Barn was approaching on the left and they pulled into the parking lot. The restaurant was either a converted barn or a replica, it was busy inside and the hostess informed them that there would be a half hour wait. They could book a table now and go into the bar. Mike asked for a non-smoking table and the hostess said she would come for them when their table was ready.

'Let's get a beer,' said Mike.

They found a table near the bar, sat down and a waitress came almost immediately. Mike ordered two Buds and took off his jacket.

'So what are you going to write about?' asked Jamie.

'I'm not sure, I'm still getting ideas.'

'A thriller maybe?' she asked.

'Give me some ideas then.'

'Well let's think,' she said and paused to light up a cigarette. 'A disappearance,' she continued.

'Is that it?'

'No, the girl doesn't change into a monster, but she kidnaps the guy and holds him against his will in her house deep in the woods.'

'And…?' he replied.

'You're the writer, use your imagination.'

'Tell me about yourself,' said Mike.

'What do you want to know?' she asked in a more serious tone.

'Tell me about Boston.'

'How do you know about Boston?'

'Jenna Kirshaw, she said you went to college there. What did you study?'

'An economics masters degree.'

'Economics. That explains why you run such a good hotel.'

'No, my father is responsible for that.'

'Did you enjoy it there?'

'Yes, I had a great time, met some good friends.'

'Do you still see them?'

'No, most of them came from Maine.'

'Didn't you keep in touch?'

'Well you know how it is, Mike; people come and go don't they.'

'Yes, I only kept in touch with one of my college friends. I see him about once a year; he's married and got kids now.'

'What about you, Mike?'

'Kids? No never had time.'

'Are you married?' she asked in a cautious tone.

'Divorced, six years ago.'

'What happened?'

'Just drifted apart, work mainly – probably my fault. Anyway we're talking about you. What are your plans?'

'Here come the beers,' she said, derailing the conversation. The waitress gave them the Buds and handed Mike the cheque. Jamie quickly took it away from him.

'On me, Mike, and thanks for asking me out, it's been a while.'

'You're welcome.'

'To your book,' she said raising her bottle.

'Thanks, now where were we?'

'I'll get a menu. Don't go away,' she said and stepped off the barstool. She walked to the desk where the hostess had greeted them. Mike tried not to stare at her as she looked at him from across the other side of the room. He drank his beer and looked at the décor around him. The bar was open to non-diners too and it was as he looked around the room to take his eyes off Jamie that he noticed the man with whom he had almost collided in the Pied Piper sitting across the bar. Their eyes met and they nodded to each other like two men who had made a truce. Then Jamie began to walk back towards their table.

'Excuse me while I go and freshen up,' she said as she returned. 'Here are the menus.'

'Will I ever get a chance to talk to this girl,' he thought. Perhaps all she wanted was a meal, some company and small talk.

The waitress came over again. Mike ordered two more Buds and gave the waitress a ten-dollar bill. As he was alone he allowed his mind to wander and he began thinking about Hank Jebson. Maybe he would take up Hank's offer to call at his home and have further discussions with him. Mike also thought about others he could speak with to help him with his research. There was Jenna Kirshaw for one. She seemed to know a lot about what was going on in Ashbury Falls; maybe she could point him in the direction of people who could give him material for consideration. There was her friend Carla too, and even Jamie might have some interesting things to say. The waitress disturbed his concentration as she returned with the beers and he left the change as a tip for her.

'Thank you, enjoy your meal,' she said.

A minute later, Jamie walked back into the bar and sat down at the table.

'Shouldn't be much longer now, does anything take your fancy?' she asked.

He remembered the menus she had left.

'I think I had better take another look,' he replied.

They each reviewed their menus and didn't speak for a while. Jamie noticed a couple a few tables away looking intimate. She stared at them for a while and then turned her attention back to Mike. He was still busy studying the menu. She had not been asked out on a date for a couple of years now and felt very content being in this man's company, even though she knew little about him. He was a mystery, a writer even, and this drew her to him in a way she could not quite fathom out. He was attractive she thought to herself, but there was something else.

'Your table's now ready,' said a voice suddenly.

'OK, thanks,' said Mike as he looked up from his menu.

They both stood up and headed into the restaurant area. It was dimly lit, providing a cosy atmosphere. The hostess led them to their table and told them she would be back in five minutes to take their order and so Mike decided to do a little probing.

'So, is there much to do around here that allows a hard working hotelier like yourself to unwind of an evening?'

'Only the mall. There's a movie theatre and bowling centre next to it and a few restaurants. That's about it. Not much there.'

'So what do you like to do?'

'I'm usually too busy, but when I do relax I enjoy a good book and a glass of wine in the comfort of my apartment.'

'Do you know of anyone or anywhere that might give me some inspiration for my book?'

'Yes, you can go and talk to Reuben Stein!' she said jokingly.

'Who's he?' Mike asked inquisitively, cleverly concealing the fact that Hank had mentioned him earlier. He was keen to find out if Jamie's view of this individual married with his.

'The town weirdo! He tried to get me to invest in a new hotel complex outside of town once. I wouldn't, but he would keep coming back and then he asked me out on a date. I think I upset him big time when I said no.'

She began to giggle.

'What is it?' asked Mike.

'Nothing, it isn't funny really.'

'Is it about Reuben?'

'The guy's had a rough time, everything considered. It must have started at school. The other kids picked on him, you know. Then at high school he could never get a girlfriend. People can be cruel, Mike.'

'Yes they can.'

'I know that he desperately wanted to be part of the football team to please his father who had been quarter back for the school in his day. Even though he worked hard and got reasonable grades, they weren't good enough for Reuben senior. His father would constantly remind him that he needed to be smarter than the other guys if he wanted to cut the big deals, you know what I'm saying?'

'Yes, go on.'

'He had hoped that Reuben would become a top financier like himself so that he could have a big house, a big drive and the best cars, but all that Reuben wanted was a normal life. As he reached his twenties I think any desire to be what he had wanted to be had been brutally driven out of him.'

'A sad case,' said Mike.

'He did eventually make it to a good college near Portland, Maine, but only because his father had contacts there. By the time he graduated he didn't care what his father thought anymore. Life had been relatively easy at college compared with high school and the highlight of his period there was the one and only time he had been truly happy.'

'What happened, did he get a girl?'

'Yes, for eighteen months he had been dating a girl named Sarah Milton and as the relationship turned a year they had started making plans for their future. Six months later for no reason she ditched him for an older guy. It took Reuben a long time to get over that.'

'You seem to know a lot about this guy.'

'Things I've heard from various people and things he's told me over the years.'

'So you're friends then?'

'Not really, he would tell me about himself when he'd call by. I think he's lonely and there's nobody he can really talk to. I think there's an emptiness inside of him that torments him constantly.'

'What happened afterwards?'

'His parents sold up and moved to Portland when he was twenty-seven. He stayed in Ashbury Falls, living in a rented house and working for a real estate company in a nearby town to supplement the money his mother and father had left him to see him on his way. Disappointed as he was in Reuben, his father had compassion enough to deposit $75,000 in a bank account before they left to ease his conscience.'

'That was good of him.'

'As time went on, Reuben became determined to prove that his father had been wrong about him. I guess he wanted to show him, Sarah Milton and the world that Reuben Stein Junior could cut the big deals. He must have learned a lot from his apprenticeship in real estate because by his early thirties he began borrowing to invest in properties around the area and renting them to his contemporaries. From there came buy-ins to property development deals and leisure complexes. He must have been so intensely occupied that the rest of the world just drifted by. He had had no real substance to his life as Carla Dempster had once intimated to him many years after they had been at high school together.'

'Are you sure you never dated him?'

'No honestly, as sorry as I am for him he gives me the creeps. Sometimes I feel like I've been in this town too long. You get to know too much about people. Maybe I should have gone back to Boston when I had the chance.'

'Why didn't you?'

'Bad memories I guess.'

'I thought you said that you enjoyed it there.'

'I did, but I met my fiancé there.'

She was opening up now, rather unexpectedly in Mike's view.

'You were engaged?'

Jamie halted the conversation momentarily as she took her jacket off and put it over the back of her chair.

'Yes, when I was twenty-six,' she continued. 'I met him at college, but we didn't court until after we both left. We were friends and we kept in touch, and then we met up and started seeing one another. He moved to Manchester and so we weren't far apart.'

'What happened?'

'He got offered a management position in one of the Boston banks, but I didn't want to go, because of the hotel and my parent's health and all that. So it was the job or me, and he chose the job.'

'I'm sorry to hear that.'

'I didn't get over it for a long time.'

'Did you ever contact him?'

'Yes, and he asked me to come down to Boston and see him, but I refused, what was the point?'

'Was that it?'

'No, a girlfriend of mine from college who also got a job there asked me over for a week. This was a year later and while I was there I decided to look him up, hoping maybe we could go to the movies or something and see how we both felt. I was so dejected when I knocked on his door and this girl answered. I got invited in and saw Malcolm again, stayed for a cup of coffee and small talk. I couldn't wait to get out. He introduced Anna to me and from then on I had to just pretend we were old friends from college and that I had just called in to say hello, you know how it is.'

'Must have been upsetting for you,' he said sympathetically.

'I cried all the way back in the car to my friend's apartment. What an idiot!'

'Perfectly natural,' said Mike.

'That started me smoking again. I'd given up for three years before that. He never liked me smoking.'

The conversation was interrupted momentarily as the waitress returned and took their order. When she had gone Mike resumed.

'Are you over him now?' he asked.

'Does anyone ever get over anybody until they meet someone else?'

'I think you can,' said Mike.

'Are you over your ex-wife?'

'Yes.'

'You don't meet many decent men in this quiet corner of New Hampshire. Most are a lot younger or they're married, if they are my age.'

'Why don't you go to Boston, Jamie, catch up with old friends, sell up, start a new life? I'm sure a girl of your talents can get a decent job.'

'I don't know, Mike.'

It was just after 10 pm when Mike and Jamie arrived back at the hotel.

'Thanks for a great night,' she said as they walked into reception.

Stella was just ready to leave.

'I've filed that paperwork and put up your morning list,' she said.

'Thanks, Stella,' said Jamie.

'Did you have a nice evening?'

'Yes thank you.'

'Well I'll be off then, see you tomorrow.'

'Goodnight, Stella.'

They were left alone in reception.

'Do you want some coffee or something?' asked Jamie unzipping her jacket.

'No thanks, I'd better get upstairs and do some work on the laptop before I turn in.'

'OK,' she replied.
'I had a good time,' he added.
'Me too.'
'Goodnight, Jamie.'

5

Mike pulled into the sidewalk outside of 1154 Cambridge Road. It was a cool overcast morning, the air was still and an eerie quietness pervaded. Hank Jebson's house was small and quaint unlike the ones he had seen in the neighbourhood on the way to the Farrington Hotel. Hank had stars and stripes hanging from a diagonal flagpole waiting for a breeze to gently ripple it. He stood for a little while inspecting the house and then decided to ring the doorbell and wait for Hank to answer. Observing the neighbouring houses, he noticed on one side an elderly man cleaning his porch, another tending to his front garden. He smiled politely at the first, and the neighbour nodded in acknowledgement before returning his attention to the white paintwork he had been so diligently working on. Mike rang again but there was no answer.

'Hank is usually out at this time,' called the other neighbour from the end of his garden.

'OK, thanks, I'll come back later,' he replied.

'You'd might as well wait,' called the other. 'He's usually back by about 11.30 for an hour before he goes to the Pied Piper for lunch.'

'Guess I'll wait then.'

If Hank didn't arrive by 11.35 he would have to try another time. He had been up late in his room last night working on his laptop after his night out with Jamie. Now was a good time to talk to Hank and he hoped he would return soon. The neighbours watched as Mike returned to his car. When they realised he was not going to leave they returned to their tasks.

After about five minutes, Mike began to feel awkward as he sat in the car, conscious of the fact that Hank's neighbours were probably wondering who he was and what he wanted. To look less conspicuous he decided to walk back up to the neighbour tending to his porch to introduce himself.

'I'm Mike Fabien,' he said as he held out his hand.

The man put his cleaning rags down, wiped his hand in his jeans and then shook hands with him.

'Curtis Gerard. Are you from welfare services?'

'No, I'm just passing through and thought I would look up Hank. Have you lived here long?'

'Thirty-seven years.'

'Nice town.'

'Peaceful now, that's how I like it.'

'So Hank's a regular at the Pied Piper then?'

'I guess he likes the company and conversation. I'd rather eat at home myself.'

'Have you got family here?'

'Just my wife, my son Robert and his family. He owns the drug store on Wilson. Do you take vitamins, Mr Fabien?'

'Sometimes.'

'Well Bob will do you a good deal this week, if you buy in bulk.'

'Thanks, I'll remember that.'

'Here's the man you're looking for, home early.'

Mike turned to see Hank pull up in his pickup truck.

The old man clumsily wobbled out of the vehicle and staggered slightly across the lawn.

'Well, Mr Fabien, why did I somehow think I'd be seeing you today?'

'Hello, Hank.'

'Still cleaning that porch, Curtis?'

Curtis Gerard ignored him and carried on working.

'Come in, son, I'll get some coffee going, some real coffee.'

'Thanks.'

'Always cleaning that damned porch,' muttered Hank as they went into the house.

'He's been a neighbour of yours for a long time then.'

'Curt's OK, his son's a bit of a case though, owns the drug store on Wilson. Sit down, son.'

The lounge was full of old furniture and memorabilia that Mike studied for a minute or so. Hank was in the kitchen whistling to himself. There were many pictures of him and his wife and ones with a teenage boy who must have been his son. Mike studied them long and hard – it was like seeing all of Hank's life in a single photo exhibition.

'That's Rosa and my boy Ronnie.'

'You've got a lot of memories here, Hank.'

'That's right I have,' replied Hank as he handed Mike a mug of coffee.

'Sit down.'

'Thanks.'

'There's not much left for an old man at my age except memories and conversation.'

'Is that why you go to the Pied Piper every day?'

'No, I just can't stand my own cooking!'

Mike laughed.

'Your coffee's good though.'

'Rosa was the best cook in the world, you ask Jack Dempster.'

'That's Carla's husband right?'

'We've known each other for a long time. Jack moved to Ashbury Falls back in 1977 to work for his uncle in Dempster's Hardware Store. I went into the store late one afternoon and had bought some goods. Can't remember what they were now, but I recall his Uncle Pete telling him to run an errand and help me carry them home. I asked him if he wanted to come in for a glass of lemonade. You should have seen the smile on his face when I opened a bottle of ice-cold beer for him. After that he'd come around regularly. Jack was very fond of Rosa; she always made a fuss of him. I think

Jack felt almost as deep a loss as me when Rosa died six years later. She had cancer. He spent a lot of time with me after that and a special bond grew between us.'

'You must have loved Rosa very much.'

'I did, but she's gone now.'

'Jenna runs a good shop down at the Pied Piper,' said Mike changing the subject.

'I like the company, it's good for me and I'm not ashamed to admit that. At least you can talk about things that matter. Too many folks around here are just interested in talking about the roses or what so-and-so said to so-and-so last week, never getting down to anything of any substance, you know what I'm saying?'

'Yes, Hank, I do.'

There was a momentary silence.

'Good, because you didn't come here to talk about the roses did you?'

'No the reason I'm here is because I need to talk to real people too, people with real lives, real experiences, people like you, Hank. Is that your parents in that photograph? '

'Yeah, taken back in 1940 when my father was in the US army. My mother was always proud of that picture, standing next to him in his uniform. I was just in my teens when my parents moved here. Then the war started and my father went away. I can remember getting a job in the log mill just out of town. Ben Cooper, the owner's son, would pick me up when I wasn't at school. They needed timber for the war effort; it gave me extra money in my pocket. I didn't know what that crazy war was all about until I came home from the mill one day and saw my mother crying with a piece of paper in her hand. It was then that I realised that I wasn't going to see my father again and it cut me deep, real deep. Then I knew what it was all about. I ran out the house, fast as I could all the way to the river, down to the jetty. I stayed there all night, didn't even think about my mother and the pain she was going through, just thought of myself and then I realised it was time to go home and face life without him. And that is the very chair I saw her crying in.'

Hank pointed to an antique rocking chair in the corner.

'This was your parent's house then?' said Mike.

'I brought Rosa home here on our wedding day. She was a woman with a heart, Mike. Most girls wouldn't want to be living with their husband's mother, but she did. My mother had nobody, just me. Rosa nursed her until she died back in '65. Rosa was a fine woman, never said a hurtful thing to anyone and she sure looked after Ronnie and me.'

'You must miss her very much.'

'I do. She died back in '83. She took Ronnie's death real hard though.'

'Your son died?'

'Back in '77. We had him late you see. He was our only child and I can't help but think that the grief and the shock had something to do with the cancer, but who can tell anyway. They were my family, Mike, and then they were gone.'

Hank topped up Mike's coffee and then poured some more out for himself.

'Why did you come here, son?'

'I wanted to hear your story, Hank.'

'No, son, why did you come to Ashbury Falls?'

'I'm writing a book about a small New England town and how the lives of the residents are entwined by events that happened some years back. I don't know how the plot will develop and how things will turn out but that's the fun of being a writer, you just don't know where the words will lead you. I need ideas, Hank.'

'And you expect me to believe that?'

Mike became uncomfortable.

'Yes I do,' he replied.

'Well let me tell you what I think. You're a reporter and I think you know things about my son. Like I already told you, the place was crawling with them. I never understood why a kid drowning could cause such interest.'

'I'm not a reporter, but I am interested in knowing what happened.'

'I guess I'm just weary of strangers who turn up asking questions.'

'It was a long time ago, why would anyone want to bring it all back now?'

'I don't know, son, you tell me.'

'I lost my mother at a young age, Hank, and I never wanted to talk about it. The kids at school taunted me at first. They'd say things like "Mickey ain't got a mom anymore" or "where did your mother go Mickey?" I know what it's like to lose someone close, Hank.'

'You married, son?'

'Divorced.'

'There was no one else for me, only my Rosa, and there never will be,' said Hank, and then he paused. 'Can I trust you, Mike?'

'Yes, Hank, tell me what happened to your son.'

'My Ronnie was a kind hearted boy, spirited at times though. He had a slight limp that made his walk look a little clumsy.'

'How did that happen?'

'I built him a tree house,' said Hank pointing to a large oak at the bottom corner of the rear garden. 'It's still there; I never had the heart to take it down.'

'Go on.'

'One day when he was ten, he was playing some spy game with his pals. Guess he thought he was some hero in the CIA or something. He was playing dangerously. I kept warning him about it, he nearly fell off but he caught hold of a branch just in time. It didn't seem to bother him, he just carried on, but then about half an hour after I heard a cry and a yell, I didn't see anything. I ran out as fast as I could, Rosa got all hysterical like mothers do, and he was lying on the ground. Broke his arm or so we just thought. It wasn't until he complained about his leg that we realised that was broken too. The arm healed fine, but the leg took a while and he always had that limp as a result. His friend said that he hit another branch with the top of his leg on the way down, so it must have broken his fall, probably stopped something worse from happening.'

'Sounds like he may have damaged his hip,' said Mike.

'Who knows, anyway it never bothered him, he just took it when the other kids made fun of him, well most of the time anyway. If he had taken after me...'

Hank paused for a few seconds, and then turned his head towards Mike realising that he had been staring out of the window during the account of the tree house.

'Well things got better as he grew into his teens, he became more confident, had a couple of girls who had a claim on his time, I even think the limp got better, but not enough for him to be in the school football or baseball teams. That bothered him, but not for long. I got him a guitar from an old friend, one of those Telcaster things.'

'A Fender Telecaster?'

'Yeah, one of those, white it was. Anyway he got a band together, playing R&B with some pals at school and they did a few gigs, so that kind of made up for things. Mind you, the number of times his mother had to tell him to turn the noise down!'

'I wouldn't mind some more of that coffee, Hank. I don't usually drink the real stuff,' said Mike interrupting the conversation.

'Ronnie never had plans to go to college and if he had gone, he would have needed a scholarship,' said Hank pouring some fresh coffee. 'He just wanted to get a job. Learning wasn't his thing. We tried to help him, his grades were OK and the principal said he had a lot of potential. Hell, kids, you can't tell them what's for their own good can you?

Still you'd be about Ronnie's age wouldn't you, so I guess your folks did the same. Did you go to college?'

'Albany.'

'Well anyway Ronnie stayed in high school...'

'Are you OK, Hank?' asked Mike.

'Yes, just give me a moment will you,' he replied as he stood up and walked to the other side of the room. 'Do you drink whiskey?'

'No thanks,' he replied as Hank poured out a small glass and quickly emptied it into his mouth.

'I lost my family, Mike. It should have been me first. What hurts me most is that I wasn't there.'

'What happened to him, Hank?'

'No one knows for sure and that's what eats me up. I know he drowned in the river but it doesn't make sense. He was a good swimmer, I taught him from a young age.'

'Tell me what happened, Hank.'

'Why do you want to know?'

'Hank, if this is too painful we can stop right now. It's like I said to you before, I'm just doing research for a book.'

Mike got up to go.

'You didn't answer my question, son.'

'I've taken enough of your time, Hank. Research can be a dangerous thing; you can ask too many questions. Maybe I'll see you again at the Pied Piper. That place does have its attractions doesn't it? I guess Jenna chose an appropriate name. Thanks for the coffee, you take care now.'

Mike opened the front door and walked out across the lawn down to his car – Hank watched him all the way.

'You still haven't answered my question,' he called.

'Another time, Hank,' said Mike quietly to himself as he got into his car.

6

Mike parked his car in the public parking lot in the centre of town and made his way across to State Street. The streets seemed a little less busy than they had been the previous day and he was finding his way around with ease now. Ronnie Jebson's death was on his mind. Hank had twice mentioned now that reporters had been around at the time. A teenager had drowned, but why all the interest? His next visit to Hank would he thought, shed more light on this. Hank was hooked now and would be forthcoming next time. Carla Dempster was next but a little detour to a certain drugs store mentioned by Hank's neighbour would be needed first. As he turned into Wilson Street the building in question appeared a few yards down on the left hand side. It was a long narrow store with fully stacked shelves and neatly assembled displays all around. Behind the counter the large figure of the store's owner was busy opening boxes and delayed in greeting Mike as he approached.

'Just a moment please.'

'No hurry,' replied Mike as he studied the store whilst the man finished removing the contents of the last box.

'I need some multi-vitamins. I hear you've got an offer on,' said Mike.

'Six months' supply for $29.95 any good to you?'

'Fine. Can you tell me where I can find a good hardware store?'

'Dempster's on Howard,' replied the owner placing the pot of vitamins in a bag. 'Comes well recommended, I've been a customer of the Dempster's for years, nice couple.'

'Would that be Jack and Carla Dempster by any chance?'

'Yes, do you know them?'

'Kind of. Friends of a friend really. How is Carla?'

'She's getting those blackouts again.'

'Oh yes, I had heard that she's had some problems in the past.'

'I've known them a long time and she's had to cope with a lot.'

'My wife fainted once after we'd got married,' said Mike.

'I hear it's more serious than that but Jack's keeping things close to his chest.'

'I'm passing through so I'll pay them a short visit. Thanks for your help.'

Howard Street was wide and spacious unlike Wilson. There were a number of parked cars, a truck delivering office supplies and people browsing the stores that lined both sides of the road. Dempster's stood out. It had a bright coloured sign and looked appealing even for a hardware store. A man was fixing the doorbell at the entrance and Mike assumed this must be Jack. He nodded as Mike passed him and when Mike reached the counter he got down off his stepladder and approached him.

'How can I help?' he said placing his screwdriver down.

'Hi, my name's Mike Fabien...'

'Hello, Mike,' called Carla as she emerged from the stockroom.

'You know each other?' asked Jack sounding a little surprised.

'Jenna tells me you're doing research,' she continued, ignoring her husband.

'Jack Dempster,' he said cutting in.

Mike reached over and shook Jack's hands.

'I met your wife at the Pied Piper the other day, great place.'

'Can we get you something, Mr Fabien?' asked Jack.

'No thanks. The reason I've called is that I was wondering if you were both free this evening for dinner? I'd like to interview you.'

'Why would you want to talk to *us*, Mr Fabien?'

'Please, it's Mike. I seem to have developed writer's block and I'm trying to think of new ideas. I came to Ashbury Falls to get input from people who live here. I've done this kind of thing before and it allows you to write without any pre-conceived ideas. I've found that talking to people like you gives me inspiration.'

'Come on, Jack, it's not every day that you get to talk to a writer and help them with a book, it might be fun,' said Carla.

'I'll buy dinner,' added Mike.

'Mike Fabien? I've never seen any books by a Mike Fabien,' said Jack.

'When do you read books anyway?' asked Carla.

'There are many writers in America. I'm just one of them, not a best-selling author, but I make a living.'

'So what sort of fee are we talking about?'

'Jack! Don't pay any attention to him, Mike, we'd be happy to talk to you. Why not come around to our place for dinner.'

'I don't think that's a good idea,' exclaimed Jack.

'It's OK; another time maybe, I'm sorry to disturb you. If you don't ask…'

'Please, Jack, I'm sure Mike's got some interesting experiences to tell us too,' said Carla calmly, reeling inside at Jack's lack of hospitality and narrow mindedness.

'I don't know, Carla; things have been a bit stressful lately…'

'OK, maybe I'll catch up with you folks some other time,' said Mike trying to leave the store quietly.

'Well thanks for calling,' said Jack as Mike left the store.

'What is wrong with you?' shouted Carla, incensed.

'We hardly know him!' replied Jack angrily.

'So, what's the harm? I'm going to apologise to him,' said Carla assertively.

'Whatever, but he's not probing me for ideas for his story book, OK!'

Carla marched out of the store, almost slamming the door behind her.

'Mind the bell!' shouted Jack.

Carla chased after Mike and called out to him. He had already walked some distance back down the street and turned to her as she speeded towards him.

'I'm sorry about Jack,' she said. 'He can be unwelcoming at times.'

'It's OK.'

'Listen; meet me at the Pied Piper tomorrow morning about 10.30, I'd like to tell you about my life, Mike, really I would.'

'Are you sure, what about Jack?' asked Mike.

'Never mind him – 10.30 OK?'

'I'll be there.'

'Thank you. I have to go now.'

Carla hurried back to the store leaving Mike on the sidewalk. He watched her disappear inside, and then smiled. His plan had worked.

7

Reuben Stein gazed at the wall before him with exhausted eyes as he sat at his desk. He had been losing sleep in recent nights, reliving long suppressed and fragmented memories of a fateful day in September 1977 when his best friend Ronnie Jebson had drowned in an accident down at the river. He had not witnessed the incident, but remembered that he was one of two people who had been the last to see Ronnie alive. He remembered another boy who had been hanging around in the parking lot at the top of the walkway that led to the jetty. He had noticed him on his way back towards the road and wondered if he had seen anything of the accident. He had neither known him nor could he remember his face.

It was time to make an important call, so he stood up with the intention of going into his secretary's office to instruct her to get his lawyer, Morgan Stevens on the phone. He liked to keep an eye on her from time to time to make sure she was being productive and that he was getting his money's worth from employing her. As he approached the door he began to lose his balance. The room seemed to tilt slightly, the walls started to bend and the door seemed to move further away. Without warning blackness enveloped him and he collapsed to the floor like a felled tree in a distant forest.

He could hear an echo around him, then a voice, distant but just recognisable.

'Mr Stein.'

It became louder, then clearer, there were lights, and a face began to take form out of the chaotic blur before him. In a few seconds he could see the face of a woman.

'Mother?'

His secretary Rita was knelt over him as he began to regain consciousness.

'What happened to me?' he slurred.

'Are you OK, Mr Stein?'

'Mustn't blow the deal,' said Reuben as he tried to catch his breath.

'I heard you fall, Mr Stein,' said Rita nervously. 'I thought I should come up. Do you want me to call a doctor?'

'I'll be fine, please just get me a glass of water.'

Reuben sat up and loosened his tie. Rita soon returned with some water, which he gulped down in seconds before getting to his feet, staggering as he did so. Impulsively he hurried back to his desk and started to make a neat pile of the letters that he had opened earlier. His hand shook and the pile fell apart. Just as before he started to make the pile again, being meticulous in ensuring that they were back in the correct order, his eyes fixed intently on the task as Rita stood helplessly watching him, not knowing what to say.

'Are you OK Mr Stein?'

'Do I look like I'm OK?' he replied sternly. 'It should never have happened,' he continued, his voice trembling.

'What shouldn't have, Mr Stein?'

He looked up at her in surprise.

'Nothing. Please get me Morgan Stevens on the phone will you.'

'OK, Mr Stein,' she replied nervously.

Reuben waited anxiously for Rita to put his lawyer through to him. Each second seemed to drag on and on as the tapping of his fingers became louder and more pronounced.

'Rita, what's going on?' he asked quietly.

'Mr Stevens is with another client at the moment.'

He raced over to Rita's desk and snatched the phone from her hand.

'Get me Morgan Stevens now please, it's very urgent,' he said trying to remain composed.

'I'm sorry, sir, but as I explained to your secretary, Mr Stevens is with another client at the moment, can he call you in about an hour?'

'What's more important than the Logan development deal?'

'I'm sorry, Mr Stein, please let me get him to call you back.'

'One hour, no longer.'

Reuben handed the phone back to Rita.

'Damn that Moreland,' he muttered.

He walked back into his office and shut the door behind him. Rita stared at the closed door in shock. She had been working for him for about nine months now, and never a day would go by without her being on the end of his mood swings. At first she had regarded him as someone socially inept, now he was beginning to frighten her. She stopped working on the letter she was composing and started a new one.

Reuben had received a letter from his lawyer stating that the Logan development case was finally going to court in early November. Charles Moreland's lawyers had been effectively stalling things while they made their case watertight and everything appeared to be going in their favour. The deal was going very badly and the greater the delay in the work starting, the more money the investors were losing, and Reuben stood to lose everything he had invested. As a result of the sleepless nights and the amount of time and energy he was putting into this deal, other areas of his business were suffering. He was getting a steady income from his investments and home and store properties he was renting, but half a million dollars was a lot to lose, and he had already started planning the deals that the return from the Logan development was going to fund. The Ashbury Falls mall was expanding and Reuben wanted to get his share of the stores to be built and subsequent revenue from the rent that that would bring. This and other deals were going to get him in league with the big players, just like his father.

The phone rang.

'Stevens?'

To his dismay it was one of his business associates making an enquiry about rent revisions. He would never employ associates in his firm, so he would contract out some of the less interesting work to other agencies.

'Don't call me about this now, I'll speak to you later,' he replied and put the phone down.

Disturbed from the silence of the past twenty minutes, he began the tapping again with one hand and the rotating of his pen through the fingers of the other. Another ten minutes passed and nothing happened. Then another ten; now Reuben was becoming uncomfortable. He knew in his mind that it would be an hour before the all-important call would come, but he couldn't wait.

He pressed the intercom on his desk and asked Rita to get Morgan Stevens again. There was no reply.

'Rita, get me Morgan Stevens please.'

There was still no reply.

'Rita!'

With that he got up from his chair and hurried to the door. Rita was gone.

'Rita?' he called again.

He looked in her desk diary to see if she had any appointments but there were no entries. Then he noticed that her PC was switched off, the desk very neat and tidy and everything filed away. Maybe she had finished for the day. She would always ask him if she was going somewhere or taking the day off. What was different about today? It was then that he noticed the envelope on the desk, simply addressed to 'Mr Stein'. He opened it, unfolded the note and began to read it. When his eyes had finished reading the cold words written on the paper he composed himself, screwed the note up into a ball and threw it into the trash bin under her desk.

It was the afternoon and Mike returned to the Farrington Hotel. As he walked into the reception area there was nobody around, so he went straight up to his room. He opened the wardrobe and took out a bottle of Jack Daniels that he had brought for the visit before slumping into the armchair by the window. He poured himself half a glass, sat back down and put his feet up on a stool, contemplating his next encounter with Hank. Hank would tell him what he wanted to know eventually, it was just a matter of when and under what circumstances he would do so.

To overcome Hank's suspicion of him he reached over to one of the drawers of the desk in his room. He opened it and pulled out a book. It was a paperback novel entitled *Scenes of Yesterday* with the author's name in large print at the bottom of the cover; MICHAEL FABIEN. He placed it on the bed next to him and then took another gulp of his Jack Daniels. As he rested back in his chair, he allowed his eyes to wander around the room and considered whether to check out the local beauty spot at the centre of the controversy that Hank had mentioned.

As he cast his eyes back to the desk, he noticed what looked to be a small thin box wrapped in blue paper with a white card attached. He got up to inspect it and saw the card with the words 'THANKS FOR LAST NIGHT – JAMIE' written on it in blue ink. He opened it to find a black box with a lid on it. Inside was a gold-plated razor neatly set in a red velvet décor surround. He examined it and smiled trying to remember whether he had shaved properly last night. There was a knock at the door. Mike placed the razor back in its box and proceeded to answer. It was Jamie.

'I hope I'm not disturbing you,' she said.

'No I was just taking five,' he replied. 'Thanks for the razor; it was a nice thought.'

'You're welcome,' she replied.

'Do you want to come in?' he asked.

'No I just came up to ask if you like Italian.'

'Yes.'

'I'll cook us something then.'

'OK,' he replied surprised. The night at Howie's must have gone well he thought.

'See you downstairs at eight then,' she said and closed the door.

8

The next morning arrived in a blaze of sunshine. It had rained the previous night and the roads glistened with the residue of surface water as Mike drove into the Pied Piper for his rendezvous with Carla. He had skipped breakfast; Jamie had won his heart with the pasta dish she had served up the previous evening and he wasn't feeling at all hungry. The tyres of his car splashed through the remaining pools of water as he pulled up near to the entrance. He was pleased; there didn't appear to be many customers inside. Jenna greeted him with a smile and brought him some coffee. There was no sign of Carla. He checked his watch; it was now 10.35 and so he decided to wait a while and see if she was going to turn up. To avoid suspicion he ordered a light breakfast; he did not want to appear to be waiting for someone.

By the time he had eaten it was 11.14 and there was still no sign of her. He would wait another fifteen minutes and then leave. Perhaps she had told Jack about their meeting and he had talked her out of it. Maybe she had cried off. Either way he was very keen to talk to her, as keen as he was to talk to Hank Jebson again.

'Can I get you anything else?' asked Jenna as she took his empty plate away.

'Just some more coffee please.'

Another two customers entered the diner and Mike began to feel uncomfortable. It was approaching lunchtime and the diner was going to get busy. Being a creature of habit Hank would soon be in and that would complicate things.

11.35; she wasn't coming. Mike got up and went through the archway that led to the restrooms before leaving. One minute later Carla's car turned into the parking lot. As she got out Jenna could see that she was in some kind of rush. She walked briskly into the diner not even thinking to look for Mike's car; she had already assumed that he had gone by now. Jenna mustn't have any inkling she thought. She had planned to say a brief word or two to Mike as though they had met by accident. She would then leave promptly and get Mike to follow shortly thereafter. She did not want Jenna or anyone else to see her with Mike. If Jack found out what she was doing he would crack. He was already fuming because Sheriff Conway had informed him that morning that he didn't have proof enough to make any charges against Ritchie Templeman.

'Not stopping then?' asked Jenna, watching as Carla looked around the diner.

'No, not today.'

'Are you looking for someone?'

'No,' said Carla abruptly. Her nerves were starting to show. As much as she wanted to ask Jenna if Mike had been in, she couldn't.

The door opened and in walked Hank Jebson. He smiled at Carla and Jenna and then sat down at his usual table.

'Be right there, Hank,' called Jenna.

'I've got to go,' said Carla.

'Did you want something?' asked Jenna.

'No, nothing I'm fine. I'll see you later,' replied Carla and then left the diner. A perplexed Jenna walked over to Hank's table and she took his order as Mike returned from the restrooms. Hank nodded at him.

Carla put the keys in the ignition. It wouldn't start. She tried turning it over again several times but it wouldn't fire up. She tried once more, finally with success. She put the stick in reverse and drove out of her parking space turning the wheel as she did so. She stopped, put it into drive and then there was a tap on the window. She was startled as she looked up to see who it was. It was Mike and so she quickly wound down the window.

'Are you standing me up?' he asked her.

'Mike!' she said with absolute relief. 'I'm really sorry, I just couldn't get away. If Jack knew I was here he'd blow his top!'

'I figured that.'

'Look, I am going to drive out of here and then stop at the other side of the lights around the corner. Get in your car and meet me round there, then follow me. I know a great park out of town where we can talk. I've got one hour.'

'OK.'

She drove off. Mike waved to appear to be saying goodbye. He glanced back at the diner as he got into his car and noticed Jenna looking suspiciously at him from inside. Carla could never hide things from her and her little act had been pointless.

As Mike turned right at the lights, Carla pulled out to allow him to follow as planned. They drove through the east neighbourhood until the houses became trees and they had reached the town limit. Mike saw Carla indicating to turn left at a sign saying 'Wood Spring recreation area'. As he drove up the tree-lined road he noticed a few people walking on the explorer paths before reaching the parking lot. Vehicles were sparsely parked and so he decided to leave his a good distance from Carla's.

'There's another picnic area about a quarter of a mile along that walkway,' said Carla pointing to an opening behind them. 'Let's take a walk up there.'

'OK,' said Mike.

The path led them through a tree-lined grove that partially shadowed them from the sun. The leaves were showing signs of turning but it was too early in the fall for anyone to fully appreciate the colours they would eventually display. They walked a few yards before Mike opened up the conversation.

'Thanks for meeting with me, it's useful when people like yourself can spare me the time, I am very grateful.'

'I'm sorry we couldn't do this over dinner. It's nothing personal; Jack's not very adventurous at the best of times and he's not that warming to strangers. It's probably better that we talk without Jack being here. Jack and I are going through a rough patch at the moment and it's mainly my fault. I wanted to talk to you because in some strange way I think you can help me. You're a writer; I want you to write about me.'

'Why?'

'When I was a girl my parents told me that I had the world at my feet; my high school principal said that I would make a great head of advertising one day. I was creative you see. I was going to work for one of those big corporations – they had it all planned out for me but I flumped college, came home and got married, had a kid and worked in my husband's hardware store. Their high hopes vanished into thin air.'

'Why didn't college work out?'

'I worked hard, but I couldn't concentrate.'

'Mind on other things?'

'No, I would just get these periods when I just couldn't take anything in. It affected my grades, my coursework, in the end the college principal called my parents in and suggested that they seek medical attention for me and that I leave college.'

'Sounds serious.'

'I'm forty years old, Mike, and I've been married for twenty of them. He's a good husband and I love him—'

'But?' interrupted Mike.

'There's no but, Mike.'

'I think there is, Carla, or you wouldn't be speaking to me.'

68

'Have you got kids?' she asked.

'No kids, I was married, but we split six years ago.'

'Did you want kids?'

'We never really talked about it as we were both too busy really. What about yourself?'

'We've got a daughter, Joaney. We were over the moon when we had her, but we couldn't have any more after she was born.'

'I'm sorry to hear that.'

'Sometimes I wished we had travelled places, experienced life, but Jack wanted to concentrate on building up the business and that was that. He always dreamed of owning a chain of hardware stores, but as you can see, the dream never became a reality. I'd sell up tomorrow and move on, but the store represents twenty years of Jack's life and it's like a part of him, even though he moans about it sometimes.'

'So you'll be staying in Ashbury Falls for a while longer then?'

'I guess so.'

'Are you happy, Carla?'

'What is true happiness, Mike? Is it meeting the right person, falling in love, having children, having a nice home?'

'I think people who have those things have got the basic ingredients of a good life'

'Isn't there more though?'

'Well some have interesting careers whilst others just have jobs. Life's like trying to bake the perfect pie. The opportunities are there for adding all the needed ingredients in the correct measure, but only a few people in this world get it just right and taste the perfect pie, others eat, taste and if they think about it long enough they realise that somehow that pie doesn't taste as good as they would like it to.'

'Is that the case with you, Mike?'

'I guess my work makes up for a lot of things, but yes; sometimes the pie could taste better.'

'But it is enjoyable?' she asked.

'Yes it is.'

'Then as long as it doesn't taste bitter...'

'You said that things weren't good between you and Jack at the moment. You need to make them good, believe me; you're talking to someone who knows.'

'It's me; I feel empty, Mike, have you ever felt that way?'

'No I haven't, what do you mean?'

'Empty, robbed, I don't know how to put it into words. I don't even know what I really feel.'

'Are you talking about not being able to have had any more children?'

'Maybe. Jack isn't sure what it is. That's the problem; he keeps telling me to move on, get over it, whatever IT is. That's all I think he can deal with. I've been to counsellors but I don't take well to what they're saying.'

'Did you get treatment after you left college?'

'Yes, but it didn't work and they could never get to the bottom of the problem.'

'So do you still suffer from it?'

'In a big way, Mike, but it's different to what it used to be. It developed into minor dizziness and fainting and then got worse after Joaney was born. I still get very bad spells and it's not a nice experience, but the blackouts have returned.'

'How often do you get them?'

'I don't know, once, maybe twice a week sometimes more, it depends on what I'm doing. I had a couple of weeks not long ago when nothing happened.'

'Can the doctors trace it back to anything; do they know what caused it?'

'No, not really, they gave me drugs but that only stopped it getting worse, stabilised it I suppose. I guess I'll just have to live with it, but I just have this awful feeling that one day a spell will come when I'm in the car or I'm crossing the road or something. Jack says I should spend more time at home to minimise their frequency, but I don't want to live like that, doing nothing. What sort of books do you write, Mike?'

'Fiction.'

'Could you use my experiences?'

'I want to help you, Carla.'

'Help me?' she said puzzled.

'Fulfil your dreams,' he said smiling.

'Of course… dreams. I have many,' she replied.

'I think we should head back soon,' said Mike. 'We don't want anyone getting suspicious, particularly your friend Jenna.'

'She won't know,' said Carla confidently.

'If you could put some other things on paper for me that would be useful.'

'I will.'

'Meet me in the Pied Piper on Friday. Just call in for a chat with Jenna at about noon, I'll be there at 12.30, that way nobody will notice us. I'll ask you to join me OK?'

9

The square in the centre of downtown was unusually quiet. A few people were walking their dogs but for the most part it was empty. It was often used as a thoroughfare. Cutting diagonally through well-kept lawns was a path lined with benches that was a very useful shortcut. A cool breeze brushed through the trees and gently blew the hair of a man sitting on one of the benches as he gazed into space and rocked back and forth in a clockwork motion. His hands were covering his face and his tie loosened. An elderly lady walking by asked him if anything was wrong.

'I'm fine,' replied Reuben, meaning that is was no concern of hers.

She moved on promptly, muttering something to herself to the effect that younger people had no time for anyone these days. She walked a few steps and then looked back at him with a puzzled expression.

Reuben stared at his office across the road that was situated on the first floor above a real estate agency. He had owned the building since 1989 and had rented the ground floor to them for the past three years. It was small-time business in his view. What Reuben had worked for all these years was in real danger of collapsing around him; something he was finding very hard coming to terms with. He imagined his father standing in front of him laughing at his incompetence, telling him that he wasn't smart enough when it came to playing with the big guys. The Logan deal was all that mattered right now. There must be something he could do to defeat Charles Moreland and his band of cronies. Nobody makes any money in this world by being soft, by worrying about beauty spots and dead men's bones, he thought to himself. He couldn't pull out of the deal now nor find some other way of salvaging half a million dollars. He was counting on the returns to back-fill for funds that he had put into other projects he had committed to. If the Logan deal fell through, his capital base would collapse and bring the whole house of cards down with it.

His concentration was disturbed by the sound of footsteps in the distance. The footsteps turned into the sound of a woman's boots and as they approached he looked to his right and saw someone he recognised.

'Jamie Farrington. I haven't seen you for a while,' he said.

'Reuben!' she said nervously as he stood up.

'What brings you down from your little castle and into town?' he asked.

'Just a few things to get, that's all,' she replied.

'Well it's good to see an old friend again.'

'Likewise, Reuben,' she replied asking herself why she had decided to cut through the park in the first place. Now she would have to humour him if she had any chance of him leaving her alone; it had been this way in the past when he had tried to date her.

'How's business?' she asked.

'Business is great; the Logan deal is going to come off.'

'The Logan deal?'

'Haven't you heard? They're going to build lots of very expensive homes on an old Indian burial ground and it's going to bring in a great yield.'

'I hope it works out for you, Reuben. Look I am in a hurry, so maybe we'll bump into each other again!'

'You're going to wish you'd accepted my offer to be my girlfriend, Jamie.'

'I'm flattered, really,' she replied nervously.

'Surely you've got time for an old friend? What have you been up to?'

'Busy with the hotel.'

'That's good, Jamie. I've been thinking about you a lot you know. About what it would be like if you and me... you know,' he said putting his arms around her waist.

'Reuben, you're holding me, please let go.'

'Still looking like a biker chic then?'

'I don't think so, Reuben,' she replied. Now she was worried.

'Still got that rose tattoo on your left shoulder?'

'How do you know about that?'

'I decided to pay a visit to that biker joint once myself!'

'That was a long time ago, Reuben.'

'You're shaking, Jamie. Don't worry I'm not angry. You changed when you started seeing Rooster – that was his name wasn't it?'

'Yes it was.'

'Well now you're back to the way I like you, Jamie, well almost. I hope you're not still smoking. My father told me that only bad girls smoke.'

'Reuben, please I...'

'You can still be my girlfriend if you want, Jamie.'

'I don't have much time for relationships these days,' she said clumsily.

In her mind she was begging for someone to walk into the square, but nobody was around. A feeling of helplessness overwhelmed her. She had to do something.

'Reuben, it's been good talking to you, but I really have to go.'

'Just a while longer, Jamie, we haven't talked for a long time, whatever it is that you're in a hurry to do can't be more important than this' he said as he stroked her face. 'What are you in a hurry to do, Jamie?'

She froze, unable to answer the question.

'Nothing that important, I thought so.'

'Reuben I...'

Suddenly she saw somebody enter the square out of the corner of her eye and she fixed her gaze at them. Reuben was muttering his feelings for her but she wasn't listening. She was desperately hoping that the figure would walk this way and her prayer was answered as her anxiety turned to sheer relief. As she looked over Reuben's shoulder a man was walking towards them. Reuben did not see or hear him approaching. All his attention was fixed on Jamie – he didn't even notice her eye movements. As the man approached she smiled and pulled herself out of Reuben's clutches.

'Mike!' she said in unprecedented disbelief.

'Hi, Jamie,' he said looking a little perturbed.

'Well, Jamie, we'll talk again,' said Reuben, seething inside.

Mike could tell that he had arrived just in time and Jamie said nothing as Reuben walked away and headed back to his office. When Reuben was out of view, Jamie grabbed hold of Mike and squeezed him tightly, resting her face in his chest.

'Are you OK, what happened?'

'To say that you're my knight in shining armour is the understatement of the year,' she told him trying to take a deep breath.

'An old boyfriend?' asked Mike.

Jamie was shaking.

'Let's go and get a cup of coffee,' said Mike pointing to a small café across the square. Jamie wouldn't let go.

'Jamie?'

'I'm OK,' she said. 'Just give me a minute.'

She composed herself and unzipped her jacket to cool herself down. He put his arm around her and they walked out of the park. From a distance Reuben watched them, his face lit up in rage, his eyes fixed on their every move.

'Are you OK now?' Mike asked Jamie as he brought the drinks over and sat next to her.

'That was Reuben Stein,' she said.

'Oh. I see.'

'He had his arms around my waist, Mike! He's never touched me before.'

'Was he going to hurt you?'

'No, Reuben wouldn't do that, I don't think so.'

'You look scared.'

'He even knows about the tattoo!'

'The tattoo?' said Mike a little shocked.

'When I dated Rooster.'

'Rooster?'

'Yes, the biker guy. I was a biker chic once!' she replied; now feeling uncomfortable and embarrassed. She wished she had not mentioned that.

'It's OK, calm down.'

'I'm sorry. I dated a biker called Rooster once. Reuben must have followed me one night to a biker joint that Rooster used to take me to. I was all mixed up then, Mike. Rooster wanted me to look the part and I... it doesn't matter anymore; that's all in the past. Just forget I said it.'

'OK.'

'I'll never forget one of the times Reuben asked me out on a date,' she continued, starting to laugh.

Mike looked at her. She was clearly shaken and this was obviously a pretence.

'He nearly passed out!'

'Passed out?' replied Mike as he homed in like an eagle that had spotted its prey.

'Yes he went all dizzy and weird. I may be a femme fatale, but I didn't think that turning him down would have that effect on him!'

She hoped that Mike would laugh at the joke. He didn't. He looked deadly serious.

'What exactly happened?' he asked her in an interrogatory tone.

'I don't know, Mike, I can't remember. Why is it so important?'

'Never mind.'

'Why, Mike? Why do you ask?'

'It doesn't matter,' replied Mike as Jamie led back on the cushioned corner of the sofa and suddenly took a strangely relaxed posture.

'Are you sure you're OK?' he asked again.

'Does the tattoo bother you, Mike?' she asked calmly.

'I'm not your boyfriend, Jamie. What I like or dislike doesn't really matter.'

'Really?' she replied unimpressed.

'Shall I take you home, I'm heading back to the hotel,' he asked.

'I've got my own car, Mike.'

'I'll walk you over to your car then,' he insisted.

'You don't have to,' she replied coldly.

When they finally left the café they headed towards the parking lot that was just around the corner from the square. Jamie fell silent and Mike said nothing either. When they reached Jamie's car she unlocked it and was about to get in. He gently caught hold of her arm and she turned around and looked at him.

'That Italian was great last night,' he told her.

'Maybe we'll do it again sometime?' she asked.

'Maybe. Are you OK now?'

'I'll be fine. Mike I—'

'Jamie, I'm only here for a short time.'

'I understand; no personal attachments right?'

'It's not like that—'

'Then what is it, Mike?'

He didn't answer.

'I'll see you later,' he said and walked over to his own car. She looked on as he strolled over and opened the door.

'Thanks for saving me from the Morlock,' she called out and watched him drive away.

She got into her car and lit up a cigarette.

'Reuben was right, I've got to give these damned things up,' she said to herself.

As she started the engine she pondered over Mike's reaction when she had told him about Reuben. Maybe there was something he wasn't telling her, she thought.

Mike was the first to arrive back at the hotel. Taking off his jacket he threw it onto the bed and headed over to the desk to pour himself a Jack Daniels, and booted up his laptop. He opened a file that brought up dossiers on a number of men of similar age and appearance. He browsed through the file for several minutes and then came to a man named Connor Newman aged thirty-nine. He stared at the photograph of the man for a while, examining the facial features closely before reading through the file text. He recognised the face.

'I still need to talk to Hank,' he thought to himself. It had to be tomorrow after his next meeting with Carla. He needed more information on Ronnie's death.

10

Jamie opened one of her eyes to see the sun's rays penetrate through the trees and in through the window of her bedroom. She quickly turned over; her bedclothes in a mess, her body slumped to the end of the bed and her right arm dangling over the edge. As she raised her head to check the time it throbbed with pain as she realised that it was way past the time she would normally get up. She quickly got out of bed, forgetting her delicate condition and allowing the hammer to come down hard on the bell again. She went into the bathroom to get a glass of water and some pills and looked at herself in the mirror. Her hair ran down the side of her face partially covering her eye, she was still wearing her make-up and her mouth felt like a septic tank. Even Mortisha Addams has looked better, she thought. Then she noticed that she was still wearing her underwear and mini skirt she had worn the previous night. Her denim jacket and blouse lay sprawled on her bedroom floor.

Her friend Heather must have bundled her out of the cab, got her to her room and partially undressed her before putting her into bed.

She gulped down a large glass of water and swallowed two pills as she pulled back the curtains to observe the outside world. As she did so she had to pull her hands over her eyes like a vampire who had forgotten about the sunrise. She had certainly drunk too much, smoked too many cigarettes and she dearly hoped that she hadn't done anything foolish as well. She had called Heather Johnson, an old friend whom she had not seen for quite a while and they had decided to go out and catch up with things. For some strange reason they had caught a cab to the old biker joint where

Rooster used to take her. She could remember most of the evening, the smoky room, the dance floor, the loud heavy metal anthems blasting out of the jukebox and a few bikers who had been chatting them up. Whilst looking in the mirror she looked down at the rose tattoo on her arm. Entwined around its stem was the word 'Rooster'. 'I've got to get rid of that one day,' she thought.

She switched on the coffee machine, gulped down another glass of water and picked up her clothes from the floor – it had been some years since she had got as drunk as she had the previous night. 'Why are things so complicated?' she thought as she opened her wardrobe trying to find something normal to put on that was intermingled with all the biker gear she had bought during the period she had been dating Rooster. Tired, she took off the rest of her clothes and put on her dressing gown. The coffee was like nectar to her parched mouth. By now she was waking up and contemplating the day ahead, still wondering what had happened the previous night and why she had allowed herself to drink so much. She then recalled that the last time this had happened was when she and Rooster had split. As the last mouthful of coffee slid refreshingly down her throat, she got up, went back into the bathroom and turned on the shower.

Mike sat in one of the rowing boats on the river that he had untied from the jetty and had decided to borrow for the afternoon. He was drawing a map in his notebook. It detailed the course that the river took on its route through Ashbury Falls and all sorts of other details that he felt were important. He had been there for well over two hours and had seen only two or three other people walking along the bank as he studiously examined his surroundings.

Carla had not turned up at the Pied Piper as they had arranged, so he had had to engage Jenna in conversation over coffee and muffins. The hardware store had been closed when he had driven past so he guessed that Carla must have been spending the day with Jack. He put his book in the inside pocket of his jacket and continued rowing downstream until he reached a footbridge that spanned the river some twenty foot above the bank. He steered the boat towards the bank as he sailed under the bridge and moored it about a hundred yards away by tying it to a post that jutted out of the water.

The bridge was of sturdy roped suspension and wood plank design. It swayed slightly as Mike, looking up, observed a man crossing it with his dog until the afternoon sun blinded him. It looked a little unsafe if someone were to get too near the edge as there were only two guide ropes on either side. He opened a can of Coke and then his notebook. The bridge was not far from the sloped access that led out onto Eastfeldt so he imagined that was where it could be accessed. As he looked across the flowing water he noticed the near stillness of the surface as it seemed to glide peacefully along in the tranquillity of the afternoon, but he knew that the current was deceptively strong. His arms were beginning to ache a little from all the rowing he had been doing and he was beginning to feel tired. He had been out of shape lately and had not rowed a boat for some time. As he looked downstream from the bridge he noticed that the water became very turbulent as it negotiated its way around a series of boulders close to the opposite bank. One boulder was particularly large and he could see that the current was strong around the rock cluster. The air was still and a strange silence filled it, only the flutter of a flock of birds could be heard.

He decided that he would stay there a while to rest up before heading back to the jetty to pick up his car and drive to the central library. He wanted to look through the old newspapers and see if he could get any more information on Ronnie Jebson's death. He lay back in the boat and began to feel sleepy. Half an hour passed before he realised he had dozed off. He got out of the boat to untie it from the mooring post, but the knot had fastened too tightly so he knelt down and began to attempt to loosen it. It was no use. He took his pen out of his pocket and tried to drive it into the knot between the cords. If he could just loosen it slightly, he could then wriggle the cords until they eventually loosened.

He heard voices from above him and looked up. A couple came into view and began to walk over the bridge, talking together arm-in-arm but he couldn't see their faces because of the sun. Then the woman stopped, pulling her partner back.

'Mike, is that you?' said the woman.

'Hello?' he replied.

'Mike, it's Carla and Jack.'

'Hi.'

'It's a beautiful day isn't it,' called Jack trying to be polite.

'Yes, I picked a good time to get a boat out,' replied Mike. 'I was just going to head back into town but I'm having problems untying it.'

'Need a hand?' asked Jack.

'No, I think it's coming soon, thanks anyway. Enjoy your walk and don't forget the offer of dinner still stands.'

'Sure,' replied Jack in a neutral tone.

Jack continued across the bridge and then stopped just past the middle to rest his arms on the guide ropes as he admired the view upstream, leaving Carla looking down and conversing with Mike.

'Are you coming, Honey?' called Jack, his back still turned.

As Carla turned to catch up with him, Jack didn't notice her beginning to stagger on the bridge. On the bank Mike had his back to the river trying desperately to loosen the knot to free his boat. Suddenly Carla fell through the guide ropes of the bridge and plummeted into the river, letting out a loud yell before she entered the water with a force. Jack spun around and saw that Carla was gone. Mike turned to see Carla splashing desperately in the water.

'HELP ME!' she cried.

'My God, Mike, she can't swim!' shouted Jack from the bridge.

Mike dived into the water, but the current had already taken Carla some distance away from him. He swam as fast as his aching arms would allow him.

Carla disappeared momentarily under the water before resurfacing. She splashed and waved her arms violently around her.

'HELP ME!'

Mike was getting nearer. He stopped, briefly remembering that he had seen some rope and a life buoy attached to the pillar of the bridge.

'Jack, get down to the bank and grab the rope and life buoy... QUICKLY!'

Jack felt a terrifying panic overcome him and froze momentarily before realising that his wife was going to drown. He rushed to the other end of the bridge and clambered over the edge, tumbling down the muddy slopes to the bank of the river, almost colliding with one of the trees that covered it.

'Over there!' cried Mike pointing to the equipment and continued with all his might to reach Carla. He then noticed to his horror that she was heading straight for the boulders. Carla went under again, this time for longer. Only her waving arms could be seen above the surface of the water. Then she re-emerged gasping for breath.

'Hurry, Jack!' cried Mike, desperate for him to provide a lifeline. Jack's hands had gone limp with the shock and he was having problems getting the rope and life buoy off the hooks.

Mike realised that if he swam to her they would both be plunged onto the rocks. Then he noticed the large boulder rock that was jutting out of the river and headed straight for it. Jack came running along the bank.

'What are you doing, Mike, you can't leave her!'

'It's OK, I know what I'm doing, trust me!'

Mike was in danger of missing the boulder himself. As he got to it, his hand missed an abutment that he wanted to grasp and he was flung around its edge towards the rock cluster. Just in time, he managed to grab hold of another part of it and pull himself up, grazing his knee badly as a jagged edge tore through his jeans. Carla was fast approaching.

'Throw me the rope, Jack, NOW!'

Jack's aim was bad; it missed, so Mike had to act quickly. He dug both his feet into a recess on the other side of the boulder and hung himself over with just enough room to plunge his arms into the water on the other side. As Carla floated by she stretched out her arms, her face frozen in terror. As she was about to hit the rocks, Mike swung his right arm around the top of the boulder and grabbed her forearm. He felt her hand lock against his arm and then a jolting of his body as the force of the turbulent water pulling Carla along pulled him over the boulder. It was down to Jack now.

'Jack, throw me the rope, I can't hold her for long!'

Jack tried again and missed. He desperately pulled the rope back into the bank to try again. This time he threw it with such force that it landed on Mike's back. With his left hand Mike began to pull the rope around him and then tried to arch his stomach to pull the rope between his body and the rock.

'I can't hold on any longer!' cried Carla.

'Hold on, Carla, please hold on; you've got to hold on!' pleaded Jack from the bank. He knew there was nothing he could do now except hope that Mike could tighten the rope around himself and that he would have the strength to pull them both to the bank. Mike had to arch his body again to slot the rope underneath it. It was still not around him so he had to do it again, his body reeling with pain as he fought against the force of the current. As he finally tucked the rope under him, he felt Carla's grip loosen.

'Hold on, Carla, don't let go, just a little longer!'

Pulling the rope around his side he fastened the clamp at the end around the rope and called to Jack to pull it tight.

'Jack, dig your feet in and pull hard when I say.'

Jack acknowledged and Mike grabbed the collar of Carla's coat and was about to pull her onto the boulder when she let go and almost collided with the rocks. He grabbed her arm again in a split second and held it tightly almost crushing it. With a final surge of energy he pulled her up onto the boulder so that only her hips were in the water, and then dragged her over him until she was out of danger. She fainted. Turning himself slowly around and nearly slipping off the boulder he laid Carla on top of him with her back on his chest and his arms firmly around her.

'Now, Jack, pull, pull hard!' he shouted as he jumped into the water on the other side of the boulder.

Jack pulled vigorously until Mike and Carla were safely on the bank and then Mike laid Carla out flat and scrambled out of the water. He pulled her onto the grass and looked for her vital signs. She was still breathing but unconscious. Jack slumped to the ground trembling and held Carla tightly.

'She's OK, safe now,' said Mike as he got to his feet. Jack remained on the muddy bank and began to sob gently with Carla still in his arms.

11

In the far corner of Pine Drive Jack Dempster stood gazing out of his window into the garden trying to reason out the events that had taken place that afternoon whilst Carla lay upstairs in bed still traumatised. Mike sat at the kitchen table in one of Jack's dressing robes with a hot drink and nursing his cuts and grazes.

'Do you need something stronger, Mike?'

'Only if you do,' he replied.

Jack reached into the cabinet and pulled out a bottle of scotch whiskey and two glasses. Sitting at the table across from Mike, he poured out two large measures and gave one to him.

'To you, Mike,' he said.

'No, to both of us,' Mike replied.

'You saved her life; I'm in your debt. I only turned my back for a moment, Mike, what happened?'

'I didn't see either.'

'Maybe she leant on the guide rope and misjudged it somehow,' Jack continued.

'Maybe she had one of her blackouts,' said Mike.

'How do you know about those?'

'Jenna told me.'

'Did she tell you how bad they've been?'

'No, just that she gets them frequently.'

'She's had them for the last twenty years, Mike. No doctor can put a finger on it. She desperately wanted a second child too; we've only got Joaney you see. No therapist can help her with that. I just don't know what to do.'

'I'd like to help you, Jack.'

'I know you would, Mike, but there's nothing you or anyone can do.'

'No, Jack, I'd like to help you.'

'What do you mean?'

'I can't tell you right now, but I want you to trust me.'

'OK,' replied Jack sceptically.

'Let's just say I've come across this condition before.'

'With Reuben Stein?' asked Jack.

'Among others.'

'It's funny,' said Jack gulping his whiskey, 'Reuben and Carla are about the same age and grew up in this town. The more I think about it there must be some link but I've never really had any idea what it could be. Do you know something Mike?'

'It's like I said Jack, I've seen this condition before and I have a friend in the medical profession who may be able to shed some light.'

'What are you proposing?'

'I need to contact him, and then we'll talk again.'

'Anything would help me right now, but what makes you think he could help?'

'He's got experience in these types of disorders. I'm not promising anything, but it's worth a try.'

'Your clothes may be dry now, I'll take a look,' said Jack as he went into the utility room. 'No, still a little damp.'

'Don't worry, I'll manage. I need to get back to the hotel anyway so I'll take a shower and change when I get back.'

'OK,' said Jack bringing in his clothes.

'I'll give you a lift back to your car. Just let me check on Carla.'

Jack went upstairs and entered the bedroom. Carla was asleep and breathing normally so he adjusted the blankets around her so that she would be a little warmer and then stood there, looking at her.

'I nearly lost you today,' he whispered and then leant over and kissed her.

Jack drove his four-by-four into the parking lot by the walkway to the river where Mike had left his car.

'Thanks for the ride,' said Mike as he climbed out and shut the door.

Jack drove off leaving him alone in the dark trying to find his notebook. It was still in his damp jacket pocket. He pulled it out and felt the ruffled pages, wondering if his notes were still readable and leaned back against the side of his car, brushing his fingers through his damp knotted hair. He decided to head down the walkway and stopped towards the bottom looking down onto the jetty. The moon's reflection lit up the river turning it a haunting silvery colour. There were small lights on some of the posts of the walkway to allow visitors at night to find their way down. Even the jetty was lit up. As he turned to go back, the lights went out and he assumed that they must have been on a timer.

Mike pulled into the Farrington Hotel and parked his car around the back. As he headed for the front of the building he noticed Jamie sat out on the porch swinging slowly on a wooden chair and gazing out onto the dark of the night. She looked around at him in surprise as he called to her and then she noticed he was wet, his jeans were torn and his hair a mess.

'Mike, what on earth happened to you?'

'Carla Dempster.'

'What about her?' replied Jamie getting up from the swing.

'She nearly drowned, I saved her.'

'What happened?'

'She was walking with her husband Jack across the footbridge near Eastfeldt and fell over the side.'

'Is she OK?'

'Asleep when I left the Dempsters.'

'You'd better let me take a look at those cuts.'

'I'm fine. I need to take a shower and then I have to go out again. I'll see you tomorrow.'

'Where are you going?'

'I need to talk to someone.'

'OK,' she said suspiciously.

'Maybe we could go out some place tomorrow night?' he asked her.

'Sure,' she replied.

There was a knock at the door of 1154 Cambridge Road. Hank wondered who it could be at this ungodly hour. It was around ten-thirty. To Hank, anyone calling after 9 pm was an intrusion but he opened the front door anyway.

'Oh it's you! I knew you'd be back, you'd better come in.'

Mike entered with a six-pack of ice cold Budweiser, sat down, opened one and handed it to Hank.

'Thanks, son. You still up at the Farrington place?'

'Yes, Hank.'

'How's that Jamie?'

'She's good... I mean she's fine.'

Hank grinned.

'It's nothing like that, Hank.'

'You think you can fool me?'

'I'm not trying to fool anyone, Hank.'

'So you've come back to find out about my son haven't you?'

'I thought you might have had a change of mind, Hank, and anyway you wouldn't have let me in if you didn't want to talk would you?'

'Who are you, Mike?'

'Someone who can help you, Hank.'

'Why would you want to do that?'

'Because since I've been in town I've found out a few things which don't seem to add up and I need some help from you.'

'You are a reporter aren't you?'

'No, Hank, I'm a writer, but my research has gone a little too deep,' he replied opening his briefcase. He handed a book to Hank.

'*Scenes of Yesterday*, Michael Fabien,' said Hank reading the cover. He turned it over to look at the back and then flicked through the pages. On the inside cover was a photograph of Mike.

'I wrote that about two years ago.'

'Not much of a reader myself,' said Hank handing the book back to Mike. 'So you're a writer. That still doesn't explain why you want to know about my son.'

Mike took a drink of his beer.

'If I could help you find out what happened to Ronnie, would you talk to me?'

Hank looked Mike straight in the eye.

'I would do anything to find out what happened to my son. But can I trust you?'

'Trust is a funny thing, Hank. I'm offering you something you've wanted for the last twenty years. How badly do you want it, Hank?'

'Badly,' said Hank wiping beer away from his face.

'Then really you have no choice than to trust me.'

Hank took another large gulp of his beer and threw the empty can into the trash bin.

'I'll have another one of those,' he said. 'It looks like you've got me on the ropes. OK where do we start?'

'Before the accident, had Ronnie changed in any way?'

'Changed?'

'Personality changes, emotional problems, that sort of thing.'

'No, he was his usual happy self as far as I remember, well all kids get attitudes sometimes don't they?'

'Was he sick, did he have a medical condition at the time?'

'No he was just fine.'

'What do you recall from the day of the accident?'

'Well it was a Saturday. He said goodbye to us at about 11 am and said he was going into town to meet his friend Reuben Stein. He came into my workshop, I remember him saying he wouldn't be home for dinner. I was working that day to get a table finished for someone. I used to make furniture for a living. That was the last time I saw him.'

'Why, Hank? Didn't you have to identify the body?'

'There was no body to identify.'

'Then how did you know that he had drowned?'

'Two reasons. Firstly Reuben told us that they had been down by the river just before it was getting dark. He said that he and Ronnie had had some sort of argument and that he had left him down on the jetty. Nobody saw what happened. The police were asking Reuben a lot of questions after the accident. Anyway they didn't take it any further. Reuben insisted that he had passed some other guy on the walkway back up to the parking lot, but they never found him, if he ever really existed.'

'What was the second reason?'

'They never found the body until two weeks later, way downstream out of town they said. Told us that Ronnie's dental records matched that of the body. But we never got to see it. Rosa wouldn't have wanted to, but I wanted to see him, I wanted to see my son.'

'Hank, has there always been a sloped access to the river from Eastfeldt?'

'Yes why?'

'No reason, I just noticed it when I was down on the river today. I took a rowing boat out to pass the time.'

'I wanted to find out more, I wanted to know what had happened, but it was like the police wanted to close the case as soon as possible. Not long after, a stream of reporters came flooding into town trying to talk to me. I turned them away, Rosa and I were too distressed to talk to them and then it got me thinking. Why all the interest? There's something else too, we never got to see the body before he was cremated.'

'Why?'

'They wouldn't let us.'

'They wouldn't let you?'

'No. We protested, my God we protested, it was then I knew that something was wrong about all this. Every time I went to the police, and I knew the sheriff then, he would be very uncooperative. I remember calling around his home one night pleading with him as a friend to tell me what he knew. I remember his words to this day. He warned me to let it go and stop asking questions. He looked worried himself like there was something he couldn't tell me. What's this all about, son?'

'I don't know, Hank. Look it's getting late, I'll put the rest of these beers in the refrigerator. 'Is there anything else you can remember, Hank, anything unusual?'

'No, son, it's all a big mystery.'

'Well if you think of anything, even if you don't think it's that important you call me immediately OK? I don't care if it's in the early hours.'

Mike handed Hank a card that he had picked up from the hotel reception.

'OK, son.'

'Thanks for your time, Hank, we'll talk again I'm sure,' said Mike walking to the front door.

'I want to know what happened to him, Mike.'

Mike noticed a sorrowful look on Hank's face; something he had not seen before, as though a sense of hopelessness that had filled Hank's soul for the past twenty years had been uncovered.

'There's always hope, Hank, remember that. I'll let myself out.'

Hank watched from his porch as Mike walked out into the cold night air towards his car. All that Hank had told him had confirmed his own suspicions; a cover-up, but why? He turned around and waved back at Hank before getting into his car. He sat there for a moment before starting the engine, and then drove back towards town.

12

Stella was doing an afternoon shift at the hotel the next day. She wasn't that busy and was trying to find something to do to assist Jamie. As it turned out she had missed the coach party that had arrived that morning. Jamie had dealt with everything. The next three days were going to be busy and catering for a party that was on a tour of New England was no easy task. She was relieved when the bell on the front desk rang and as she emerged from the office Carla was stood waiting.

'May I help you?' she asked.

'Yes, I've come to see Mike Fabien, I believe he is staying here.'

'May I take your name?' asked Stella as she picked up the internal phone.

'I'm a friend,' replied Carla emphatically.

'I see,' said Stella, 'very well.'

She dialled Mike's room and waited for a reply that was long in coming. When it did she informed Mike of his visitor and he told her he would be down shortly.

'Mr Fabien's on his way, have a seat,' said Stella pointing to the sofa over the other side of reception.

'What room is he in please?' asked Carla impatiently.

'Well, it's No. 3 at the front of the…'

Carla rushed up the stairs before Stella could finish. She scouted around the landing trying to find the door and eventually found it, discovering that it was the first room she had passed. As she was about to knock on the door, Mike opened it.

'Carla, I thought it might be you,' he said.

'May I come in?'

'Please. How are you?' he asked closing the door.

'I'm fine now, my arms ache a lot and my chest is a little sore, but I'm fine. I had to see you, to thank you for saving my life.'

'I'm very glad you're still with us, Carla.'

'No I really mean it, Mike, if you hadn't been there, I would have drowned in that river.'

'You can't say that, Carla, Jack would have saved you.'

'No he wouldn't have, Mike. He would have tried and given it his all, but he wouldn't have saved me.'

'You don't mean that.'

'No, Mike, I'm only alive today because you were there yesterday. It seems that your coming to Ashbury Falls is like... well I can't explain it.'

'Then don't try to,' said Mike.

'They say when you save someone's life you become responsible for it,' said Carla.

'And they also say that everyone walks their own path,' added Mike.

'Yes, but those roads cross sometimes don't they, Mike?'

'How's Jack taking it?'

'He's upset, but he's been comforting.'

'What happened on the bridge, Carla?'

'I got dizzy, I think, it's difficult to remember.'

'Were you OK driving over here?'

'Yes.'

'Do you want some coffee?' he asked.

'Mike, please hold me.'

'Is that a good idea, Carla?'

'Right now, yes.'

'Are you OK now?' asked Mike holding her.

'Yes, thank you.'

'Look I've got a bottle of Jack Daniels in the cupboard, would you like some?' he asked after a few moments.

'Yes please.'

Mike let go of Carla and poured them both a large glass.

'That'll make you feel better,' he said.

Carla took a large gulp.

'How long will you be staying here, Mike?'

'I'm not sure, I told Jamie a few weeks, but I may stay for longer.'

'How's the research going?'

'Fine.'

'Mike, I want to see you again.'

'About the book?'

'No, I want to see *you* again. I feel something, Mike.'

'Are you really sure about your feelings right now, you know you've just been through a very traumatic experience.'

'I felt this way before the accident.'

'Well, Carla, what can I say?'

'How you really feel, Mike.'

'Carla, I'm here to do research for a book and I'll be gone soon. You're married to a man who clearly loves you and is trying desperately to get through what must be very difficult times, and I don't want to get involved, well not in that way anyway. You're an attractive woman and a good person, Carla, but get rid of any feelings you have for me.'

'I'm sorry, Mike, I've made a fool of myself.'

'No you haven't and I'm very flattered.'

'I'd better go now as Jack will be worried,' she said as she picked up her bag.

She gave him a tender kiss on the lips and headed for the door.

'See you, Carla, I appreciate you coming over.'

'Bye for now,' said Carla as she left the room. Mike closed the door and drew a deep breath.

'What have I done?' he thought to himself.

The town hall was situated directly opposite Reuben Stein's office, the other side of the park. He could just see it from his office window and noticed that a large crowd was walking towards it. It must be a public meeting he thought and paid no further attention to what was going on in the square.

He was working late as usual, trying to catch up on all the things he had neglected due to the problems with the Logan deal. Reuben had been obsessed with it for weeks now but suddenly realised that he would lose everything if he didn't keep the other areas of his business in check. Rita had not called and he had finally realised that she was not coming back. He would have to hire a replacement soon or the business would suffer. But at the back of his mind eating him up inside was another crisis; Jamie Farrington had rejected him again and she would be sorry for that – very sorry.

The town hall began to fill up with people from all cross-sections of the community. There were storekeepers, the local minister, real estate agents, construction workers, families and a group of lawyers sat at the front to name but a few. There were even a few children sat there with their parents, wondering why they had been dragged there when it was TV time.

'This concerns you too,' said one woman to her bored and frowning son. 'Listen and learn,' said another to his daughter.

Towards the back sat Ritchie Templeman. He had never been to a public meeting before, but the subject interested him. He looked at his watch. It was 19.45 and suddenly the sound of chatter gently died down as the speaker with two grey-suited men walked onto the stage. They sat either side of him as he stood at the rostrum. The speaker was Charles Moreland; a stocky man in his fifties, his hair grey as stone. Many had hoped that he would run for Mayor but he had stated publicly that he was only interested in politics when something dear to him was threatened and this he claimed, was why he had called a series of meetings of which this was the third.

'Ladies and Gentlemen, I would like to thank you for taking the trouble to be here this evening. We are here because we realise that even in this fast moving world where money and self-gratification seems to be the most important things, respect for sacredness and the beauty of this great country of ours must never be forgotten.'

There was a loud applause that gradually faded as Moreland signalled for it to be abated.

'Chakowah Park will not be turned into a housing development. Those of our Indian brethren that have been laid to rest will not be disturbed from their peace, neither will one of New England's most beautiful recreation areas be ruined just because a minority of greedy men want to make a fast buck.'

Outside in the square Reuben could hear the applause coming from the hall as he made his way across to his car. It was then that he noticed a large Lincoln with a chauffeur in the front reading a book. He recognised the car and immediately ran towards the hall. Inside Moreland continued his speech to the adoration of those present and to Ritchie Templeman who remembered how he had spent many days as a child and young teenager in Chakowah Park. This was a big issue and meant something.

'So I can say with great confidence that when this case goes to court next month, we have very strong legal grounds for winning. All avenues have been explored and our case is watertight.'

'DEAD MEN'S BONES!' shouted an angry Reuben as he burst into the hall.

Moreland looked down from the rostrum in shock. He had not expected anyone to turn up who supported the Logan deal. 'You want to stop a multi-million dollar deal because of dead men's bones?'

'Your case is weak, your motives self-orientated. You and the rest of the investors in this Logan deal will have to learn a painful lesson. Drop the case, Mr Stein, or it will cost you dearly.'

'Then we'll take you down with us, Moreland!' he shouted and began to lunge forward towards the platform.

Ritchie sprang out of his seat, ran forward to the platform and grabbed hold of Reuben Stein's arms to hold him back.

'GET YOUR HANDS OFF OF ME... NOW!!! cried Reuben. Ritchie held his grip and began to pull Reuben back. There was a struggle. 'GET OFF ME, GET THIS MAN OFF ME!!'

'Get him out of here, now,' said Moreland from the platform. 'You're finished, Stein, you and the rest of those greedy investors!!'

The applause was deafening for Reuben as he continued to struggle with Ritchie. By now two other men had joined him and were dragging him out of the hall.

'We'll get you for this, Moreland!'

The doors flung open as the three men dragged Reuben out of the hall. Once in the foyer, Reuben calmed down and they let go of him.

'Your face, I won't forget it,' he told Ritchie.

Reuben's evil stare made Ritchie uncomfortable. He glared at him from over his shoulder as he hurriedly descended the steps to the sidewalk. He then paced off tidying his jacket and adjusting his tie as he went.

Ritchie nervously went back into the hall to hear the remainder of the meeting. As Moreland ended his speech Ritchie applauded with all his heart, very appreciative of this noble cause of which he in some small way felt a part. As the hall emptied, Moreland came down off the platform and began conversing with the lawyers and a few of the more prominent members of the Ashbury Falls community. Ritchie stayed in the hall in view of him, wanting to shake Moreland's hand but felt somewhat reticent and out of place. He nervously looked around the hall trying to appear disinterested in Moreland and the lawyers but then he caught Moreland's eye.

'Excuse me for a moment,' said Moreland.

Ritchie saw this as his cue to approach Moreland.

'Great speech,' said Ritchie with his hand outstretched.

'Thanks, and thank you for restraining that protestor,' said Moreland.

'No problem,' replied Ritchie.

'And you are?' asked Moreland in a superior tone.

'Templeman, Richard Templeman.'

'Well thanks again,' said Moreland and turned back to his colleagues.

Ritchie now feeling more than awkward knew it was time to leave. As he walked down the steps of the town hall, Reuben drove past. Their eyes met again and Reuben gave him another glare before accelerating down the street and out of view.

13

Mike was pondering over what to wear. He hadn't packed a comprehensive set of clothes for the trip so the contents of his suitcase were mainly casual, neither had he anticipated going out on any dates. At least he was shaven, his hair was set right and he smelled good. He was nervous; he wasn't used to doing this kind of thing. It was now 6.45 pm and he had originally arranged to meet Jamie in reception at about 7.30, but Stella had given him an envelope late in the afternoon that had been left for him in the pigeonholes. At first he thought Carla had left it, but when he opened it, he discovered that it was a note from Jamie. He was to get a cab to a location called Rendezvous 9 at 7.15. The cab company would know the place and he was not to be late. He decided on the other pair of Levi's, the black cap-sleeve T-shirt and the black sports jacket.

When Starlight Cabs finally arrived at 7.40 Mike was on edge. He would be late now and made his feelings known to the driver.

'Sorry for the delay, sir,' said the attractive blonde in the front as the cab drove off. 'So it's Rendezvous 9 then.'

'Yes, wherever that is,' said Mike.

'It's not a place we usually take customers, sir.'

'Oh and why is that... sorry I didn't catch your name.'

'Cindy. Sit back and enjoy the ride.'

'Thanks, I will.'

Mike had spent the last few days exploring Ashbury Falls and was becoming familiar with the geography of the area, but he had absolutely no idea where Cindy was taking him. Now he was becoming suspicious.

'So does Starlight cabs specialise in mystery tours then?' he asked.

'We take people anywhere they want to go, sir.'

The journey took around twenty minutes. Eventually the cab pulled up by a phone box in the middle of a street with a string of bars along it.

'Well, sir, here we are,' said Cindy.

Mike gave her twenty dollars and after the cab had driven off he looked over to the other side of the street looking for a sign for Rendezvous 9. The phone rang in the call box. He ignored it at first but when it continued to ring for nearly a minute longer he knew that it must be for him and now he would have to play along with Jamie's little game. He got into the call box and picked up the phone.

'So you made it then,' said a voice, but it wasn't Jamie's.

'I did, whoever you are.'

'Take a look back across the street,' said the voice.

'OK,' he said and turned around.

'What do you see?'

'A bar.'

'What's it called?'

'Rendezvous 9,' he said.

'Very good, Mr Fabien, so you'd better hurry and get over here. Find table 17.'

'May I ask who this is?'

'Table 17 or you'll never see the girl again!'

The phone went dead. It must have been Jamie disguising her voice. He was intrigued.

Mike got out and walked over to Rendezvous 9. It was an old house that had been turned into a bar with blue neon signs in the window. He entered the bar. It was busy but not too crowded, inviting and yet could be a little overwhelming for someone who just wanted a quiet drink. The jukebox could have been turned down a little and there was a dance floor over in the far corner. Mike searched for table 17 like a child on a treasure hunt. The tables were large, round and high up, as were the chairs. He caught site of what must have been table 17 and saw a dark-haired girl sitting facing the opposite direction. He hurried up to her.

'Jamie.'

The girl turned around. It wasn't her.

'Sorry, I thought you were someone else,' he said and then noticed the small round brass disc that told him this was table 17.

'Mike isn't it,' said the girl.

'OK, where's Jamie.'

'She'll be here. I'm Candy, sit down.'

'Candy! Well there's a surprise, I just met a Cindy not half an hour ago.'

'That's right, Mike, you did,' said Cindy as she appeared from behind him.

'OK so there's no Starlight cabs right?'

'With a name like that? No!' giggled Cindy.

'And what are your real names?'

'She's Heather,' said a voice from behind that he recognised. 'And your chauffeur this evening was Cindy.'

'You had me worried,' said Mike as he turned to Jamie.

'Here's the twenty back,' said Cindy.

'Keep it, and thanks for the ride. Get Heather a drink as well.'

'Time to go,' said Cindy to Heather. 'Enjoy yourselves!' she added as they left for the bar.

Jamie was dressed provocatively and no one needed to spell out to Mike where the evening would be heading. Her capped sleeve top revealed the small rose tattoo that she had told him about and her leather mini skirt had a silver studded belt around it.

'Heather suggested coming here as we used to hang out in this place a lot in our younger days. It was called Rusty's back then,' said Jamie.

'Has it changed much?'

'A little,' she replied.

Heather and Cindy waved to Jamie from the bar and then turned around to talk to the bartender. She tried to ignore them.

'Nice friends,' said Mike.

This was not going to be as easy. Howie's barn had just been dinner; this was a real date.

'Let's dance,' said Jamie.

'I'm not so good these days,' replied Mike.

Jamie got off her chair, caught hold of Mike's hand and led him to the dance floor. In Mike's eyes dance floors were for dancing not for conversation so she had made it easy for him. Losing herself in the rhythm she got closer to Mike as her body moved in a controlled and elegant motion. Mike responded and began to mirror her movements as though being hypnotised by a cobra. The faces and voices around them gradually became distant as they moved and stared into each other's eyes. Mike felt Jamie pull his arm towards her and rest his hands on her hips as her eyes were fixed on him with a penetrating stare. They had made first contact and Mike felt like easy prey. He had known about Jamie's feelings for him since the incident with Reuben Stein in the park. Without any resistance he put his arms around her and they danced as though they were one, with everything and everyone round them melting into a blur. They didn't know how long they had been dancing together before there was a tap on Mike's shoulder. It was Cindy.

'Look after her,' she said.

'Don't worry,' he replied before realising who it was. It felt like he had been woken from a dream just as you get to the best part.

'We're off,' said Heather. Jamie waved in acknowledgement.

'Shall we get a drink?' asked Mike.

'OK,' replied Jamie.

They headed back to table 17. Mike took off his jacket and placed it over the back of his chair. A waitress walked by and so he asked her for two scotches.

'You're a great dancer, Jamie.'

'You're not bad yourself.'

'It's been a while since I danced like that or with someone so beautiful.'

'Do you mean that, Mike?'

'Yes I do.'

Jamie said nothing.

'Anyway, Miss Farrington, where the hell are we?'

'That's for me to know and you to find out and you're not going to!'

They laughed.

'Just tell me that when they finally kick us out of here we're not walking.'

'We'll see,' she replied. 'How's the research going?'

'I don't want to talk about that now – I'm more interested in my current project.'

'I see,' she said smiling.

When they had finished drinking, the tempo of the music slowed.

'Shall we?' asked Mike taking Jamie's hand.

He walked her to the dance floor again and they put their arms around each other.

'Mike.'

'Don't talk,' he said as he put his finger on her lips. 'Treasure the moment.'

He held her close and they said nothing as they let the music envelope them and take them to another world.

By eleven, they had drunk several more whiskeys, danced for longer than they had done for years and had talked like they had always known each other.

'Let's get out of here, Jamie,' said Mike finally.

'OK,' she replied and slipped her jacket on as Mike left a tip on table 17 for the waitress.

They left the smoky atmosphere of Rendezvous 9 and walked out into the cool night air. He held her hand tightly as they walked down the street and out of sight of the bars. In the distance the road became a bridge and, as they approached it, they saw that it spanned a busy highway. They stopped on the bridge as the lights of the cars flashed past beneath them and the breeze flowed through Jamie's hair. Mike put his arms around her waist and brought her close to him. She put her arms around his neck, and then he kissed her tenderly as he held her tight.

Jamie could no longer stifle her feelings. She began to kiss Mike passionately and clung to his body. Mike responded letting down all the barriers he had tried to put up since he had first laid eyes on her upon his arrival at the hotel. After a couple of minutes they stopped and looked at each other.

'What's happening here, Mike?' she asked.

'I don't know, Jamie, but I know one thing...'

'What's that?' she asked.

'Right now I don't want to be anywhere else.'

'Neither do I, Mike.'

14

Mike rubbed the sleep from his eyes and sat up in bed as Jamie kissed him and handed him some coffee.

'I'm taking the day off,' she told him. 'I know a great spot up state; it will only take us a couple of hours to get there.'

'I'd like that,' he replied.

'Shall I fix us some breakfast? Then we can get going.'

Mike nodded and looked at the clock. It was approaching ten so he got up and went into the bathroom to put on his dressing gown.

'I'll be down as soon as I can,' he said and then he kissed her. When she had left he got into the shower. The jets of hot water massaged his face and woke him up. He would have stayed in there for quite some time had it not been for the sound of the phone ringing in his room. He quickly turned off the shower and wrapped himself in his dressing gown. Taking the towel he quickly rubbed it through his hair and walked over to the phone.

'Must be Jamie,' he thought as he picked up the phone. It was.

'Don't worry, I'm on my way.'

'Mike, it's Hank Jebson,' she said. 'He says it's urgent.'

'OK, put him on.'

'Hank, is everything OK?'

'Yes, son, listen. I've been doing some thinking since our conversation the other night. When you're as old as I am, your memory doesn't work as well as it used to. Anyway I got to thinking about what you said about whether there was anything strange about Ronnie before the accident.'

'Go on,' said Mike.

'Well, a few months before, he started to get these dizzy spells. Very strange because he never suffered from anything like that before. I remember him coming in one night and falling over the table. I asked him if he was drunk. I was angry, but he said he hadn't been drinking, and then it happened a few more times. You don't think that maybe he had a turn when he was down at the river do you, Mike?'

Silence hung in the air as Mike digested what Hank had just told him.

'Mike, are you still there?'

'Yes, Hank, thanks for the call… I'll be in touch.'

He immediately dried himself and got dressed. Then he dug out his suitcase and holdall from the wardrobe and began packing his clothes and belongings.

'Hi, come through to the apartment,' said Jamie as Mike hurriedly entered reception.

'Is this part of the original house?' he asked.

'No we used to live in the main building, but I had this built on after my parents died. I wanted my own place and it freed up some rooms which have more than paid for this.'

'What about the rooms around the back by the rear parking lot?'

'My parents had them built as separate accommodation for passers-through who needed a room for just the one night, well that was the idea anyway.'

'Jamie. I'm sorry to have to spoil the day, but I have to leave town this morning. Something's come up.'

'What is it, Mike?'

'Just business.'

'Well when will you be back?' she asked.

'I'll be gone for about four maybe five days. I'll be back. Then we'll spend the day together. I promise.'

'OK,' said Jamie despondently.

'I'll pay you what I owe you so far, plus extra to keep my room whilst I'm away.'

'You don't need to do that, Mike.'

'Yes I do.'

'You're not coming back are you?'

'Of course I am.'

'What did Hank say?' she asked, now suspicious.

'I will be back, I promise.'

'I'd like to believe that.'

'I'd better be going.'

Mike went out into the main hotel building and up the stairs to his room. He put his jacket on, took his car keys out of the ashtray and gathered his bags together.

He took a last glance around the room and was about to leave when he noticed that he had forgotten the most important thing.

'Laptop!'

He quickly unplugged it, closed it and put it into its case. After a couple of trips to the car he locked his room and went back to reception. Jamie was clearly both annoyed and perplexed.

'Call me?' she asked. He didn't reply and that disturbed her. 'Just go and then hurry back,' she added.

She kissed him as Stella walked in.

'Just saying goodbye to Mike,' she said, embarrassed. 'He's leaving town for a few days. Keep his room will you.'

'Here,' he said handing her a cheque for five hundred dollars. Now she was certain he was leaving for good.

Jamie came out of the office to see Mike's Nissan disappear down the sloped drive.

'I hope you know what you're doing,' said Stella.

'So do I,' she replied, realising that he had left no contact number.

15

Jack and Carla Dempster sat at their kitchen table just finishing lunch. Carla smiled appreciatively at Jack for the way he had cared for her the last couple of days. They had not spoken much about the accident as Carla had been trying to suppress the memory and carry on with her life as normal. Jack was reluctant to bring up the subject as he was feeling like he was treading on eggshells at the present time and he knew that Carla would bring it up in her own time if she wanted to. Carla's thoughts were on Mike Fabien.

'Have you seen Mike Fabien since the accident, Carla?' asked Jack.

Carla froze with guilt. He must have found out somehow, she thought to herself.

'Are you OK?'

'I'm fine,' she said calmly.

'Only it's just that I wondered if he had said anything to you. When you were asleep the night of the accident, we were talking.'

'No, why what did he say?' replied Carla relieved.

'He thinks you may have had a blackout when you fell off the bridge.'

'How does Mike know about this?' she asked putting on a pretence.

'He said that Jenna had told him.'

'Maybe she did.'

'Anyway the strange thing is, he told me he'd seen your condition before and that he might be able to help.'

'Help me?'

'Yes, he said he has some doctor friend who knows about these things, but I don't know much more than that because he wouldn't be drawn.'

'Well, let's see what happens then shall we,' said Carla sceptically.

'I'm sorry, I didn't mean to upset you,' said Jack.

'I don't want to talk about this at the moment,' she replied.

'OK.'

'I need to go into town, thanks for doing lunch, Jack.'

'You're welcome,' he replied sensing that something wasn't right.

Carla did not go into town. She drove straight to the Farrington Hotel to see Mike. Her car sped up the sloped drive and turned sharply into one of the parking spaces at the front of the hotel. Stella was at the desk as she had been the last time Carla had visited.

'I need to speak to Mike Fabien now,' she said trying to catch her breath.

'I'm sorry, but Mr Fabien checked out earlier.'

'He did what?'

'He checked out.'

'When?'

'Just an hour ago.'

'Can I help, Carla?' said Jamie coming out of the office.

'No, it doesn't matter now.'

'She wanted to see Mr Fabien,' said Stella.

'I gathered that,' said Jamie looking straight at Carla with a piercing glare.

'She was here the other day, Jamie.'

'I know, I saw her. Thank you, Stella, would you please excuse us?'

Stella looked puzzled but then disappeared into the dining room.

'Carla, I know you went up to his room, I heard you from the landing, what's this all about?'

'Why do you care, Jamie? He's just a guest, isn't he?'

Jamie said nothing. That was enough.

'Oh, now I understand,' said Carla.

'I know he saved your life the other day,' said Jamie in a less aggressive tone.

Carla turned and clenched her fists on the front desk.

'He told Jack he could help me and now he's gone!'

'Help you?'

'Yes, he knows someone who might help me regarding my blackouts.'

'He said that?'

'Yes!'

'Carla, you've had this problem for twenty years, you've seen umpteen doctors, how on earth can Mike help, he's just... a writer.'

'Yes, twenty years of hell, Jamie. Reuben Stein has had the same, and even poor Ronnie Jebson, but we'll never know how bad he might have got.'

'He would have been about your age if he'd lived wouldn't he, Carla?'

'Yes and Reuben, funny isn't it?' replied Carla angrily.

'What's Mike got to do with all of this?'

'You tell me, Jamie,' said Carla as she left.

Jamie was about to call out to Carla and inform her that Mike had planned to return, but held her tongue at the last. She wasn't even convinced of that herself. Then she remembered the way Mike had reacted when she had told him about Reuben, when they were in the café on the square in town.

'There's someone I need to talk to,' she thought to herself and went back into the office.

Hank Jebson sat in his armchair looking through his photograph albums. On the table beside him was a pile of black vinyl covered volumes with ornate gold coloured braiding around the outside. As he turned the pages of the one on his lap, pictures of him, Rosa and Ronnie on the beach at Cape Cod when Ronnie was five years old came alive. The memories of those happy years flashed through his mind like a locomotive train passing through a station without stopping.

'Better days,' he thought to himself.

The next volume contained photos of Ronnie as a teenager. One in particular brought back fond memories. It was a photograph of Ronnie when he was fourteen, leaning against Hank's pickup truck and holding a pitchfork in his hand. It was the day that he and Hank had spent helping his uncle, Hank's brother Tom to gather the hay at his farm. The next photo had all three of them with Ronnie in the middle. Hank and Tom had lost touch in recent years and the photographs reminded him that he ought to give Tom a call sometime.

He put the last photo album on the table and picked up the remote controls of his TV. He decided to watch a movie before turning in for the night. As he flicked through the channels, he came across an old western starring John Wayne but wasn't sure exactly which one. He had only been watching it two minutes when there was a knock at the door. He switched off the TV and got up out of his chair, wincing slightly as he straightened his stiffened back. A look of complete surprise came to his face as he opened the front door.

'Jamie? Jamie Farrington?'

'Hello, Hank, I'm sorry to intrude like this.'

'Not at all, my dear, I haven't seen you for a while. You don't visit the Pied Piper much these days.'

'No I don't, Hank.'

'Well come in, don't stand there in the dark.'

'Thanks.'

'Want some coffee?'

'No thanks.'

'Say, you remind me so much of your mother. How's the hotel?'

'Fine, business is good.'

'Sit down, my dear.'

Jamie sat on the sofa opposite Hank, looking a little uneasy.

'Well then, what can I do for you, Jamie?'

'You may think this a little strange, Hank, but I've got a guest staying at the hotel. His name is...'

'Mike Fabien?' asked Hank.

'Yes, that's right,' said Jamie, her eyes widening.

'The writer.'

'Yes, Hank, have you met him then?'

'Came to the Piper a few times, and he's been here, the last time was a couple of nights ago.'

'Do you mind if I ask you something, Hank?'

'No, my dear, fire away.'

'Have you been helping him with his research?'

'If that's what you want to call it, then yes.'

'What do you mean, Hank?'

'He says he's a writer, he even showed me one of his books, but he was asking a lot of unusual questions, probing you know.'

'Probing into what?'

'Ronnie's death.'

'That's awful, Hank!'

'No, my dear, I think he knows something about it. He said he could help me find out what really happened to my son as long as I could trust him.'

'Do you trust him, Hank?'

'Do *you* trust him, Jamie?'

'Why do you ask?'

'Because you wouldn't be here talking to me about him. Not unless you wanted to trust him too.'

'How can he help you, Hank? I mean he doesn't even know you, why does he want to help you?'

'He knows something; I believe he's sincere and I trust him. I don't know what this is all about, Jamie, but if he can help me get answers...'

'He left town today.'

'Is he coming back?'

'I don't know, Hank.'

'Do you want him to come back?'

Jamie didn't answer. She was confused and upset enough and didn't want to reveal her true feelings to anyone on the matter. Only Stella knew how she felt and that was enough.

'You do, don't you?' said Hank.

'I should be going now,' she said.

'Never be afraid to take chances, Jamie, life's too short.'

'I'll remember that, Hank. Did he mention anything about Carla Dempster?'

'No, why?'

'No reason.'

'Take care now, Jamie.'

'You too, Hank.'

'I hope he returns, for both our sakes.'

Jamie smiled at him and opened the front door.

'Hank, there's one more thing.'

'What is it?'

'When you rang him this morning...'

'Yes.'

'What was it all about?'

'I just told him about Ronnie before he died.'

'What about him, Hank?'

'Well he just kind of started having fainting fits or something, you know similar to Carla and Reuben for that matter. That's all I told him, Jamie. He knows something. He knows about the town, the other cases, I'm sure of it.'

'What other cases?'

'Get yourself home now, Jamie, OK.'

'Goodnight, Hank.'

'Goodnight, my dear.'

Hank closed the door as Jamie walked out into the darkness. She placed her hands into the pockets of her jacket and walked towards her car. The neighbourhood was quiet and still. The streetlights omitted a dimness that captured the air of loneliness she was beginning to feel. Then a single car drove slowly by, slower than necessary. It passed her parked car as she walked towards it and as it did so she noticed two men in it. The passenger looked at her for an inordinately long time before the car drove off. She shuddered. She quickly got into her car but didn't turn the engine. She waited until the other car had disappeared into the distance and then drove off taking a different route home than she would normally have taken. As she drove back to the hotel she began to notice headlights in her mirror. She ignored them at first but then began to realise that they had been behind her for longer than she had wanted. She turned off the road down a shortcut that she knew would come out near the road to the hotel. The car behind followed her. She was frightened now and stepped on the gas to get some distance between her and the car behind, but the headlights didn't get smaller in the mirror. She began to think the worst. It must be the two men she had seen drive by outside Hank's place. She put her foot to the floor to get more distance but then another set of lights appeared behind her and began flashing with the sound of a siren.

'Thank God,' she said and pulled over.

The other car drove past and disappeared into the darkness. She jumped when she heard a tapping at the window. She wound it down and a police officer shone a flashlight into the car.

'May I see your driver's licence ma'am?'

'Sure it's in here, thank God you arrived!'

She fumbled her hand around nervously in the glove box spilling things out onto the floor. She found her licence and handed it to the officer and he looked at it with his flashlight.

'Going way too fast there, Miss Farrington.'

'I'm sorry officer, but someone was following me, really.'

'Then you'd better get off home quickly and watch your speed, I'm giving you a caution this time.'

The police officer left and Jamie drove off shaking a little. She reached the end of the shortcut road and saw the lights of the police car in the distance behind her before turning onto one of the main roads that lead to the hotel – there was only a mile or so to go. Suddenly a car pulled out from the side of the road and began to follow her. She dared not put her foot down again so she calmly drove at normal speed watching her rear view mirror more than the road. The agony of her fear wrenched through her stomach as her whole body stiffened and her hands clutched the wheel as though she was trying to bend it. Eventually the hotel appeared in the distance and as the entrance approached she skidded into it, her wheels squealing as she turned up the sloped driveway and into the parking lot.

She raced out of the car and into the hotel reception. Grabbing the keys to room 3, she darted up the stairs and went into Mike's room that overlooked the front of the hotel. Leaving the light off, she raced to the window and hid behind the curtains, peering out so that no one would see her. She could see the road from the window. The car that had been following her was parked opposite the hotel entrance, its engine still running. She noticed a puff of cigarette smoke come from the passenger side. Whoever they were, they now knew where she lived. They waited there a while, presumably to see if she was coming out. After ten minutes they drove off and as they did so she noticed the man in the passenger seat put his arm out of the window to get rid of his cigarette. Luckily the hotel sign was bright enough for her to just see for a split second that it looked like he was wearing a suit jacket. She put her hands to her face and tried to comprehend what had just happened before slumping onto Mike's bed and lay there for the next thirty minutes alone in the darkness of his room.

16

At the end of a long secluded road a man sat in a dimly lit room at the back of an old abandoned house surrounded by woodland. The house must have been a good mile or so off the highway and was just habitable. Some of the windowpanes were smashed or cracked, damp had set in, and the white paintwork was starting to dry up and fall off the exterior walls.

It was around 11.30 in the evening. He decided to walk around the side of the house and began gazing into the distance to see if there was any sign of lights coming up the roadway. He checked his illuminated watch to see how late his visitor was and realised that fifty minutes had passed since the time he had arranged to meet with him. His own car was parked in the garage around the back, out of site. As he turned to go back into the bedarkened house he heard a cracking sound in the distance. Instantly he turned around and took his gun from inside his jacket. Someone was there but he couldn't see who and what worried him most was the fact that whoever it was could probably just see him against the backdrop of the dim light coming from the room at the rear of the house. He immediately put his back against the wall to move into the darkness. It was then that he noticed the outline of a fox moving briskly across the driveway and disappear into the trees to the side of the house. He breathed a sigh of relief and went back to the front of the house to see if anyone was coming. He noticed some light between the trees in the far distance, which gradually became brighter until he could see the headlights of a car driving up the road towards the house. As the car approached, the man's figure was silhouetted by the full beam of the headlights until it swerved past and drove around the side of the house, coming to an abrupt stop just before the derelict garage entrance. The man went back in the house as the light from the headlights of the car vanished, leaving the darkness of the night to re-envelop it. The door of the car opened and the driver got out, briefly viewing his surroundings as he did so. He looked back for a moment or two to ensure he had not been followed.

There was an eerie feeling about this house; it was in transition from being neglected to becoming derelict, almost although the occupants had left suddenly, determined never to return. It felt as though nobody should live there again. The driver of the car walked along a corridor to a door with a dim light behind it and opened it. As he entered the room, shadows danced across the ceiling, caused by a slight movement of the light which hung low from it, and which cast its shallow rays evenly across a square table in the middle. Sat on the opposite side of the table was a dark-haired man staring into a laptop.

'Nice place you've got here, Jennings.'

The man at the table looked up.

'Fabien, sit down and make yourself comfortable.'

'You call this comfortable!' he replied as he pulled up the other chair. 'How did you find this place?'

'You can find anything if you ask the right people.'

'Is it secure?'

'Of course.'

'No, what I mean is, will the ceiling still be above us by the time we conclude this meeting?'

'Very funny,' said Jennings with his eyes remaining fixed upon his laptop.

'You've dragged me all the way out here, so what have you got for me?'

'Some very interesting findings, Fabien.'

'Go on.'

'Well as you quite rightly suspected there is a link between your friend Carla, Reuben Stein and the late Ronnie Jebson. Your e-mails have been very descriptive you know.'

'That's the writer in me.'

'Moving on – they were all born within about six months of each other, they were all born in Ashbury Falls, New Hampshire and were all in the same high school grade.'

'And?'

'They all have something else in common too.'

'Which is?'

'Have you ever heard of the Sterling Medical Research Corporation?'

'I think so.'

'That means that you haven't then.'

'OK, what about Sterling?'

'I checked your friends' medical records, the real ones that is, and discovered that when they were all about the age of seventeen, they took part in some sort of medical research.'

'Carla never mentioned that to me.'

'That's because she didn't know that she had, none of them knew.'

'How is that possible? Did they slip a pill into her soda or something?'

'Really, Fabien, do you think that's how they used to work? Think, did Carla ever give you any information on any immunisation she may have had or can she trace her problems back to a visit to a doctor or something?'

'No she didn't.'

'Well I'm not saying that's how it happened, whatever 'it' was, but it had to be a cleverly concealed experiment of some kind and that I'm afraid, is the missing puzzle piece. We have a list of names of seventeen-year-old kids from all different states that were selected to take part in something called The Ascension Project back in the mid-seventies. There were others from Ashbury Falls too.'

'Where on earth did you manage to find out that sort of information?'

'Government funded and traced back to Sterling Medical Research, that's all we know.'

'You must have friends in high places.'

'And some who would rather this didn't go any further. I'm walking a fine line here, Fabien. You're lucky that I managed to get as much as I have. Questions were being asked, someone must have found out as further information was suddenly not forthcoming.'

'Are you saying that someone's onto you?'

'I don't think so. Look, Fabien, this is big and dirty and I don't think anyone would want this one uncovered.'

'I need more.'

'Well that's where you come in, my friend.'

'What do you mean?'

'That missing piece, you're on your own with that one.'

'OK, never mind about that for now, what about the dossiers you sent me, any leads?'

'Possibly, we think we may have identified your missing link.'

'Connor Newman?'

'Yes, he could be the one.'

'Keep working on it.'

'Are you sure this is a wise move?'

'Just keep on it, Jennings, this is very important.'

'If this is all tied in with your friends from Ashbury Falls, my retirement fund is on the line, you know what I'm saying? You owe me one, Fabien, a big one. Anyway, this missing piece of the puzzle lies with Sterling Medical Research. You've got to get information on The Ascension Project, find out what it was all about. That's the only way you can help your friends back in Ashbury Falls know the truth. It's down to you now.'

'Why me?'

'Because someone needs to break into Sterling and look at the computer records if they still have them, and download them. It's not going to be me, Fabien. I've done enough already to get my butt kicked until I retire!'

'You are kidding, right?'

'No, I'm deadly serious; it's the only way. This one's your baby, Fabien.'

Jennings handed Fabien a floppy disc.

'Load this on your laptop and read it carefully. It's a file on Sterling's computer and security system. You'll need it if you're going to stand any chance of getting those files. I've a question for you; why are you doing this?'

'I have my reasons.'

'I hope you know what you're doing. One more thing, what's the deal with the girl from the hotel.'

'Have you been following me, Jennings?'

'Watch your back, Fabien, you're on thin ice here, and I don't just mean with the girl.'

'Thanks for the advice, now I suggest we disappear. I'll e-mail you in due course and we'll meet again, somewhere else next time, hey Jennings?'

'We better leave separately.'

'OK leave ten minutes after me.'

'See you soon then, and try not to get caught will you.'

'I'll try not to,' Fabien called out.

'And if you do, don't mention my name, OK?' added Jennings.

17

The reception area of the Sterling Medical Research Corporation was a hive of activity. It was situated on the ground floor of a state-of-the-art building about ten miles out of Boston. It had been built back in 1989 when Sterling decided to move their research operations and head office out of the greater Boston area from a building which by then had outlived its purpose. The corporation had outgrown the fifties build complex which it had occupied since its beginning some forty-three years previous. The new building was of circular design in the centre, with four large rectangular wings jutting out from it. From the air it looked like someone had carved out a large 'X' in the middle of a field. Its grounds were superlatively landscaped to provide a serene setting for the many scientists, technicians and support staff who worked there. The reception area could be seen from all floors of the circular section and its central atrium reached all the way to the glass ceiling sixteen floors up. A number of the floors had extended balconies that acted as employee recreational areas.

Down in reception a group of visitors was beginning to increase in number as they entered the building via the rotating doors at the front. The three female receptionists were becoming flustered as they tried to keep tabs on individuals as they reported to the desk to obtain their temporary passes. The visit by hospital doctors from the surrounding states to view the facilities had clearly been over-subscribed and reception had not been given accurate numbers. They had been expecting a party of around twenty – now at least forty had arrived.

Amidst the crowd, one of the visiting doctors finally managed to get through to reception. He had light brown hair, a moustache and glasses. He was wearing a dark pin-stripped suite and carried a briefcase in his left hand. One of the receptionists turned to him and immediately her eyes became focused on the rather large scar that spread across his left cheek. Realising that he must have now noticed that she was looking at it, she quickly looked him in the eyes and smiled.

'Dr Meriden from Manchester, New Hampshire.'

'OK, sir, one moment please,' said the receptionist as she checked through the register.

'I'm sorry, Dr Meriden, but your name doesn't seem to be here.'

'Really, are you sure?'

'Yes, sir.'

'That's strange.'

'Let me check again... No it's not here.' She turned to her colleague. 'Susan, do you have a Dr Meriden from... from where did you say, sir?'

'Manchester, New Hampshire.'

Susan checked her list.

'No he's not down on my list. Can I help you, sir?' she continued as she spoke to another visitor.

'You don't appear to be registered,' said the first receptionist.

'That's not possible. My secretary faxed the forms through three days ago before she went on vacation.'

'Well we didn't get them, sir.'

'No, wait a moment... someone told me the fax machine was out of action. I assumed she must have used the one in Emergency. She's done it again; she forgot to sort it out before she left. I really need to talk to her about her organisational skills. She's not been with us long you see.'

Suddenly a voice called from behind the crowd.

'Ladies and gentlemen, can I please have your attention.' The noise abated a little. 'Good afternoon. It's my pleasure to welcome you all to Roxman House, the national headquarters of the Sterling Medical Research Corporation. The tours will start in about five minutes so can you please report to your respective tour guides and they will give you further instructions. Thank you.'

'Look I'm really sorry for the mix-up, but I've driven all the way down from Manchester and I've been dying to see these facilities for a long while now.'

The receptionist looked at her colleague. Visitors were still pouring in and things were getting out of hand. She nodded briefly before seeing to the next visitor.

'OK, sir, what's your full name?'

'Dr John Meriden,' he replied.

'OK, here's your pass, please report to Diane over there on the left.'

'Thank you... Jaclyn,' he replied looking at her lapel badge.

'You're welcome.'

'Jennings you're a genius,' said Mike in an undertone as he walked towards Diane his tour guide. She was standing near one of the elevators signalling for visitors to assemble.

There were four guides in total situated evenly around the circular reception area eagerly waiting to start their respective tours. By the time everyone had settled into their groups Mike observed that there were sixteen persons in his party, doctors ranging in age from their late twenties to early fifties.

'Hi, I'm Peter Larssen from Boston,' said one of the party reaching out to shake his hand. Mike acknowledged him reservedly.

'Great place isn't it?' said Larssen.

Mike nodded.

'Where are you from?' asked Larssen.

'Manchester,' replied Mike. Now he was feeling uncomfortable and was desperately hoping this guy would go away. Then a welcomed voice began to speak.

'OK everyone we're going to begin our tour.'

At that moment Peter Larssen, his short balding friend shuffled his way towards the front of the party, no doubt to ask lots of questions, thought Mike.

'OK first I'll take you through the evacuation procedures in case there is a need to invoke during the tour. On each floor you will see the fire escapes marked...'

At this Mike switched off and took a few moments to look up at the various floor levels and get a feel for the building. He visualised in his mind the schematics that Jennings had given him two nights ago and hoped that the tour would take him somewhere near to the records department which was situated in the rear east wing of the complex. He was on the wrong side at present. When the elevator arrived they filed in and Mike positioned himself at the back of the party to avoid being noticed. Once they had arrived on the third floor the party settled and Diane stood in front of them.

'Welcome to the Sterling Medical Research Corporation. Dr Robert Sterling and his partner Dr James Roxman founded the corporation in 1954. Both men were respected surgeons in the Boston medical community, indeed they became noted nationally within the medical profession for their papers on the immune system and their theories on such matters as influenza, measles and other such conditions. If we turn to our left we can see some of the labs where leading edge research is taking place right now as we speak into some of mankind's most perplexing conditions such as AIDS and some forms of cancer. Please follow me and we can take a look.'

Peter Larssen asked to look inside but to his disappointment Diane informed him that it would not be possible. They could however view activity through the observation window. The group moved over to look. Inside could be seen men and women in white coats, some in masks working on what looked like very hi-tech equipment and computer systems. Mike looked around him. There was no obvious place where he could slip away on this floor so he had to hope that the tour would take them somewhere near the rear of the east wing. Diane continued her discourse but he wasn't listening. He was looking up to the ninth floor across the far side of the circular atrium. Towards the end of that corridor was the computer records department.

'OK, we're going up to the ninth floor now to the computer department, so if you'd like to make your way back to the elevator...'

'Good,' thought Mike as he mingled back into the centre of the group, ready to get into the elevator. Peter Larssen stood next to him.

'Amazing what advances they're making in this field of medicine, don't you think?'

'Sure,' said Mike trying to ignore him.

'I mean, that SRX application software is something else isn't it, the amount of information the database can hold and process...'

Mike didn't need this. As before, Diane was the last to get into the lift. People were beginning to converse a little which to Mike's relief gave his friend Peter the chance to talk to someone else. The journey to the ninth floor was endless.

'This, everyone, is the computer complex. We process millions of instruction per seconds on the mainframe, which is situated in a secure room in the centre of the complex. So for all you computer enthusiasts, I'm going to swipe my security pass here and we can go in and look at some of the peripheral hardware.' This was his chance or so he thought. 'For security reasons I need to count you all in and out so no lagging behind anyone.'

The group entered into the complex that contained a mass of computer hardware surrounded by a walkway with railings. At intervals there were gaps presumably to allow the hardware engineers access to the systems.

'I'm going to introduce you to Jeff Cunningham our Ops manager who's going to tell you all about the equipment here... Jeff.'

There was no way out for Mike. He would have to grin and bear all the boring technical talk about mainframes, midrange servers and modems. As long as he kept a low profile it should be easy for him to slip away at some point after they got out.

He followed aimlessly as the group were taken around to view everything from network front-end processors to data storage devices.

'So any questions, folks?' asked Jeff Cunningham. There was silence. Not even Peter Larssen spoke up.

'OK, well thanks, Jeff, It seems our distinguished visitors have seen enough computer hardware for the day!' joked Diane. The group laughed quietly.

'OK, let's go see the commercial side of the business and then we can get some coffee and sit out on one of the balconies in the Atrium.'

The commercial block was over on the rear east wing, exactly where Mike needed to be to access the computer records. As the group made its way through the circular corridor that took them around the other side of the Atrium he looked through the large glass panels that allowed him to see the reception area nine floors below him. When they reached the other side Diane called the elevator. They had to go up to the twelfth floor to see the commercial block and Mike thought it would probably be best to see it through and then slip out when the others were taking refreshments. He quickly looked around him and noticed that the restrooms were situated in the same place on this floor as they were on the third. He deduced that they must be the same on the twelfth floor and fortunately for him they weren't too close to the rest area.

The commercial block was a pleasant contrast to the labs and the computer room. It was open planned and spanned all of the rear east wing on the twelfth floor with all sorts of business people working on their desktops, in offices or in conference rooms. Mike was surprisingly interested to see the marketing department and samples of literature that were produced for various institutions including the US State Department.

After about forty minutes Diane called the group out to the circular corridor.

'I hope you've enjoyed the tour so far. We're going to take a break now. The rest rooms are situated over there, and if you want coffee, water or soda you can get it on the balcony. We'll reconvene in thirty minutes... and please don't wander off!'

Mike slipped quietly out of view from the others and headed for the restrooms. Luckily some of the others went to the restrooms on the other side of the Atrium so nobody would see him going in and out of the ones on the east side. Inside he looked in the mirror for a moment and adjusted his tie before leaving. He cautiously opened the door and seeing nobody from his own party in the immediate vicinity, he quickly headed for the elevator. He pushed the button and waited. The elevator took an inordinately long time to come but when it finally arrived Mike stepped in and promptly closed the doors. As they did so and the elevator began its descent, Peter Larssen came around the corner and walked past. A few seconds' delay and Mike would have been spotted.

The doors opened on the ninth floor and he got out. He walked over to a floor plan to check that Jennings' schematics were correct. They were. Computer records department was down the far end of the corridor on the left. As he walked down it a few people passed but took no notice of him. He suddenly remembered that he was wearing his visitor's badge with his swipe card tucked behind it in the plastic wallet. He took it off and took out the visitor's card leaving the swipe card showing before clipping it back onto the breast pocket of his suit jacket. As he approached the entrance to computer records he noticed the door was card activated. His visitor's pass would not let him in and he didn't want to risk trying it in case it triggered a security alert. There was a drinking water fountain nearby and so he stood by it waiting for someone to come along hoping he could tailgate and gain access. A man came out of the room a few minutes later but he needed to go in with someone so that it looked more authentic. After a while a group of three people began walking towards the door, two men and a woman. Mike bent over the water fountain and took a drink as they came closer. One of them swiped the door and opened it. At that point he walked towards them.

'Hold the door please!' he called as they entered.

'OK,' said the man last to enter.

He was in. The room was full of desktop PCs and there were a number of people sat at them, their faces glued to the screens. Mike looked around and saw an office in the corner with a tall thin man wearing glasses standing looking into a filing cabinet. He walked over and knocked on the door.

'Hello, can I help you?' asked the man.

'Yes, I'm John Meriden from NAS auditors,' said Mike as he flashed the man his ID.

'Auditors? We aren't due an audit for another three months!' the man replied.

'That's correct, Mr Clarke,' said Mike looking at the man's ID badge.

'I don't follow,' said Clarke.

'The last audit revealed some loopholes in your security system for record access to certain confidential files.'

'I wasn't informed, and anyway we use Bennington and Garrett as our auditors. I've never heard of NAS.'

'OK, let me explain, B&G have contracted us to do an impromptu audit to see if anyone in your corporation has picked up on the issues that were raised at the last one. I doubt that you would have been informed of my visit, but regardless of that I'm here to check things out.'

Clarke looked troubled.

'I'd better check with security,' he said.

'That won't do any good, Mr Clarke. They won't have any records of me, well not as an auditor anyway. The whole point of the visit is to check on the fly as it were, with no pre-warning. B&G insisted. They wanted no one informed.'

'Yes, but this is highly irregular, Mr Meriden.'

'I understand your concerns perfectly, Mr Clarke, but I need to point out that B&G are expecting absolute co-operation. It would certainly go in Sterling's favour if I put that in my report even if I were to find things amiss.'

'That's all very well but...'

'Mr Clarke, have you worked here long?'

'Fifteen years now, why?'

'I expect you are a man with ambitions and aspirations?'

'Well yes, I'm hoping to become deputy security officer in a couple of years. I've worked hard to get where I am.'

'Then it would be a shame if Bob Clarke missed out on that opportunity by inadvertently contributing to the chief security officer of Sterling Medical Research being fired as a result of a detrimental security audit report from Bennington & Garrett.'

'Yes... well I, I guess you're right.'

'Good, then would you be kind enough to let me use one of these PCs and can you please log me on using one of your auditor userids.'

'OK sure, please use this one here; I'll just get you logged on first.'

Bob Clarke went to his filing cabinet and took out an envelope that contained a userid and password. He logged on to the system and handed the PC over to Mike.

'Thank you,' said Mike politely as he opened his briefcase and took out various dummy documents, diskettes and CDs.

There was an initial menu with many different options for record selection. He chose Research and then entered 'Ascension' in the search field. As he expected, there was nothing on file. He went back to the main menu, selected projects and tried again but nothing came up. It was something unobvious he thought. He looked again. There was an option called 'Archive' so he tried this but again without success. He noticed Bob Clarke was watching him from his office out of the corner of his eye so he turned and nodded. Clarke immediately looked away and uncomfortably carried on with his work.

There were no files marked 'confidential' as such so it had to be something only restricted personnel would know about, a codeword perhaps. He looked closely through the menu again and then pretended to reference one of his manuals and make some entries in his notebook in case Bob Clarke was still watching. His eyes focused back to the screen again as he scanned the options for a fifth time. Then he noticed an option called 'Sunset' and selected it. Immediately a screen appeared and the words 'restricted access' flashed up and the password box appeared. He reached for one of the CDs on the desk and inserted it in the desktop. It loaded a standalone program that brought up a small screen in the bottom right hand corner. It flashed up alphanumeric characters at random and at terrific speed in an eight-digit box. Suddenly the first character field became static with the letter 'P' and shortly after, the second field was likewise filled with an 'A'. Gradually the word 'PAINLESS' appeared and became inserted in the Sunset password box. Within seconds he was into a screen that prompted him for a search word. He quickly entered 'ascension', clicked to search and waited for a response. Thirty seconds later, a message appeared on the screen;

YOU HAVE REQUESTED ACCESS TO CONFIDENTIAL DATA.

CLICK 'CONTINUE' TO ACCESS, OR 'ABORT' TO TERMINATE.

He clicked on 'continue' and again had to wait for about fifteen seconds. Another password request came up and so he activated the password decoder software that he had just used. The word IMMUNISE appeared and was entered for the password. To his surprise it was rejected.

PASSCODE FAILURE, PLEASE RE-ENTER.

He reactivated the decoder in encryption mode and after running for well over a minute, a new screen appeared.

PROJECT ASCENSION – CLICK ENTER TO CONTINUE.

He clicked 'enter' and a menu appeared with fourteen options. He quickly loaded another CD and activated a program called 'ISPY'. The words 'SEARCH FOR ENTIRE SOURCE DATA?' appeared. He clicked 'yes'.

SOURCE DATA LOCATED ON
Q:/SUNSET/RESTRICTED/ENCRYPT/ASCENSION.PPX
INSERT DOWNLOAD MEDIA

He inserted another CD.

CONTINUE DOWNLOAD?

He entered 'yes'.

DOWNLOADING.

DOWNLOAD COMPLETE, A 2ND COPY REQUIRED?

He inserted another CD and repeated the process.

DOWNLOAD COMPLETE, A 3RD COPY REQUIRED?

'Better be sure,' he thought as he entered a floppy disk in the 'A:' drive.

DOWNLOAD COMPLETED, A 4TH COPY REQUIRED?

Mike entered 'no' and terminated the ISPY program. Trying to act in a composed manner he slowly put the CDs and the diskette into his briefcase and exited the applications on the desktop before tidying away his fake documents. He logged out and walked back over to Bob Clarke's office.

'OK, I'm done here, thank you, Mr Clarke,' he said.

'Did you find what you were looking for?' asked Clarke.

'It'll be in the report. I've logged out, goodbye now.'

Mike walked out of Clarke's office and remembered that he could not get out of computer records unless he could tailgate somebody on their way out. So as not to draw attention to this he pretended to inspect the area whilst waiting for someone to either leave or enter.

Eric Marshall sat at his desk in systems security. He was reading a book and facing away from his computer screen with his feet up on the side of his quadrant workstation. Nothing eventful had happened so far today as was the case most days, until now. Engrossed in the book he hadn't noticed the message that had begun to flash in red on his computer screen about five minutes earlier. When he put the book down to reach for his drink something on the screen finally caught his eye.

'What now?' he grumbled and looked closer.

ALERT: RESTRICTED FILE SEARCH IN PROGRESS

He typed in a command to determine what was being accessed. The system responded:

DATA ACCESS: PROJECT ASCENSION

He entered a further command to determine who it was. The system again responded:

ACCESS ID: EXAUDIT8: LOCATION: ER9F2

'That's an external auditor ID,' he said to himself. 'Why would an external auditor be accessing restricted information?'

He paused for a moment and then picked up the phone.

'Hi, Sam, this is Eric Marshall from systems security here. We've had an alert. Someone using an external auditor ID in computer records is accessing data for something called Project Ascension.'

Sam Pearson put down the phone.

'What's up?' asked a colleague.

'Someone's accessing Ascension. Nobody accesses those files especially not auditors and I wasn't informed of any being on site today. I'm calling security.'

He picked up the phone again.

'This is Sam Pearson, get your men up to computer records, ninth floor, now! We may have a severity one intruder alert. I'll meet you there.' He put the phone down and turned to his colleague. 'They should have destroyed those records years ago,' he said as he picked up his jacket.

'You're the chief security officer, why don't you tell them?' asked his colleague.

'I've been trying to tell them for years. Call computer records will you and tell them to secure the block – nobody leaves.'

Mike was becoming uncomfortable. Someone had to access the door soon. The phone rang in Bob Clarke's office. Mike looked over as Clarke picked it up and began speaking into it. Moments later Clarke looked over, shock written all over his face. Mike knew that something was wrong. Clarke came out of his office and was about to call over to him as the door opened and two women and a man walked in. He rushed for the door.

'Excuse me, ladies, I'm in a hurry,' he said as he brushed past them. As he did, he collided with the man, grabbing the lapel of his jacket as he did so and sped out into the corridor.

'Stop him! Stop that man!' shouted Clarke, but Mike was out.

He sprinted around the corner and out of view of computer records but slowed to a brisk walk when an entourage of security guards came into view. They looked at him briefly before heading around the corner to computer records. He heard Bob Clarke shouting hysterically in the background.

'Calm down, Clarke, who was he?' said Sam Pearson sharply.

'He left a moment ago, he was wearing glasses and... a scar, yes a scar on his face, quickly, you must have passed him.'

'The guy in the corridor, quickly get back and find him!'

Pearson dialled his mobile.

'Secure the elevators, we have an intruder. Clarke – a fuller description please.'

'Suit, um... light brown hair, carrying a briefcase um... moustache, moustache.'

'Guy with glasses and a scar on his face, light brown hair, suit and a moustache.'

Pearson turned to Clarke.

'So what's the story, Clarke?' asked Pearson angrily.

Clarke stood there looking hopelessly incompetent.

'He said he was an auditor hired by B&G...'

Mike heard the guards coming. He darted down the corridor and again slowed down, trying to act normally as he saw people coming out of the offices. He had to think quickly; the elevators would be useless and so would the emergency exit stairs. Then he saw a door labelled 'Janitor'. He entered, closed the door, and a moment later the security guards arrived in the section of corridor he was in.

Down in reception another group of security guards was assembled and stood at the main entrance. Sam Pearson was questioning the receptionists as the elevator doors opened at various locations and the tour guides came out followed by their respective parties.

'I'm sorry, folks, but the tour is over, there seems to be some kind of security issue. Can you please remain together so that we can account for everybody. Thank you for your co-operation and I do apologise for having to cut the tour short,' said Diane.

A disappointed Peter Larssen objected and informed Diane that he would make a formal complaint. She ignored him.

'I think we're missing someone,' he added. 'Well I haven't seen Dr Meriden from Manchester since we took coffee in the Atrium.'

'I had better report this,' said Diane. She walked over to the reception area where Sam Pearson was checking the signing-in book. 'Excuse me, Mr Pearson, but it appears that someone from my party is missing.'

'What's his name?' asked Pearson.

'Dr John Meriden from Manchester,' said a voice from behind them.

'And you are?' asked Pearson.

'Larssen, Peter Larssen.'

'OK, Mr Larssen, what can you tell us?'

'Well he wasn't very talkative when I tried to speak to him. He wouldn't tell me his name, but I managed to get a look at his visitor's pass during the tour.'

'Very helpful, Mr Larssen but what I would really like to know is what he looked like!'

'Oh yes, well he was tall, well by my standards anyway. He was wearing a suit and he had glasses.'

'Anything else you can tell us?'

'He had a moustache, and what a scar on his face, not a pretty...'

'That's him,' said Pearson turning to his security team.

'Listen carefully. The intruder is going under the name of Dr John Meriden. He joined one of the visitors' tours. This gentleman will give you a full description. He must be somewhere in rear east ninth floor. Find him, he has classified information that must not, I repeat must not leave this building.'

Pearson turned back to the receptionists and then checked the visitor's book.

'He's not on here, why did you let him in?'

'Well he said the fax confirming his booking never arrived.'

Pearson looked at them both in disbelief.

'This is a security nightmare! First I have receptionists letting in a visitor without verification, then he tailgates someone to get into computer records, and I have a security officer giving him access to the system on a plate. I'm not saying anymore in case I get fired, and I probably will after this. There will be a major review of security procedures after this, you mark my words!'

The Janitor's room was small and dark with a washbasin and a series of storage cupboards. The only natural light came through a small window up near the ceiling. Fabien dared not switch on the electric light for fear of attracting attention to the room. He had to act quickly, for he knew that the security guards would be searching all the rooms on the ninth floor. To his amazement there was a pair of janitor's overalls hung up on a peg and so he quickly took off his suit jacket and tie, and bundled them into a black bin liner that he found in one of the cupboards and put the overalls on. Next he took the CDs out of his briefcase, put them inside two other cases and then inserted them into the inside pockets of his overalls. Reaching into his trouser pocket, he pulled out the security pass he had acquired during his hurried exit from computer records and took it out of its plastic wallet. Opening the briefcase again, he took out a small passport photograph of himself, pulled off the transparent film on the back and stuck it over the top of the picture on the security pass.

'This will have to do,' he thought.

He had to hide the briefcase. Looking around he noticed an upper compartment to one of the cupboards and so he placed it inside, concealing it with rolls of toilet paper. He ruffled his hair a little and then took off the glasses and placed them on the basin. Next he began to pull off his moustache. He winced; the adhesive had been stronger than he had expected. Then he pummelled his face until he found the edge of the scar and pulled it off as well. He wrapped the glasses, the moustache and the scar in a small plastic bag and placed it at the bottom of a large trash bin. Finally he filled a bucket with water and disinfectant and grabbed a mop out of the broom cupboard. Opening the door he made his way down towards the elevator.

There was a security guard posted at the entrance and so he acted as though nothing was happening. He was just the janitor now.

'Where are you going?' asked the guard.

'Nasty incident reported in the male restrooms on the ground floor, bit of a clean-up needed if you know what I mean!'

'Let's see your pass.'

Mike handed it to the guard who examined it for a moment and then handed it back to him. He summoned the elevator and waited. More of Pearson's security team were pacing along the corridor and opening every door they could find. The doors of the elevator opened and he made his way inside, the security guard watching him as he entered. When the doors closed he began his descent. The lift stopped on the fourth floor and a small group of people got in. They looked at him and then began to feel uncomfortable with the smell of the disinfectant in his bucket. They reached the ground floor and got out of the lift. He was within sight of the exit but as his eyes surveyed the reception area, amongst the commotion he noticed the man whose pass he had borrowed speaking with the security officers.

'Sam, he's got a pass that will let him out of the building,' said one of the officers.

Pearson picked up his radio.

'All units, he has a stolen security pass, check everyone leaving the building, no, double-check everyone.'

Mike cautiously walked through the crowd towards the male restrooms, opened the door and went inside. When everyone had left he dumped the bucket and mop and headed back out and began walking towards the front entrance. There was a queue of about twenty people mainly visitors from the tour that he had caused to be aborted, waiting to leave and being checked and searched.

Two security officers entered the janitor's room on the ninth floor and turned on the light. They scanned the room, opened the cupboards and looked around the floor. One of them opened the cupboard where Mike had hidden the briefcase. There were some empty boxes in the bottom compartment and just toilet rolls on the top.

'Nothing in here,' he said.

'Check the bin,' said his colleague.

'Nothing.'

'Wait, what's that?'

'What?'

'That bag.'

'It's just a bag.'

His colleague stooped down and picked it out of the bin. When he opened it inside was a pair of glasses, a fake moustache and a scar.

Mike approached the security guards and showed them his pass.

'Leaving early?' one said to him.

'No, I'm just going out for air. I just had to clean up a nasty mess in the men's room and I'm feeling a little queasy.'

'Shouldn't be a janitor then if that's the case,' said the other.

'I'm between jobs.'

The first guard examined the pass closely and then looked at it again before glancing up at him. Everything had gone to plan; the exit was within feet of him but the last hurdle looked insurmountable. The other guard began to frisk him and felt the CDs in his overalls.

'Take them out.'

Mike handed them over.

'Well, Mr Johnson, this pass looks a little...'

'Hey, I love Bruce Springsteen!' said the other guard.

'These two are my favourites, 'Nebraska' and 'Born in the USA', listen to them all the time when I'm working. It passes the time you know,' said Mike. Little did the guards know what was actually contained on them.

'You've got good taste!' replied the guard handing him back the CDs.

The security officer in the janitor's room got onto his radio.

'JANITOR! repeat, he's disguised as a Janitor.'

'I think I'm going to throw up!' said Mike lunging pass the guards. 'The mess in the toilets...'

Mike entered the revolving doors, ran out onto the grass, faked a vomit and then darted around the corner.

'JANITOR! STOP THE JANITOR!! cried Sam Pearson.

The guards realising that they had just been duped ran out of the entrance and out onto the grass. On the ground lay a pair of janitor's overalls.

Mike rushed to his car, got in and drove off towards the entrance. Others were leaving at the same time and he found himself in a queue of vehicles moving slowly. Finally he reached the gate and quickly turned out onto the highway leaving Sterling Medical Research behind him. He noticed in his rear view mirror that the barrier had remained down and that no other vehicle was being allowed to leave. His had been the last one.

18

Another tourist party had checked into the Farrington Hotel which was one of a number in New Hampshire that was registered with the New England tourist centres and described as 'highly recommended'. Many of the tour operators would use the hotel for parties and this provided a regular income for Jamie, particularly in the fall. Early November would see the peak of visitors and there were usually very few vacancies at the hotel at that time. At around 13.00 a coach departed from the hotel to take the party on a mini-tour of New Hampshire and would not return until much later that evening. The hotel felt as empty as Jamie did.

It had been over a week since Mike had left and she had resigned herself to the fact that he wouldn't be returning. The incident the night she had visited Hank still played on her mind and she could not reconcile it with anything that was going on in her life except for Mike's arrival. His sudden departure was too coincidental and aside from this it had caused her to do some self-examination. It had raised questions to which she finally began to feel that she had some answers. The hotel had been her life. She had carried on the business where her parents had left off and it was as though they had passed over the torch to her to keep their life's work alight. The hotel was a proud legacy that Jamie had inherited and she had continued to maintain the high standards her parents would have wanted. But now what she really wanted was a life, her own life and someone to share it with. Maybe it was time to move to Boston, get a job, sell the hotel, buy an apartment and live a bit.

She walked down to the edge of the lawn, sat down and looked back at the hotel. If she remained there, she knew she would have a home and financial security for the rest of her life. Did she really want to give all that up? But what kind of a life would it be? Maybe she should keep the business and employ a manager to run it for her while she lived in Boston. Stella would be the ideal candidate and of all people would understand the way she was feeling. The thought of planning a trip entered her mind. Maybe she could look up some old friends, stay for a couple of weeks and check out some job vacancies, she thought.

The sudden noise of a car speeding up the drive pulled her away from her thoughts. It was a Nissan Primera and the driver parked it by the entrance of the hotel.

'Great day for a picnic,' Mike called out. 'I told you I would only be gone for a week, well maybe eleven days.'

'I didn't think I'd be seeing you again, Mike Fabien.'

'Well I'm here now, and as far as I remember we had a date didn't we?'

'I guess I'd better rustle up some food then,' she replied feeling guilty that she had distrusted him.

'Let me dump my bags in my room. I still have one don't I?' he asked.

'I saved it for you, but I nearly let it go this morning. I'll see you down here in thirty minutes,' said Jamie as she walked back into the hotel and disappeared out the back.

Mike slung his bags on his bed and then opened the wardrobe. He carefully placed his laptop holder in the corner and closed the doors. He had checked into a motel on his way back to Ashbury Falls from Boston, and for a few hours he was half expecting a police patrol car to pull into the parking lot and two armed officers burst into his room and arrest him. But as the evening had advanced he had begun to realise he was home and dry and had set about checking that what he had actually downloaded was readable. It had been a nerve-racking experience as three times he had attempted to read the data from Sterling onto his laptop without success. To his relief, on the fourth attempt it had loaded, and he had spent the rest of the night reading the information. At one point he really did think that the police had arrived when there was a loud knock on the door, but it turned out to be the laundry lady bringing him towels she had forgotten to leave in the room prior to his arrival.

Now back at Ashbury Falls he needed to contact Jennings for a second meeting, but he knew he owed Jamie his time now and so today he would spend it with her and relax after what had been a very intense week.

He left his room, hurried downstairs and out to his car. He got in and waited for Jamie to arrive and then began checking the glove box and the floor to make sure he had cleared out any evidence of his activities of the past week in case Jamie spotted anything and started asking awkward questions. She finally arrived with the picnic basket and a blanket and so he got out and opened the trunk for her to put them inside.

'Where are you taking me?' he asked.

'Chakowah Park.'

'Didn't you mention something about that place to me?' he asked curiously.

'I think so. Come on let's get going and I'll tell you on the way.'

They pulled out of the hotel and Jamie directed him back towards town.

'It's only a few miles out on the other side of the river,' she said. 'It's a beauty spot that folks in the town and surrounding communities have enjoyed for years, but it's a hotbed of controversy at the moment.'

'Yes I think I heard something about that,' replied Mike.

'Apparently there's a development company called the Logan Corporation who are planning to build a new housing estate on it, and there are various local and national investors who have put a lot of money into it. We're talking million dollar homes here, Mike, and Reuben Stein is in on the deal.'

'What else do you know?' he asked.

'I heard that a guy called Charles Moreland and his supporters are claiming that it's an ancient Indian burial ground and are legally challenging the development.'

'Interesting.'

'I've never been one for politics, but it is a very beautiful place. I'd hate to see it ruined.'

'A paradise for the privileged. I'm looking forward to seeing it,' he said.

They eventually reached Chakowah Park and as Mike drove up the entrance road he knew that Jamie had not been wrong when she had said it was a beauty spot. The trees and landscaped gardens seemed perfectly arranged to the point that you could catch a glimpse of the lake behind them that reflected the sky and surroundings as though a huge mirror had been laid on the ground. He parked the car in a clearing and they got out, opened the trunk and took out the basket and blanket. The tranquil ambience of the park pervaded as they walked towards the lake, and to Mike it seemed that the area could almost be described as a miniature national park.

'Over here,' said Jamie.

They walked through the trees and came to the shore of the beautifully still body of water that had seemed to be inviting them from the moment they had entered the park. Its placid waters were barely disturbed by the waterfall that was running into it in the far distance.

'Let's sit over here,' suggested Jamie.

Mike followed her to the designated spot as she neatly laid the blanket on the grass for them to sit down.

'What a beautiful place,' said Mike noticing a few couples dotted around the shore and a few cyclists on the pathway. 'This is a large area, where are they planning to build?'

'I saw the plans once at a public meeting. I think mainly around by this lake. We all know that in the end it comes down to money don't we, so I think people will just have to enjoy it while they can, unless Charles Moreland gets his way.'

Mike seemed suddenly distant to Jamie. As she looked up at him, she saw his searching eyes gazing into the distance, surveying the area as though he was looking for something.

'Sit down, Mike.'

'Sorry, miles away,' he replied and then sat down on the blanket next to her.

'It's good to see you again, Jamie.'

'You too. Now you can tell me what the hell's going on.'

'I don't follow.'

'I visited Hank after you left. I had a very interesting conversation as it happened. Then I was followed home when I left. To say it scared me to death is an understatement. And by the way Carla Dempster came looking for you. She says you know about her condition. Who are you, Mike?'

'Things have got out of hand, Jamie, that's all,' he replied. He had gone over this in his mind as he had been expecting Jamie to question him sooner or later.

'I had no idea what sort of impact my research would have, so now I've finished I won't be speaking to any of them again. I think they've misunderstood a few things. It's true I have seen their condition before – I have a friend who is a doctor and he was telling about it a few years ago.'

'Who followed me and why does Hank think you know about his son's death?'

'Hank is old, confused and scared by what happened. I was just trying to comfort him. He's mistaken that for probing. He thinks I'm a reporter!'

'Are you?'

'No. Did you get a good look at the people who followed you? It was probably kids getting a high on frightening a lone woman.'

'One of them was wearing a suit.'

'So did you call the police?'

'No. This happened after you left. Coincidence?'

'I have no idea what this is about, Jamie. I think you should report it. I'll come with you if you like.'

'There's no point. I haven't seen them since. Anyway I'm thinking of moving to Boston.'

'That's good,' replied Mike.

'Maybe it's time I got a life of my own.'

'Seize the day, Jamie, you deserve it.'

'Can I trust you, Mike?'

'Yes.'

'Then why did you leave straight after Hank called you?'

'My publishers wanted a meeting. They e-mailed me and told me to meet them in Boston immediately. Like I told you, just business that's all. Can we quit all the questions now?'

Before she could answer he grabbed her, pulled her close and then began to kiss her. They lay together under the autumn sun while a gentle breeze cooled by the lake brushed across them, occasionally lifting Jamie's soft brown hair on and off her face. As she lay there, she began to feel like a teenager with her summer love that she had met on camp, knowing that soon her parents would be packing up the car and telling her it was time to say goodbye and leave for home.

Mike woke up and to his surprise dusk was falling on Chakowah Park. He must have nodded off after they had kissed and rested on the blanket. As he got up he saw Jamie sat at the edge of the lake, her slender body silhouetted against the blue and red sky and the shimmering of the lake. He got up and walked over to her.

'I'm sorry, Jamie, I nodded off, no reflection on your company. It's been a busy few days.'

'That's OK, it's good you are back.'

'I came back to see you,' he said and put his arms around her. She felt secure again.

'Beautiful evening isn't it?' she said.

'It is, wish we could just stay here.'

'We'd better pack up and go, the park Ranger will be locking the gates soon.'

'I've got something for you,' said Mike reaching into his bag. He pulled out the copy of *Scenes of Yesterday* that he had brought with him to Ashbury Falls and handed it to her.

'Hope you like reading,' he said.

She took it and opened it to the first page. There she saw handwritten the words...

Thank you for being here.

Mike

'I do, thank you,' she replied and kissed him on the cheek.

'We'd better get going then,' said Mike as he began packing up their belongings.

They returned to the car and packed their things back in the trunk. There were no other cars around so it was clearly time to leave. They quickly got in and drove off back down the entrance road towards the gates at the bottom. The Ranger was waiting for them and bid them goodnight as they passed him on their way out. As they turned out onto the highway he shut the gates behind them and locked up.

'How long are you staying now?' asked Jamie.

'Another week. I'm done with the research. It was clearly a mistake coming here, but you've made up for that.'

'Will you send me a copy of the new book?'

'Sure,' he said as he smiled at her gently.

Jamie reclined the passenger seat and snuggled comfortably into it as Mike drove them back to the hotel.

'You do remember the way back don't you?' she asked.

'Yes, I think so,' he replied.

The car turned into the hotel and up the slope before Mike pulled into the parking space he had used when he had arrived earlier that day. They got out and Mike started to head inside.

'Mike, wait.'

He turned around.

'You not coming in?'

'Stay outside with me for a while, it's a beautiful night.'

'OK.'

'Let's sit on the swing over there.'

They sat down and Mike put his arm around her as she cuddled up to him. She would make sure that over the next seven days she would live the moment. Even if she never saw him again, she wanted them to be special and become indelibly marked in her memory. There would be no more questions. Would the truth be better than the fantasy, she wondered?

From a distance a car pulled up slowly down on the road below, the lights were dimmed and then the engine was cut. Two men sat in the car staring up at them on the lawn from behind.

'That's his car,' said one of them. 'And that's definitely the girl.'

The other picked up his mobile phone and dialled a number.

'Henderson,' said a voice from the other end of the line, a few moments later.

'We've located Fabien.'

'Bring him in.'

'Understood.'

He ended the call and placed the phone back in its holder by the radio.

'Tomorrow,' he said turning to his colleague.

19

Mike was sat at his desk in his room. His laptop had just completed its boot-up and so he clicked on his e-mail icon and began to compose a note to Jennings with instructions for their next rendezvous. It had to be a different location from the last one, just as a precaution, besides he wondered if the old house in which they had met a week ago would still be standing. He had just finished typing the details of the time and place when there was a knock at the door that he recognised as probably belonging to Jamie. For some reason he forgot to perform a save as draft, therein leaving the note visible on the screen.

'I've brought you something to try. I think you'll like this,' said Jamie, waltzing into the room. Formalities had ended long ago.

'It smells like coffee, what is it?' he asked.

'It's something special, take a sip and find out.'

'What if it's drugged?' he asked grinning.

'Drink!' she said.

'That tastes good, what's in it?'

'My secret. Now put it down on the desk and come here.'

As he put the drink down she moved in closer and put her arms around his neck and then looked over his shoulders. She noticed the e-mail right there on the screen.

'Who are you writing to?' she asked.

'Oh nobody.'

She began kissing his neck, causing his body to tingle, whilst at the same time quickly glancing at the screen at intervals. Then as she reached her hand out, the drink toppled over and spilt over the desk and underneath his laptop.

'I'm so sorry!' she said. 'Quickly, there are some rags in the closet out on the landing,' she added with faked urgency as she grabbed his laptop.

Mike hesitated. He had never left his laptop unattended. Now it was in the hands of Jamie.

'Mike, quickly, the rags, this is expensive carpet!'

When Mike went out to the landing to fetch the rags the expression on Jamie's face suddenly changed. She gleefully smiled, satisfied that her plan had worked. She looked down at the screen and read the message on his laptop.

Jennings,
Tonight. 22.00 at the old river mill house off Eastfeldt in Ashbury Falls. Bring the files on

'That place is closed to visitors at 6 pm,' she thought.

She then heard Mike returning and so she placed the laptop on the bed and turned her attention to the drips coming off the desk.

'Cheap carpet,' she thought and grinned.

Mike entered the room and came over to the desk. Surely she had not looked at it he thought as he saw Jamie knelt down holding the mug and collecting the drips.

'Here.'

'Thanks, I'm really sorry, how clumsy. I'll see to this, you check the laptop, I hope it's not damaged.'

'It's fine, just a bit wet underneath; give me one of those rags.'

Mike wiped the underside of his laptop and then placed it down on the other table.

'Jamie, could you excuse me for a few minutes while I finish what I was doing.'

'Sure.'

'And then I'll come down for another one of those magic potion brews that I've just missed out on.'

When Jamie arrived downstairs, two men were standing in reception. She looked at them nervously as she walked around the back of the desk. Then she remembered the night she had been followed. Something was wrong.

'Can I help you, gentlemen?' she asked.

'Jamie Farrington?'

'Yes. '

'FBI. This is Agent Willis, I'm Agent Todman. You have a guest here named Michael Fabien.'

At that very moment it seemed that her endearing memories of the events of the last couple of weeks, and the very fabric of her expectations were being torn out from within her. She managed to compose herself.

'He's not here.'

'His car's parked out the front.'

'He went for a walk earlier.'

'When will he be back, Miss Farrington?'

'I'm not sure, anyway how would I know his whereabouts, he's only a guest staying here. What's this all about?'

'I think you and Mr Fabien are much better acquainted than that, I would say almost intimate wouldn't you, Willis?'

'I'd say my colleague was spot on, Miss Farrington,' replied Willis.

'So, where has he gone and when will he be back?' asked Todman again.

Before she could answer Mike came down the stairs unaware of Jamie's visitors. She looked at him, hopelessly, 'why?' written on her face.

Mike took one look at Willis and Todman and then straight at Jamie.

'You have to trust me, Jamie,' he said before sprinting back up stairs as if his very life depended on it.

'Fabien!' shouted Todman as he headed up after him.

'Willis, guard his car!'

Willis darted out the front and stood by Mike's Nissan as Todman raced after him through the upstairs of the hotel. Mike headed straight for a fire escape at the back of the landing that he had noticed during his stay. Todman was only a short distance behind as he passed a laundry cart. He stopped and pushed it in the direction of Todman sending him crashing to the floor. Shaken, Todman got up just in time to see Mike disappear out of the fire escape door. He raced down the cold metal stairs of the escape. As he reached the bottom of the stairs, Todman flew out of the door at the top and Willis came around the corner of the hotel. Mike looked around him quickly. His only means of escape was the woods and so he headed out of the hotel complex to take shelter in the trees.

'Stay in the hotel grounds,' cried Todman to Willis. 'I'll flush him out.'

Todman descended the flight of stairs at an alarming pace as though he was on a personal mission and sprinted into the woods. Mike ran through the leaves on the ground and came to the edge of the river he had seen from the hotel parking lot on his arrival. Crossing it would slow him down as he realised that Todman was gaining ground on him. He didn't want to get too far away from the hotel grounds, as he needed to get to his car and quickly. Instead he followed the river back around to his left which he figured would take him back towards the road. The ground was bumpy and full of leaves and dead bark which made it awkward to run through. As he ran he kept tripping over the debris as he frantically tried to get a good distance between himself and Todman. There was a slippery slope that led up to two large oak trees, which contained a clearing between them. He clambered up and as he reached the other side the ground dipped, leaving a clear run back to the hotel. He noticed also that there was an area of thickets to his right and so he decided to circumvent the direction he would have taken to hide and figure out his next move.

He looked back towards the oaks and saw Todman come racing through them. Suddenly Todman disappeared into the leaves as he tripped on an unseen rock that jutted out of the ground. Now was his chance. He could see the hotel through the trees and raced back towards it as Todman struggled to pick himself up. This gave him a fairly good lead as he finally reached the edge of the parking lot. He cautiously crept around the edge of the hotel and came to the front corner. He could see Willis standing by the car. He had to be quick. Todman would be out of the woods at any time so he crouched down and slid around the edge of a couple of parked cars before he found himself within spitting distance of his car. He checked his pocket for his car keys and was relieved to find them. He then pulled them out and held them tightly in his left hand.

Throwing caution to the wind he lunged forward punching the unsuspecting Willis in the face and knocking him to the floor. That was not the normal way he would deal with a situation like this, but time was against him. He jumped into his car, started the engine and quickly put it into reverse before backing out of his parking space and swerving the car violently around sending dust into Willis' face as he staggered up off the tarmac. He put the stick into drive, his foot down hard on the gas and sped off down towards the hotel entrance as Todman raced around the corner of the building and Jamie appeared from the lobby. Todman picked Willis up off the ground.

'What happened to you?' asked Willis as a trickle of blood appeared from his right nostril.

'Never mind,' said Todman as he paced over to their car and took out his mobile.

'It's Todman. We lost him. Shall we involve the local sheriff's office?'

At the other end of the line were Henderson and two others around a conference phone.

'No, let's keep this internal. He's a liability. Bring him in. Use whatever resources you need, but don't involve the police if you can help it.'

Todman turned to Jamie.

'Don't leave town, Miss Farrington, we'll be back.'

20

Mike parked his car around the back of the Aurora Motel. It didn't look like the sort of accommodation that he had been used to staying in. It was run-down, old and tatty, but it was at a comfortable distance from Ashbury Falls and off the beaten track so that his pursuers could not easily find him. He knew that this had been coming; Jennings had warned him to watch his back. His laptop, clothes and wallet were all at the Farrington Hotel, but in foresight he had left a wad of emergency cash and a spare credit card neatly concealed in the glove box of his car for just such an occurrence. After his sudden exit from the Farrington Hotel he had gone to Ashbury Falls mall and bought himself a suit, a new set of clothes and toiletries. It was the last place he thought they would be looking for him but nevertheless he had been continually looking over his shoulder during the visit.

The motel reception was dingy and hadn't had a refit since the seventies. A large balding man with a cigarette hanging out of the corner of his mouth and large tattoos on both his forearms greeted him at reception.

'Forty dollars a night, laundry is extra,' he said abruptly.

'Extortionate,' he thought. 'I'll take it,' he said reluctantly.

'There'll be fresh coffee and muffins in the morning, compliments of the house.'

'I'll look forward to that,' said Mike sarcastically.

The motel owner gave him a cold look and handed over the keys and a couple of towels.

'Room 14, out the back.'

The room was basic comprising an old TV, a table with a couple of old armchairs and a standing lamp in the corner. At least the double bed was comfortable but what of the bathroom? He walked gingerly into it to discover there was no bath, just a toilet, washbasin and a rather grotty shower cubical in the corner with a shower that looked like it was on its last legs. He quickly took a shower and changed into his new suit before going back to reception and handing a bag to the owner that contained his muddy clothes.

'Ten dollars.'

Mike handed over the money and then headed out the back to his car.

Charles Moreland's mansion was located about ten miles north of Ashbury Falls and as Mike drove his car along a quiet country road he was looking out for a turning to his right that would hopefully take him right to the house. Fortunately the data he had acquired from Sterling had given him details of Moreland's location and he had managed to memorise it. He was going to be somewhat handicapped without his laptop but he remembered enough details from the hours he had spent reading through it to give him what he needed for this visit and his meeting with Jennings later that day. He approached the turning and drove into a tree-lined road that appeared to lead to nowhere. After about a mile he came to a large stone wall with black iron gates. As he drove closer, there was an intercom on one of the gate pillars. He pressed the button and waited for the reply.

'Charles Moreland residence,' said a voice through the intercom.

'Good afternoon, my name's Tom Johnson from the Sterling Medical Research Corporation. I have to see Mr Moreland urgently.'

'Just a moment,' replied the female voice at the other end. There was silence for about a minute and then the voice spoke again.

'Mr Moreland isn't expecting anyone from Sterling Medical Research, so you'll have to make an appointment.'

'That won't be necessary. Please tell Mr Moreland that we have a code red on Ascension,' he replied.

The intercom fell silent again and within a minute the iron gates opened allowing him to drive his car up a long driveway to the Moreland house. The house was Victorian in appearance and set in picturesque surroundings with a small lake to the west side. As he parked the car on the driveway, two grey-suited men who asked for some identification greeted him. He pulled out the pass belonging to the real Tom Johnson that he had stolen during his visit to Sterling and which he had by pure chance left in the glove box. He must have missed it when he had cleared the car out prior to taking Jamie to Chakowah Park. He was then escorted into the house and came into a bright spacious hallway decked with expensive looking paintings and artefacts. In front of him was a wide wooden staircase with a red floral carpet strip running up the centre of it and spanning about a third of its width. As he ascended the stairs to the first floor and reached the landing, the size of the building became apparent. There was a long corridor down which he was escorted to a room facing at the end. When he reached the door one of his escorts knocked before entering.

'Come in,' replied a voice.

As they opened the door and escorted Mike into the room, Charles Moreland was stood by the drinks cabinet pouring himself a scotch.

'Leave us, gentlemen,' said Moreland to the escorts.

'What's your poison?' asked Moreland.

'I'm OK thank you,' replied Mike.

'It's been a long time since I've had any contact from Sterling, Mr Johnson, and now after all these years you get a code red on Ascension. You can understand how uncomfortable that makes me feel. What's the score?'

'Someone got into our computer records and downloaded most of the data on Ascension, that's all we know. I'm here to discuss contingency plans as you were one of those who funded the project and we were given instructions to contact you in the event of a breach of security.'

'If that information gets into the wrong hands there could be serious ramifications for myself and other influential persons, not to mention your own corporation, the FBI and even, dare I say it, the US State Department.'

'We are aware of that Mr Moreland; the FBI is on the case right now.'

'Well they'd better be for all our sakes.'

'We've spoken to our contact in the State Department already and have been instructed to destroy all record of Ascension; that means they'll be no returns for the investors.'

'To be honest, Mr Johnson, I gave up hope of that years ago especially after the incidents. Why it was ever kept open all these years I don't know. It's been in sunset for twelve years now.'

'There's one thing that puzzles me, Mr Moreland.'

'What's that?'

'We developed an antidote back in 1981 with further funding from yourself.'

'That's correct.'

'There are records missing on this.'

'Perhaps your hacker stole them and deleted them. Maybe they were one of the test cases plotting some revenge, I don't know. Damn it, Johnson! How could your corporation have allowed this to happen?'

'The files were not deleted by the thief, sir, they were deleted in 1982. Our I.T. department has traced the file directories back.'

Moreland's face turned pale. He marched over to the drinks cabinet, poured himself another scotch and drank it quickly.

'Then I cannot help you, Mr Johnson.'

As Moreland sat back down at his desk the telephone rang.

'Moreland.'

He listened intensely to the voice at the other end of the phone.

'Deal with it!' he said sternly and put the phone gently back on the receiver as one of his security men knocked and entered the study.

'We appear to have an intruder. What else will befall me today?' said Moreland. 'Good day, Mr Johnson, do what you have to. I do not intend to have any further contact with the Sterling Medical Research Corporation. Do I make myself clear?'

'Yes, Mr Moreland,' replied Mike.

'Escort Mr Johnson to his car,' ordered Moreland.

His aid acknowledged and the two men left Moreland's study and headed back along the landing towards the stairs. From his study Moreland called another of his aids.

'Baxter? The man who is being escorted by Roberts; let him drive out of the gates and then follow him, just as a precaution.'

As Mike began to descend the stairs to the hallway, a familiar face rushed in being followed by one of the security guards. The intruder drew a gun.

'Back – stay back!' he warned.

The security guard kept his distance as the man ran up the stairs. He pointed his gun at Roberts and then at Mike. It was Reuben Stein.

'Against the wall!' he shouted. 'Where's Moreland?'

Roberts kept silent.

'Tell me where Moreland is or you'll be the first to go!'

Roberts pointed to the door at the end of the landing as the security guard arrived at the top of the stairs.

'Back, all of you!' cried Reuben, shaking. As he was about to head for Moreland's office he stared at Mike.

'I know you!' he said.

Roberts and the security guard moved to chase after him, but stopped dead in their tracks as Reuben Stein fired haphazardly at them.

'I'd better go,' said Mike to Roberts.

Roberts nodded to him and then at Baxter who had just come to the bottom of the stairs. They parted as Mike hurried down and Roberts headed off down the corridor with the security guard towards Moreland's office.

Reuben finally made it to Moreland's office door. He was sweating and panting, and his tie was loosened. He burst into the office and pointed his gun at Moreland.

'What the hell...' cried Moreland from behind his desk.

'Shut up, Moreland, and listen to me!'

'OK, Mr Stein, you have my attention.'

'I'm finished because of you!' shouted Reuben as tears began to appear in his eyes. Moreland noticed he was shaking badly.

'I'm finished, because of you and your cronies holding up the Logan deal. To hell with you all! I ought to kill you now! You've been conspiring against me, you and that Michael Fabien!'

'I don't know what you're talking about!' replied Moreland.

'He stole my girl; he took my Jamie away from me!'

'Who?'

'Michael Fabien, the man on the landing, the man you've been collaborating with.'

'Look, you think you can just burst in here and—'

'Shut up!' cried Reuben as he steadied his hand. 'Now listen to me. You weren't content to take my money; you wanted to take my girl away from me too! You're a dead man, Moreland!'

Reuben squeezed the trigger just as Roberts and the security guard kicked in the door and lunged forward to pin him to the floor. Instinctively Moreland dived for cover as the sound of the gunshot rang around the room. Reuben groaned as Moreland's men held him to the floor using their full body weight to restrain him. As Moreland got up from the floor he looked up and noticed the bullet hole in the head of the portrait of his father that was hanging on the wall behind the desk. Roberts and the guard picked Reuben up and grabbed hold of his arms. Moreland approached him, looked hard into his eyes and then punched him with force in the stomach. Reuben reeled over in agony trying to catch his breath as he did so. Moreland grabbed his hair and pulled his head up.

'Nobody comes into my house, unwelcome, wielding a gun and making accusations. Do you understand, Mr Stein?

Reuben began to compose himself and, as he did so, his breathing started to return to normal.

'Now then, who is this Michael Fabien?'

'He stole my Jamie,' muttered Reuben.

'We'll talk about Jamie later shall we? Who is he?'

'He was on the stairs, I recognised him. He's been snooping around Ashbury Falls, asking questions.'

'About what, Mr Stein?'

'I don't know!'

Moreland winded him again. Reuben lost his breath and began coughing violently, hanging his head low and allowing his captors to take the whole weight of his body as his legs buckled beneath him.

'Please, please I swear I don't know!'

Moreland hit him a third time and he hung there between the two men, sobbing.

'Take him away and lock him up,' ordered Moreland.

The two men left the room dragging Reuben between them, leaving Moreland sat at his desk looking anxious. He poured himself another drink and sat down, lay back in his chair and put his feet on the desk as he contemplated what to do next. Then the phone rang.

'Mr Moreland, there's a Sam Pearson from the Sterling Medical Research Corporation on the line. He says it's urgent.'

'Put him through.'

'Mr Moreland, this is Sam Pearson. I'm afraid I've got some bad news, there's been a code red on Ascension.'

'Thank you, Mr Pearson, but one of your men has already been to visit me today.'

'What do you mean?'

'I have just been speaking to a Tom Johnson. I am fully aware of the situation. There will be no further contact between us. Good day.'

'Wait! I didn't send a Tom Johnson, there's no one by that name working for me!'

Moreland ended the call and then contacted Baxter.

'The man I asked you to follow, bring him in immediately!'

'I'm sorry, sir, but we lost him.'

Moreland angry now, called Roberts.

'Bring our guest back up here; I'd like another word with him.'

Four minutes later, Roberts appeared with a shaken and subdued Reuben.

'Mr Stein, It seems that you were right about our visitor after all. Please accept my apologises. You seem to be having a run of bad luck, and this Michael Fabien could also be a big problem to me. I need to speak with him and so if I was to ensure that your Jamie was taken care of and that you could see her anytime you wanted, I'm sure Mr Fabien would be more than willing to see me. Maybe we could cut a deal, Mr Stein. Help me deal with Michael Fabien and convince your fellow investors to drop the litigation on Chakowah and I'll give you the $500,000 dollars you lost on what was clearly a very bad investment, and I'll settle the legal costs for the case. Do we have a deal, Mr Stein?'

'If it means I get Jamie back, I'll do what you want.'

'Good, we'll speak again.'

'Roberts, see Mr Stein off the premises.'

When they had left, Moreland picked up the phone again.

'Madeline, will you get me Richard Templeman on the phone please?'

After a short while there was a voice at the other end of the line.

'Ritchie, this is Charles Moreland, I have a little job for you.'

21

Mike checked his watch as he sat in his room at the Aurora Motel. It was 21.30. He had been watching a re-run of one of the old *Colombo* episodes on TV, the one where Leonard Nimoy played the guilty hospital surgeon trying to cover his tracks. Viewing of this episode would have to end prematurely tonight; he had a half hour drive ahead of him to the old mill house where he had arranged to meet with Jennings and it was time to leave. He thought it would be safer to use the back roads.

As he got up to leave there was a knock at the door. He was startled. Ever since the FBI had caught up with him he had been on edge, always looking over his shoulder and waiting for the inevitable. Maybe they had discovered where he was hiding out. If they had it would have been too early in the game plan. He kept silent. Moments later there was another knock. He realised that there was no escape this time; the window was his only other exit and there certainly would not be enough time to clamber out of it.

'Hello?' said a voice.

It was not the FBI. Relieved he opened the door.

'Laundry.'

'Thanks,' he replied.

'Your jeans and shirt. That dirt was not easy to get out but they're good as new now,' said the plump lady who handed them to him.

When she had left he closed the door, put the clothes on the bed, checked his tie in the mirror and then left the room, turning the light off as he went. As he walked over to his car he noticed the motel owner sat outside the office under the light drinking a can of beer. There were a number of empty cans lying on the floor around about which came as no surprise. The man stared at him as he walked over to his car and then guzzled the rest of the can. Mike got in and drove off down the tree-lined road until he met the highway. As he turned onto it he was suddenly bathed in light being cascaded by the full moon that hung lonely in the sky above the tall pines in the distance.

Jamie zipped up her leather jacket and ran out of the hotel to her car. She had been having second thoughts regarding the merits of her decision and felt like a little girl standing in front of a door with a sign telling her not to enter. She hesitated to turn the ignition. Then voices from behind the door beckoned her. She waited; her hand ready to turn the key. She had to do this; she had to find out. The key seemed to turn by itself and before she knew it, the car moved forward and she was descending the driveway towards the main road.

The old river mill house off Eastfeldt was a working museum that had been restored to operation some twenty years ago around the time of Ronnie Jebson's death. It was down a short narrow roadway cutting into the woodland by the side of the river and had a parking lot that went right up to the edge of the building. Beyond it was a large area of marshland by the side of the river. Moonlight illuminated the building as Mike's car approached. There was another vehicle in the corner and he recognised that it belonged to Jennings. He pulled up behind it and then got out and walked over to meet him. Jennings was sat with a flashlight reading some papers.

'Beautiful night,' said Mike looking in.

'So you pulled it off at Sterling,' replied Jennings. 'I really didn't expect to see you again. I thought you'd be locked up somewhere by now.'

'Like taking candy from a kid,' replied Mike. 'Let's go inside.'

Jennings got out of his car and the two men walked over to the entrance of the mill.

'It must be alarmed,' remarked Mike as they reached the door.

'No problem, I came prepared,' said Jennings opening the door with a set of skeleton keys. He switched the light on and they found themselves in the lobby of the museum. The security alarm started its countdown and Jennings looked around the room to find the alarm box. He finally located it on the far wall and attached a small white magnetic disk to it, which immobilised the alarm.

'OK, let's sit over here,' said Mike. 'We've got a lot to discuss.'

Jamie pulled up and parked a good distance away from the two other cars near the entrance of the mill. She got out and closed the door very gently so that it made a mere clicking sound as it shut. As she walked over to the entrance she noticed a light on in the lobby. Before moving closer she looked back over her shoulder, her eyes scanning the parking lot behind her. With the most delicate of movements she crept over to the window and then crouched down. She again checked behind her before peeping over the window ledge. In the room she saw Mike and another man talking.

'This must be Jennings,' she thought.

He had his laptop open and was looking at the screen as Mike was talking to him. She could not hear what he was saying, just a faint mumbling sound. Then Mike got up from his seat and started walking around the room. He was wearing a suit; something she had not seen him in before. It made him look more attractive. Although she could hear virtually nothing that was being said, the conversation looked intense. Mike's demeanour was different from that which she had become accustomed to. He was gesturing a lot and he looked somewhat disturbed. In the course of the discussion he began to look in the direction of the window. She quickly ducked and stayed there frozen for a few minutes. When Mike did not come outside she assumed that he had not seen her. She peeped up again, her heart beating fast, her eyes wide open taking in everything she could see, with a thousand possibilities rushing through her mind.

Suddenly she heard a noise of a crackling sound in the distance behind her. She looked around quickly and then back in through the window. Mike started walking towards it. He must have heard it too. She ducked again, panting a little, and slowly slid back around the edge of the window and leant tightly up against the wall. Mike looked out for a few moments before going back to his seat. It was time to make an exit. She felt she was about to get caught up in something in which she had no business. She wouldn't see Mike Fabien again. Whoever he was, whatever he was into, it didn't matter anymore; she would live with the memories of the man she had spent two special weeks with. Maybe it really was time to go to Boston after all.

She began to retreat from the mill house, staring at the light from the window as she did so. Her emotions in chaos, she looked around to see where she had parked her car, but then she heard the crackling sound again coming from the edge of the parking lot. She quickly headed around the other side of the building that faced the edge of the river and walked down a long wooden walkway that jutted out onto it. She passed the huge waterwheel to her right and then slipped behind it and peered around the edge to see if anyone was there. She knew that someone was in the parking lot, maybe they were after Mike. She didn't want to wait around to find out. She also knew that her best chance of avoiding them was to head around the rear of the mill and back up to Eastfeldt through the marsh. From there she could walk back down the road and find a house where she could call a cab.

At the end of the walkway was a wooden gate. She climbed over it and landed on a tuft of grass behind it on the edge of the river. The clear bright night allowed her to see the water in front of her. Quickly she hid around the rear wall of the mill and peered around the corner. She was sure she could see a figure at the other end of the walkway. Turning, she could see the streetlights on Eastfeldt in the far distance between the trees so she started to run as fast as she could across the grass trying to avoid the water. A few minutes later she came to what looked like a small lake with reeds where the river had saturated a large area of the ground. It was difficult to see exactly where she was going but she paced quickly around it and then continued to run up towards the road. The ground became spongy and boggy beneath her feet and so she slowed down. The road could not be far away now, but the ground was becoming softer and so she thought it would be a good idea to alter her course. The thought that she was still being pursued caused a sudden panic to come over her; she was disorientated, scared and desperate to reach the road.

In front of her was a large log and she could see it more clearly as she stepped up to it. Then she realised that it was a felled tree with several of its branches shooting out and still intact. She stepped over it and continued at pace but soon discovered that she had entered an area of thicket which started to obscure her view. Turning in another direction proved futile. It led her into even deeper thicket and she suddenly found herself surrounded in darkness. She had lost her bearings. She knew that she had to get out and continued walking until there was at last an opening. She ran across the boggy ground. Mud began to splash up onto her legs as she became surrounded in long grass. With every step the mud became thicker as it squelched under her feet. Realising that she was heading in the wrong direction she stopped and looked around her for a moment until to her relief she caught sight again of the lights of the road. But by now her boots had started to sink into a patch of mire that lay concealed under the thicket grass she was trying to avoid. As she felt her legs sink deeper she became trapped by the squelching mud that was enveloping her boots. She was unable to move and soon realised that the mud was going to reach her knees. She struggled and tried to lift one of her legs out. Finally it emerged from the mire and she found her footing on firmer ground. She had to kneel down in order to free her other leg and soon after it slithered out.

With the road in sight she stopped again just to be sure in her mind that she was heading in the right direction, but as she was about to set off she suddenly heard something in the distance, a splashing sound. Her pursuer had caught up with her. She tried to keep very still so as not to be seen, but couldn't stop herself from trembling as she prayed that whoever it was wouldn't see her. As her eyes focused in the dark, she saw a figure of a man in the distance, standing and watching, looking for any movement, waiting for the slightest of sounds. Luckily for her, she was shielded from vision by the backdrop of the trees that lined the side of Eastfeldt road, but still her pursuer stood there as if knowing she must be somewhere in close proximity. She could feel herself wanting to scream silently and held her hand to her mouth trying to make sure that any sound she might make would be muffled. Her imagination started to run wild as she thought of the countless outcomes that she knew could and probably would befall her when he would finally catch her, but to her absolute disbelief the figure suddenly turned and ran back towards the mill house; he hadn't seen her.

She decided to wait for a while to make fully sure that he had gone. It became evident as each minute passed that he was not going to return and so composing herself she ran back towards the reedy lake and splashed her way through it in the direction of Eastfeldt road, eventually reaching the shore. The ground became dry as she approached the pine trees near the road and she wiped her wet hair from her face to enable her to navigate her way through them. She squeezed her way through towards the road as quickly as she could for fear that she may still find her pursuer on her tail.

She reached a stream that separated her from a grass verge leading to the road, jumped across it landing on the other side and then began her ascent of the verge. The climb was difficult, she was tired, out of breath and aching but finally she reached the edge of the road and crawled onto the tarmac on her knees.

The ghostly streetlights illuminated the deserted road as she picked herself up and stood there wet and shivering. She looked down at her legs; her boots were caked in mud and grass, so too were her knees and thighs. Her skirt was wet but her jacket had come off unsoiled.

She had to get to a phone and began jogging clumsily down the road to try to find a house with a door to knock. The sound of the heels of her boots on the road echoed loudly in the dark and after a while she was out of breath and slowed down to a steady walk. Then she heard a sound that made her realise that she was not alone on the roadway. She froze in her tracks.

'Who's there?' she called in desperation. 'Hello?'

Suddenly she felt an arm grab her around the chest and pull her back, and a hand cover her face with a damp handkerchief. The smell was so potent and the fumes overwhelming that she found it difficult to breathe. She tried to scream but as her head started to spin and darkness instantly enveloped her she slumped into the arms of Ritchie Templeman.

He dragged her along the road and back towards the track that led to the old mill house. His car was parked at the entrance. He laid her on the ground whilst he opened the door of his car and then pulled her in onto the back seat. He quickly opened the trunk and took out a bag. Getting back into the car, he noticed his rear seat covered in mud from Jamie's boots.

'My car!' he said to himself in an annoyed tone.

He opened the bag, took out a blindfold and tied it around her eyes. Next he turned her over and pulled her arms behind her back, binding them with a roll of tape which he wrapped tightly around her wrists. Finally he taped up her mouth leaving her room only to breathe through her nose.

'That should do it,' he said as he stepped over into the driver's seat.

He fired up the engine of his Ford Convertible and reversed the car onto the road, quickly looking up and down Eastfeldt to make sure nobody had seen him. Then he put his foot down and drove off in the direction that would lead him out of town, his rear wheels screeching behind him.

'I heard a car,' said Mike from within the mill house.

He and Jennings got up and headed outside.

'I'll get the flashlight,' said Jennings, going to his car.

Mike gazed into the darkness. Maybe they had been followed. If it had been the FBI they would surely have burst in on them. Then he noticed something in the far distance.

'Over there,' he said to Jennings, signalling him to follow as he emerged from his car.

Jennings arrived with the flashlight.

'It's a car.'

'I don't think there's anyone in it,' said Mike as he looked closely. 'Hold on I recognise it,' he added. 'Shine the light on the licence plate.'

'Whose is it?' asked Jennings.

'It's Jamie's, what the hell is she doing here?'

'She must have followed us.'

'Or she knew where we would be,' replied Mike as he remembered the laptop incident back at the hotel.

'You've got more trouble than you think, Fabien.'

'Jamie!' he called out.

There was no reply.

'Come on, Jamie, I know you're out there, it's OK you're safe, come over here, we can talk.'

The two men waited in the dark for about a minute.

'Maybe she's not here, Fabien.'

'I don't understand,' he replied.

'I think we'd better leave,' said Jennings. 'Let's go back to my hotel; we've still got work to do. There's a spare bed.'

'We've got to find her.'

'Forget it, Fabien, we've got to concentrate on Ascension, we're so close now.'

The two men left. Mike followed Jennings. As they drove to the edge of the parking lot Mike momentarily stopped his car by the side of Jamie's, wondering what had happened to her and then reluctantly followed Jennings out onto Eastfeldt.

22

The gates opened at the Moreland mansion as Ritchie Templeman drove his car up the drive towards the house. As he approached the building he parked his car outside the two large entrance doors, each containing magnificent stained glass windows. He realised that Moreland was loaded and tonight's exploits would be well rewarded. He got out of his car and rang the bell and waited for almost a minute before the doors opened and two of Moreland's aids came out. They ignored Ritchie, opened the doors of his car, picked Jamie up off the back seat and carried her into the house. One removed her boots carefully and then held her by her legs whilst the other put his arms around her chest. Ritchie followed them into the house and stood in the hallway as they carried her down the corridor and out towards the back of the house.

He felt uncomfortable; he had never been in a place like this in his life. He felt intimidated by the attitude of Moreland's men. Surely he was part of the team too, and after all he had successfully delivered Jamie Farrington to them even though it had taken him longer than planned. Following her from the hotel had been the easy part. All he had had to do was take her in the parking lot outside the museum but he had not banked on her escaping across the marsh. He had pursued her so far but then stopped when he felt the ground getting soft and decided to backtrack, knowing that she would have been heading for the road.

He stared in awe at the ornamental ceiling above him before glancing around at the paintings on the wall.

'Renaissance period replication,' said a voice from behind him.

He looked around with a blank expression and saw Charles Moreland a short distance away from him.

'The ceiling,' said Moreland.

'Oh yes, very impressive, Mr Moreland,' replied Ritchie nervously.

'A good night's work, Ritchie,' said Moreland.

'Any time.'

'And to show my appreciation…' said Moreland, handing him a brown envelope.

Ritchie opened it and saw a wad of twenty-dollar bills.

'Thanks,' said Ritchie.

'I can trust you, Ritchie, can't I?'

'Of course, Mr Moreland.'

'I expect complete integrity from those who work for me.'

Ritchie felt better, appreciated, respected.

'Well I must attend to business,' said Moreland as he walked towards the entrance door.

Ritchie followed him, realising it would not be wise to overstay his welcome.

'Good night, Ritchie,' he said as he opened one of the doors.

Ritchie got into his car, turned the ignition and was about to drive off, when Moreland put his hand on the door.

'I may need your services again.'

'Sure,' replied Ritchie and then wheel-spun his Ford Convertible away, turning it full circle before heading back down towards the gates. As he left, he checked his rear view mirror and noticed Moreland watching him from the entrance of the house as he disappeared from view.

Moreland entered a small white room containing a single chair in which Jamie was slumped. His two aids were stood guarding her. He gestured to one of the aids to untie her and then cut the tape around her wrists and pulled off the piece covering her mouth. She began to stir.

'I think she needs a little something to help her sleep longer,' said Moreland as he pulled out a needle and syringe and injected her with a small dose of tranquilliser. 'OK, take her to her room.'

The two men carried Jamie upstairs towards a large bedroom on the first floor, as Moreland walked back to the hallway and through an arch leading into his lounge.

Jamie opened her eyes slowly, and gradually a bright white ceiling came into focus. She turned her head and it began to throb, her eyes momentarily going blurred again until she managed to refocus on the huge window to her right. To the far left was what looked like a large door. She noticed the room was decorated with silver and white wallpaper, an ornate chandelier light was hanging from the ceiling and there was crimson carpet on the floor. She sat up but then had to hold her head tightly on both sides as a searing pain likened to that of having spikes driven into her temple, rippled through her head. She let out a quiet scream and after a short while it subsided as she began to regain her senses.

The last thing she could remember was climbing up a grass verge out of the marsh by Eastfeldt. Slowly she began to recall the events that had led up to the present as she climbed off the bed, but something was missing. She had no idea how she had got from being on a deserted road to some sort of quality hotel room and realising she was dressed in a silk bathrobe confused her further. There was no sign of her clothes anywhere. She caught sight of a large mirror on the opposite wall and walked over to it. As she gazed into it she felt her hair, it was a mess. It had matted where it had dried naturally, her make-up was wearing off and her eyes had dark shadows under them.

She headed over to the door and tried to open it. It was locked. She turned the handle several times, shaking it hopelessly before stepping back from the door, staring at it in derision and disbelief.

'What's going on?' she asked herself and then paced over to the window.

It was dusk outside and she could just see the large grounds of the house, but had no idea where she was. She tried to pull open the window, but it too was locked.

From his security room, Charles Moreland could see Jamie's movements on his black and white closed circuit TV monitor. The camera was hidden in the coving in the corner by the door. She sat on the bed for a while and then Moreland noticed her walk back over towards the door. She began banging on it in frustration.

'Time to greet our guest,' said Moreland.

Jamie began looking in the drawers and the wardrobes to see if she could find anything, but for what purpose she didn't really know. There was another door in the opposite corner of the room, and upon opening it she came into a luxury en-suite bathroom with a fantastic shower cubicle. As she looked around the bathroom every luxurious detail caught her eyes, but she knew that something was very wrong with her situation and as she wandered back slowly into the bedroom and seeing all the comforts she had been afforded, the memory of her last moments on Eastfeldt came into view in her mind. She remembered the hand across her face and the dreadful fumes that rushed into her head through her nose and how she felt like she was suffocating.

Suddenly a knock at the door startled her. It was followed by the sound of the turning of a key. The door opened and in walked a man she thought she knew. Everything was still very unclear to her, and she felt a weird sensation overcome her as though she had entered into some sort of alternative reality. As the door slowly closed she saw a dark-suited man waiting outside which made her feel very uncomfortable. The events that had occurred since Mike's return began to flood back to her in an instant and she knew that she was caught up in something sinister, and what was more frightening was the fact that he must be involved somehow.

'You're Charles Moreland aren't you? What's going on, why am I here?'

In his hands he had a meal tray which he placed on the table by the window.

'Hungry?' he asked her.

'I want to know what's going on!'

He picked up a plastic carrier bag and handed it to her. She took out the contents. It was her clothes, all clean and neatly folded. There was also a pack of new black underwear.

'I'm afraid we couldn't salvage the boots,' said Moreland, handing her a brown box. 'But I do hope these will be to your liking.'

In the box was a brand new pair of long black leather boots, similar to the ones she had been wearing the previous night.

'Why the locked door? Please tell me why I'm here?'

'For the moment, I would like you to consider yourself my guest, Miss Farrington.'

'Your guest! You must be crazy. Look, just tell me what's going on!'

'All in good time. Excuse me but I have work to do. Enjoy your meal.'

Moreland walked out of the room. Jamie followed him knowing full well she had no hope of getting past the door and the two men. It was shut tight and locked again. Instantly she banged on the door with both fists to show her disdain at being locked up, but soon realised it was pointless. Walking over to the window she tried to make sense of the situation. Looking at her watch she saw that it was 8 pm and realised she had been unconscious for nearly twenty-four hours. She looked out of the window as night fell, tried to open it again, but to no avail. The meal looked enticing; she hadn't eaten for ages. Pulling the curtains closed, she sat down and began to eat.

23

Stella sipped a cup of English tea as she stood in the hotel reception. She had been covering the desk for the last three days. Jamie was nowhere to be seen, her car was missing and as a result Stella was becoming very concerned. Jamie had always given her advance notice if she was needed for extra shifts and she had often filled in when she knew that Jamie would be out of town. There were no messages, nothing to give her any clue as to her employer's whereabouts.

She had known the Farringtons for many years and had watched Jamie grow from a child, through the rebellious teens and into a beautiful young woman. She had always known Jamie to be a very pleasant, homely girl with her feet on the ground, except when she had had the relationship with that 'hell's angel' as she used to refer to him. What she had seen in him or why she would want to mix with those kinds of people she had never managed to fathom out.

Everything had seemed well with Jamie in the last few years although Stella could see that behind the friendly smile was a lonely girl in her thirties who needed to find love. Over the last couple of weeks however, she had seen a change in her. She had a look in her eyes that Stella had not seen before, one when a person has choices to make. She certainly knew that this Michael Fabien had affected her in a big way. Surely she wouldn't have taken off with him without a word, thought Stella. Jamie wouldn't do a thing like that. Still, the thought had crossed her mind. Should she call the police and report her as a missing person? No, it was too early for that, there had to be a sensible explanation.

Mike and Jennings drove into the Farrington Hotel and parked the car.

'Stay here,' said Fabien. 'I don't think we've been followed, but be vigilant.'

'This is a bad idea,' replied Jennings. 'This has got to be the obvious place they'll come looking for us, don't be long.'

'I have to see her. I have to tell her what's going on; I at least owe her that.'

Mike walked into the lobby and Stella greeted him with a relieved expression.

'Mr Fabien, thank goodness you're here. Where's Jamie?' she asked. 'It's not like her to disappear like that. You must have seen her, is she with you?'

'I haven't seen her for four days. I've had some pressing business to take care of.'

'Oh my, she's been missing for three days, not a word. Do you think I should call the police?'

'No, Stella, I'm sure there's a perfectly good explanation. Come to think of it, she did mention to me that she was thinking of going to Boston, maybe that's it.'

'Oh, well, maybe,' said Stella, surprised.

'Tell her I'll see her when she returns.'

Mike hurriedly walked back towards the entrance.

'Mr Fabien…'

'Yes, Stella.'

'There's a letter for you here. Must have been put in the mailbox by hand, no postmark or anything.'

Mike walked back over to the desk and Stella handed him a plain white envelope with the words 'PERSONAL – FAO MICHAEL FABIEN' typed on it.

'Thanks, I'll see you again,' said Mike.

'Something's wrong, Jamie's missing,' he said as he opened the door and got into the car.

'What shall we do?' asked Jennings.

'Back to the old mill house museum,' said Mike as he placed the envelope in the glove box.

There were a few cars parked in the mill house as they drove into the parking lot. In the corner was Jamie's car in the same place it had been when they discovered it the night they had met there. Jennings pulled up into a parking space and turned off the engine.

'Something's happened to her,' said Jennings.

'She knew we would be at the mill house that night, so she followed us here,' concluded Mike. 'The question is who else knew?'

Remembering the letter that Stella had given him he opened the glove box, took out the envelope and quickly tore it open. There was a letter, a thin blue plastic strip and a polythene envelope containing a large clump of brown hair.

'What's that?' asked Jennings.

Mike stared at the letter and began to read it.

Michael Fabien,

Jamie is safe and well for now, but her well-being is entirely in your hands. She's mine for the present, all mine. How does that you make you feel, Mike?

Mr Moreland and I have a proposition for you. As soon as you receive this letter, break the blue strip in half and then go immediately to the phone booth on the junction of Doulton and Wendt and wait for a call. Don't be late now!

Like the souvenir? She has such lovely hair doesn't she?

R.S.

'Must be a micro-transmitter,' said Mike with a sullen expression as he broke it in half. 'Moreland's got Jamie.'

'Things are getting complicated, Fabien.'

'Drive, Jennings, we've got an appointment with her kidnappers.'

'What do you mean?'

'Just drive, I'll tell you when we get there.'

They arrived at the junction of Doulton and Wendt Street, and Mike saw the phone booth that Reuben had stipulated in his note.

'Over there,' he pointed. Jennings pulled up to the sidewalk next to it.

'OK, what now?' asked Jennings.

'We wait,' replied Mike.

'How deep are you in, Fabien?'

'What do you mean?'

'The girl.'

'You ought to know better than to ask questions like that.'

'Serious then.'

Mike ignored the comment and sat gazing out of the windshield trying to see if he could spot anything out of the ordinary. Then the phone rang in the booth.

'No hanging around,' he said as he opened the door of the car.

As he got inside the phone booth he felt knots in his stomach start to coil around inside him. He picked up the phone.

'Fabien.'

'Listen carefully. The deal is very straightforward. In forty-eight hours you will present yourself at the gates to Moreland's estate with everything you have on The Ascension Project, alone of course. I sincerely hope for Jamie's sake that you haven't divulged any such information to your friend.'

Mike paused and thought carefully before answering.

'He knows nothing. What's in this for you, Reuben?'

'Protection of my investments, Michael.'

'You wouldn't kill her, Reuben; you've gone to a lot of trouble to get her back. I rather think Moreland is in control of things don't you?'

'Correct, Mr Fabien, I am,' said a second voice 'Forty-eight hours is all you have.'

'What do you want, Moreland?'

'I want you, Mr Fabien, and everything on Ascension, that's all, it's a fair exchange. Forty-eight hours or she dies.'

The line went dead. As Mike placed the receiver back on the phone he felt a sickening feeling inside him. He was responsible for all of this and he should never have allowed Jamie to be caught in the crossfire. If that wasn't bad enough, the thought of Jamie being held at Moreland's estate with Reuben Stein made his skin crawl.

Jennings saw a worried man get back into the car.

'Well?' he asked.

'Moreland wants me in exchange for Jamie. I've got forty-eight hours. The thing is, Jennings, he knows nothing. He thinks I'm a small-time opportunist who stole some very sensitive information and found out that he's involved. So he's made the first move, a kind of pre-emptive counter-ransom demand you could say. I don't think he knows the gravity of his situation, but I'm not prepared to risk Jamie's life on that. Maybe it's time to call in the troops. We need help, Jennings, I need to get Jamie and just maybe we can deliver the prize they've been after for so long in the process.'

24

'So, Mr Stein, I hope that you have some good news for me.'

'I've done as you asked me.'

'Excellent.'

'I beg to differ.'

'Problems?'

'I'm no longer involved in the litigation, I instructed my lawyers to pull out.'

'But?'

'The other investors are sticking with it.'

'I see.'

'I'm as good as out of the Logan deal, Moreland. I hope you're satisfied.'

'Not really, Mr Stein, you obviously didn't try hard enough.'

'Damn it, Moreland, they've invested too much to give up now, do you really expect them to just pull out?'

'No, but you have, that's weakened the deal a little, let's be thankful for small mercies.'

'Now the money, Moreland.'

'Mr Stein, do you really think I'm going to part with half a million dollars for that! I want names and if I manage to convince them to drop the case as well, then I'll keep my side of the deal.'

'You promised!'

'Sit down, Mr Stein, I promised nothing.'

'You want names, here.' Reuben pulled an envelope out of his inside jacket pocket and threw it down onto Moreland's desk. Moreland picked it up, opened it and glanced through the listing inside. 'I want to see Jamie,' he demanded.

'Ah yes, Jamie. Well I did say that she was yours until I let her go. Roberts, escort Mr Stein to Miss Farrington's room.'

'Yes, Mr Moreland,' he replied and led Reuben around to the west side of the house to where Jamie was being held.

Jamie had taken a well-needed shower before going to bed and had slept soundly. Moreland had sent breakfast up to her room that morning and she had been very glad of it, as she had barely touched the dinner she had been left the night before. After a few mouthfuls she had been sick, not due to the food but probably as a result of the side effects of the tranquilliser. Breakfast went down well and, after taking another shower that morning, she felt better and decided to get dressed into her clean white shirt, her skirt and the new boots that Moreland had given her. She was in dire need of a cigarette.

Stella must have called the police, and they surely would have found her car in the mill house museum by now. What was Moreland going to do with her? What was his connection with Mike? Then she realized what was going on. Mike had come to town under the pretence that he was a writer, but he was really involved in the land development at Chakowah Park. The deal was crooked and the FBI was onto them. He, Moreland and Reuben were in league together and Mike was trying to double-cross them somehow. This had to be the reason why she had been kidnapped. She was being held as insurance. Why had she allowed herself to be deceived in that way? Mike had surely just been using her to get information. What she couldn't work out though, was why Mike had spent so much time with Carla Dempster and Hank Jebson, and why had he told Hank that he could help him to learn the truth about his son's death? Was it all just a scam to get information? Now she wasn't so sure. What she was sure of was that she had fallen for him and she had to cope with the fact that when this nasty mess was sorted out, she would probably never see him again. There was suddenly a knock on the door.

'Come in.'

Roberts unlocked the door and opened it as Jamie got up from the bed.

'You have a visitor?'

In stepped Reuben. Jamie gasped as she saw the door being closed and locked. Even Reuben looked around in surprise.

'Seems we're prisoners together, Jamie,' he said jokingly, but for a moment he wondered whether Moreland was intending to keep him locked up too.

'Reuben,' she said nervously.

'Well here we are.'

'What are you doing here?'

'Isn't that obvious?'

'Business?' she asked nervously.

'Maybe.'

'Is it to do with Chakowah Park?' she asked, trying to keep him pre-occupied with what he liked to talk about most – deals.

'Yes.'

'You were telling me about this in the park.'

'Yes, I remember now. Everything was going fine until we were interrupted by Michael Fabien.'

'I thought that Moreland was against it,' she replied trying to prolong things.

'He is.'

'So what's the deal then, Reuben?'

'So many questions, Jamie, shouldn't we talk about us?'

'There's nothing to talk about,' she replied realizing from his expression that she had made a big mistake.

'Moreland and I have patched up our differences. Things will go well for us now, Jamie, as long as you give me what I want.'

'What's Mike Fabien got to do with all this?' she asked.

'Why the interest in Michael Fabien?' said Reuben raising his voice.

'Just tell me, please!' replied Jamie, scared and confused.

'If you promise to forget about him.'

'I will.'

'That's good then. The answer is I don't know,' said Reuben laughing. 'Now, not another word about him, you promised,' he continued as the tone of his voice changed. He stared at her menacingly and she could feel his eyes caressing her. 'He'll be a dead man soon and will never come between us again.'

Jamie backed away. Reuben advanced towards her and finally pinned her against the wall, putting his arms either side of her. Then he grabbed hold of her chin. Jamie froze, wondering what he would do next and feared the worst.

'You're mine, Jamie, nothing will change that!' he said as he began to touch her.

'No!' she screamed, 'get off me!'

From the security room, Roberts was observing everything.

'Baxter, we'd better get up to the girl's room right now!'

The two men rushed down the corridor and up the stairs. They unlocked the door and burst in, to find Reuben clutching Jamie by the wrists and forcing her onto the bed.

'Stop it, Reuben, you're hurting me!' she yelled.

The two men grabbed Reuben, pulled him off Jamie and dragged him out of the room. Jamie fell to the floor on her knees. She was shaking uncontrollably, breathing erratically, gasping for breath. It was the same sensation that she remembered on the road at Eastfeldt when she had been smothered by her kidnapper. She had never had a panic attack before. She needed some air but the window was locked. She felt herself suffocating, but remembered there was a window in the bathroom. She ran in, stood on the toilet, pushed open the vent at the top, stuck her head out of it as much as she could and took a few deep breaths. Slowly the attack rescinded and she was able to draw her breath again. She climbed back down and walked into the bedroom, sat on the bed and buried her head in her hands. She had never experienced anything of this nature and had to get out somehow. Any longer in this place, and she would go insane.

Reuben was sat in front of Moreland's desk with Roberts and Baxter waiting in the wings, ready to intervene if things got out of hand. It was the next day and he had spent the night under supervision.

'Mr Stein, I'm disappointed in you, very disappointed. Treating our guest in that way, but what is worse is the fact that your co-investors in the Logan deal are willing to see this to the bitter end, and bitter it will get, mark my words. I have managed to persuade two maybe three to follow your example and pull out, but that's not enough to stop it. So you are going to have to earn your compensation, Mr Stein.'

'What do you mean?'

'I am willing to up the payment to a million. That should more than cover your losses and may even give you something to invest in a safer proposition. Tomorrow I expect Michael Fabien to arrive here as planned and you will see to it that both he and Miss Farrington are never seen again.'

'You cannot be serious, Moreland!'

'Oh, but I am, Mr Stein and I never joke about things like that.'

'But I can't, I can't.'

'One million, Mr Stein.'

'Whatever he's got on you, Moreland, it must be serious.'

'It is, so do we have a deal?'

'I need to think about it.'

'I don't think you understand me, Mr Stein. You see it's an offer you cannot refuse, it would be awful to have the death of three people on my hands, very bad indeed.'

'You're crazy, Moreland.'

'Think about it very carefully, Mr Stein. You may go and enjoy the facilities of my home but don't try to leave will you.'

Roberts and Baxter escorted Reuben out of Moreland's office. As he went through the door, he looked back at Moreland in disgust and then turned away.

Jamie stared out of the window of her room. The grounds of Moreland's estate were beautifully kept and well tended. There were a variety of shrubs and plants, fruit trees and evergreens carefully landscaped with a perfect lawn interwoven between them. She could see what appeared to be tennis courts in the distance behind a large hedge. She could also see the edge of a lake in the other direction. Coming away from the window she sat in the armchair waiting for Moreland's aids to arrive with drinks, snacks or afternoon tea, hoping only one of Moreland's men would turn up. Then she heard a noise in the corridor. She quickly went over to the other chair where her jacket lay and put it on, then hurried back to the door and put her ear up against it to try to hear more clearly what was going on in the corridor. She could hear what sounded like a trolley approaching.

'Afternoon tea,' she said quietly to herself.

The door started to be unlocked and so she stepped back waiting for it to be opened. Now was her chance. The door opened and in came a man pushing a silver tea trolley that had a hot tea service and a selection of Danish pastries on it. He had left the door slightly ajar and she noticed that the key was still in the lock.

'This looks good,' she said, and without a moment's hesitation rammed the trolley into his legs causing it to topple over as he stumbled and fell back. She quickly kicked him over and he fell to the floor crashing over the toppled trolley. She darted to the door, slammed it shut and locked it. As she ran from it she heard the man banging on it and yelling out. She ran down the corridor until she reached the balcony that looked down on the lounge area. There was nobody about and so she crept down the stairs until she reached the ground floor. The front doors were there in the far distance, but as she began to tiptoe towards them she heard voices coming from the entrance, and then two of Moreland's men enter. She quickly hid around the back of the staircase and watched the two men walk down the corridor and out towards the rear of the house, talking as they passed. When they had disappeared out of sight she moved out from behind the staircase and quickly paced across the hall to the lobby. She opened the stained glass doors to go outside and jumped as she saw Reuben staring at her from the porch.

'Going somewhere, Jamie?'

She quickly ran back into the hall with Reuben in pursuit. Upstairs on the balcony she saw the man who had come to her room, along with another who had freed him with another key.

'Stop her!' he shouted.

She changed direction, raced through the lounge and out into a long corridor that lead to the rear of the house on the far side. Reuben stopped in the lounge as Moreland's aids overtook him and pursued Jamie down the corridor. She reached a door at the end that led out into the grounds and headed for the front of the house, assuming that it would lead her to the gates. The two men rushed out of the door and ran after her as she made it to the large parking area at the front of the house. She saw the driveway that led down a road surrounded in trees, but as she ran down across the drive, Roberts and Baxter came up the road to cut her off. She was surrounded with nowhere to go.

Inside the house Charles Moreland came down from his office after realizing what had happened. Reuben met him at the foot of the stairs.

'She won't get far,' he said confidently, moments before a commotion was heard at the entrance. Roberts and Baxter entered with Jamie between them, each clutching one of her arms as she struggled vigorously to free herself.

'Is this how you repay my hospitality, Miss Farrington?'

Jamie said nothing.

'Take her to the basement.'

Reuben watched as the two men led her away.

'I'll be glad when this dreadful business is over, Mr Stein, as I am sure you will be.'

Reuben didn't answer. He began to stagger holding his head.

'Mr Stein?'

'Help me, I'm going to faint,' said Reuben as the room began to move around him.

Moreland caught hold of him just as he was about to fall and pulled him over to one of the armchairs. He sat there for a moment as Moreland looked on in surprise.

'It's nothing; I've been getting these for the past twenty years.'

Moreland's expression turned momentarily from indifference to a look of sympathy.

'You as well?'

Reuben looked up at him.

'What?'

'Nothing,' replied Moreland.

Reuben held his head in his hands and stared back down at the floor.

'There must be another way, Moreland.'

'No, Mr Stein, there isn't.'

Roberts and Baxter lead Jamie to a door at the end of another corridor. As Baxter opened it, she could see that it was pitch black.

'No!' she screamed.

They entered. Roberts switched on a light that revealed a deep staircase leading down to the basement. Jamie struggled to get free so Baxter pulled her arm behind her back. She cried out as the pain forced her to stop, and they led her down the stairs to a dark room with several doors leading off.

'This one,' said Roberts as they unlocked a large metal door.

The room was small and dingy with no windows. The only light came from a series of narrow vents right at the top of one of the walls. It looked like a storage room of some kind.

'No, please, I get claustrophobia!'

Roberts threw her in and slammed the door shut.

'No!' she screamed as they walked back up the stairs to the house. The echoes of her outcries could be heard as they coldly shut the door at the top behind them and locked it.

Fearing that she may have another panic attack she sat calmly on a wooden box and started to take deep breaths until she felt her breathing regulate. She looked around the small dark room and it brought back a terrifying childhood memory. When she was seven years old she had been playing in her father's old wooden tool shed at the end of their long garden. The shed was out of sight in a small corner of the garden behind a large hedge. She had locked herself in, but instead of leaving the key in the lock, she had taken it out and then she had dropped it. As she groped for it in the dark she had accidentally kicked it out under the door and was unable to reach it. The shed was small and dark and she had trapped herself in it. It must have been a couple of hours before her father had heard her screams. They had been sitting talking in one of their neighbour's houses across the road and had no idea that their daughter was going through such an ordeal. When her father had finally picked the key up off the grass and opened the shed, out jumped a hysterical Jamie clutching him around the neck for fifteen minutes or so, and refusing to let him go.

She knew that she would be in this basement room for a lot longer than two hours and the thought terrified her. She banged on the door as hard as she could hoping that someone would hear her, praying that her father would come, just like he had all those years ago.

25

Jennings' accommodation was considerably more comfortable than that of Mike's of late. Mike had retrieved his laptop and his belongings from the Farrington Hotel earlier that evening, but had had to listen to a complaining Stella for at least twenty minutes. She had given him a lecture on how thoughtless it had been of Jamie to just take off without warning. She had also mentioned that the police had been to the hotel regarding Jamie's car. They had insisted that it be removed from the mill house car park by request of the museum management. Stella had managed to find Jamie's spare set of keys after much searching and her husband had driven her there to pick it up and drive it back to the hotel. The police had asked a number of questions that had caused Stella concern, and Mike had had to calm her fears by explaining that it was just normal procedure. Mike had made a conscious decision not to involve the police from the start; it would complicate matters.

'It's all there except one vital missing element. We almost have everything we need to go into action,' said Mike confidently.

'What's missing?' asked Jennings.

'The antidote, but I have a theory.'

'Which is?'

'Let's concentrate on getting Jamie back, that's the priority.'

'What do you have in mind?'

'I will go to the Moreland house tomorrow evening and hand myself over in exchange for Jamie. I will arrange for them to drop her at the Aurora Motel where you will be waiting for her. You will look after her, explain who you are and not let her out of your sight until I return. Don't tell her who I am or what this is all about, that's for me to do.'

'As easy as that! What if you don't return?'

'Forget me and go into action.'

'What are you saying?'

'If I'm not back at the Aurora within twenty-four hours, I won't be coming back.'

'You're serious.'

'Tomorrow we'll split. I want you to bring Conner Newman to Ashbury Falls and book him into my room at the Farrington Hotel. If I don't return, you know what to do.'

'What about Moreland?'

'I'll have to leave that with you to follow up when this is over. You should have enough information to close in on him, but promise me you'll look after my people first and tell them what's going on. That's the reason I came here, not for Moreland, but now we know about his involvement that's a big bonus.'

There was a knock on the door.

'Pizza,' said the voice behind it.

'At last,' said Jennings getting up from the table.

He opened the door. Standing in the entrance was Todman holding two large boxes of Pizza that he had taken off the delivery boy down in the parking lot. Beside him was Willis pointing a gun straight at Jennings.

'That'll be fourteen dollars, fifty, Agent Jennings,' said Todman.

The two men entered the room as Jennings stepped back and looked hopelessly around at Fabien.

'This was bound to happen wasn't it?' said Mike in a resigning manner.

'On the bed, Jennings,' ordered Todman as Willis kept the gun on them both.

'How did you know?' asked Mike as he put his laptop down.

'Easy, you took a little trip back to the Farrington Hotel earlier and we just followed you here, and as we sat there working out our plan to bust in, along came the pizza boy.'

'I told you not to go there, Fabien,' said Jennings.

'Good advice, what a pity Agent Fabien didn't listen to you,' remarked Willis.

'Well as you're here, we might as well all eat then hadn't we. I'm hungry too. Good job we ordered the mega-size, hey Jennings?' said Fabien.

'Is your stomach all you can think about? asked Jennings.

'Yes, let's eat and then Todman can tell us all about how he's going to turn me in to Henderson.'

'You've always been the maverick haven't you, Fabien? Well now you've gone too far. I do like the writer scam though, very good.'

'Who told you?'

'That kind lady at the Farrington Hotel.'

'Stella.'

'Maybe you could have got away with whatever it is you are here for, Fabien, but breaking into Sterling was a bad move. We were contacted immediately, but I guess you would have expected that wouldn't you. We knew it was you.'

'So what's the score then, Todman?' asked Mike.

'You've opened Pandora's box and we've come to take you in, you and Jennings.'

'This is all very bad timing,' said Mike.

'It always is when you're involved.'

'The thing is, Todman, by breaking into Sterling I found out something which Henderson would just love to know about Charles Moreland.'

'Forget it, Fabien, this is just another of your scams, we're taking you in,' said Willis.

'Hear me out,' replied Mike.

'I think you'd better listen to him, Todman,' said Jennings.

'Go on.'

'We all know that the Ascension project could be very damaging to the State Department and some of our senior colleagues. We also know that when it failed, it was a closed book as it were. But certain powers in the Bureau wanted someone to take the fall for it, and they still do. It couldn't be anyone in the Bureau, so why not one of the investors. Henderson wants Moreland, but he just can't seem to pin anything on him. He's been after him for a long time. The data I stole from Sterling contained references to Henderson. It wouldn't surprise me that Henderson missed that vital promotion earlier in his career because of his failure to find a scapegoat. I think Henderson has a score to settle with Moreland, and now he can.'

'What are you saying, Fabien?'

'I have what Henderson wants.'

'Then you'd better hand it over,' said Todman anxiously. 'Get his laptop, Willis.'

'You won't find anything on there,' said Mike. 'It's all been erased!'

'OK, Fabien, what's the deal?'

'You tell Henderson that you've located me, but you tell him that my illegal operation here has uncovered something that will give him Moreland on a plate. Tell him we need reinforcements.'

'And what do you want in return, Fabien? A royal pardon?'

'Correct, but there's more, a complication that we have to deal with first.'

'So you've screwed up somewhere.'

'You can say that again!' remarked Jennings.

'Moreland has someone I care about as a bargaining tool.'

'It gets better, don't tell me, the Farrington girl,' laughed Todman.

'Tomorrow evening I have to give myself up and she will be released. Jennings will fill you in on the plan, but I need back-up. The guy is scum, Todman, and I want him just as much as Henderson does.'

'Is that it?'

'No, I came here to help some people out, victims of this dreadful mess. I intend to make sure they know about Ascension before I leave.'

'That's dangerous, Fabien. What the hell has got into you?'

'Henderson doesn't know about Jennings' involvement and it stays that way. We get Moreland, you deliver one of the biggest fishes that Henderson's been after, you let me finish what I came here to do, and then you can take me in.'

'So what have you got on Moreland?'

'All in good time. We finish my operation first, and then I'll give you Moreland.'

'And what if he kills you first?' asked Jennings.

'Then it's down to you guys. Shall we eat?'

'You can put the gun down. Willis,' said Todman. 'I don't like you, Fabien; you break the rules and always seem to come out smelling of roses. But if it means we get Moreland, I'm prepared to go along with this. But if you pull any scam on me, Fabien, I will personally see to it that you are up to your neck in paperwork and admin for the rest of your career, that is if you still have one.'

'No scams, Todman. You keep your side of the deal, I'll keep mine, and who knows, you may even come up smelling of roses yourself.'

26

Carla Dempster stood in her kitchen making a fresh pot of coffee as she looked out of the window at the garden. It needed tending, she thought, as she saw weeds appearing in the plant patch. It was early afternoon and she was expecting Jack home at any time. He had told her that morning that he would only be working until lunchtime and would shut the store early. This was unusual. He would normally take the day off and she would know why, but today he had not told her of his intentions.

Carla pondered; all the complications of her life had converged and were railroading through like never before. Her blackouts were getting worse, she was having real problems communicating with Joaney, and she was uncertain as to where she and Jack were going. As she contemplated the future, the unthinkable crossed her mind; it had been an option before. If Jack hadn't have come home early that day... she remembered, and then she heard the front door.

'Hi, Carla,' he said, kissing her on the cheek as he entered the room.

'Was it a good morning?' she asked.

'Busier than usual.'

There was an awkward silence as Jack poured himself a drink.

'Mr Grover was in this morning.'

'We haven't seen him for ages, how is he?'

'He's walking better these days. He asked after you and Joaney.'

'That's nice. Come and sit down, Jack, I've have something to say to you.'

'OK, let me dump my things a second.'

'No it can't wait – leave them.

'What is it, Carla,' he asked with a worried look.

'Where are we going, Jack?' she asked.

'I'm sorry?'

'You and me; where are we going?'

'I don't understand.'

'Yes you do,' she said sternly.

Jack looked nervous, the way he always did when he felt a confrontation brewing between them.

'Actually I've got something to tell you. That's why I've taken the afternoon off,' he said countering.

'You've decided to go for the second store haven't you?' she said in an objectionable manner.

'Look, Carla.'

'You know how I feel about this.'

'It's not like that, Carla.'

'Jack, I need a life, I can't deal with all this any more.' Now she was going to offload.

'Wait a second, Carla.'

'Jack, you never listen to me, you don't hear me, you don't see, do you—'

'Carla, be quiet, listen!' he said raising his voice. She calmed down; he rarely spoke to her in that manner. 'I've decided to sell the store,' he continued.

For once she was unable to make any reply. She stared at him in disbelief, as though it wasn't Jack who had just spoken.

'I think we should sell up and leave Ashbury Falls. It's not long before Joaney goes to college and it's time I thought about us, and not about dreams that I'm never going to realise.'

'Are you serious, Jack?'

'I've never been more serious in my life. I had big plans to get this second store, but I should have done it years ago. It's too late now. There will be no Dempster's hardware store chain in New England. To hell with it, there's more to life than selling nuts, bolts and chicken wire.'

'What's changed, Jack?'

'You, Carla. I nearly lost you down at the river the other day, and it made me realise that the only thing that matters to me is you. So wherever we end up, you'd better learn to swim!'

'I promise,' she replied with a tear in her eyes.

'The easy part is deciding what you're going to leave behind, now we've got to decide what to do. I thought about us moving to the coast, maybe getting a boat and taking tourists out on coastal tours. We could even start a little café as well, by the launching jetty, nothing big. We don't need a lot of money, Carla, we've got plenty saved. What do you think?'

'It sounds perfect. What do we do about Joaney?'

'Joaney is going to want her own life. The important thing is to mend your relationship with her now. Make her realise that you love her, and not the other child we can never have. She's not always going to be with us, Carla. Let go of the pain, please.'

'I'll try, Jack.'

'We have to try and draw a line under all this and leaving this town will allow us to do so.'

'When do we go?'

'I'll go and see the real estate agent in town next week. We'll sell the business first and then put the house up for sale.'

'Are you really sure about this, Jack?'

'Yes; it's time for us to move on.'

'This means a lot to me.'

'I know it does, Carla.'

'Let's celebrate. We'll go out for dinner tonight; you, me and Joaney. We'll tell her then. You know I've been thinking about Mike Fabien.'

'That's funny; so have I,' replied Jack.

'He left town and never returned.'

'He'll be back, I know it. He saved your life and told me he wanted to help us. That night after the incident at the river while you were asleep, we spent quite some time talking together. I don't think we've seen the last of him somehow.'

27

Three men sat around a large table in a spacious yet darkened room with the blinds partially shut allowing just enough light to enter. They were not engaged in conversation; their meeting together had a reluctant air to it. One raised his eyebrows as he looked at the clock that hung above the entrance door as another fiddled with his pen. The figure of Lawrence Henderson appeared in the doorway. He was late by five minutes, something unheard of for a man of his reputation.

'Gentlemen, thank you for your time,' he said in a sombre voice.

'What's this all about, Henderson?' asked one of the FBI officials.

'The Ascension Project,' he replied. It grabbed his listener's attention immediately. 'Yes, I thought that would draw your interest,' he continued. 'The lid has been blown off this rather sensitive matter. It appears that one of our agents, Michael Fabien, has been working independently. He has been to Ashbury Falls posing as a writer. I am not sure exactly what he has been doing but I know that he has spoken to certain individuals, one of whom is Hank Jebson. When I heard of this it caused me great concern as I am sure you can imagine, so I thought it best to brief you on the situation.'

'Hank Jebson?' asked the official.

'The father of Ronnie Jebson. You remember, subject 37,' said another.

'Correct,' confirmed Henderson. 'You must now also be aware that the Sterling Medical Research Corporation had a security breach recently.'

'I hope you're not going to be the harbinger of bad news are you?'

'I'm afraid I am, sir. The files on Ascension were downloaded. I have since instructed Sterling to delete all files on the subject. Ascension never happened.'

'Only I have authority to give that order, Henderson.'

'Sorry, sir, but that order came from above you.'

'I see.'

'I know it was Fabien. The question is why? I have two of my men in Ashbury Falls at this time and they have confirmed that they have caught up with him.'

'So you're going to bring him in then?'

'That's what I had planned to do,' replied Henderson. 'He must have been undertaking his own investigation on Ascension over the past few months whilst on other assignments but I don't know what his motives are.'

'He's overstepped the mark this time.'

'You're damned right he has!' said the other official angrily. 'We've tried to keep a lid on this for years so why has this happened now? You'd better deal with this swiftly, Henderson.'

'You're right, Jackson, but after the project was ordered closed, our superiors wanted someone to take the fall for the mess it had caused. There were several investors that put a lot of money into Ascension; one in particular was Charles Moreland. I've been after this guy for a long time now and it appears that Fabien has uncovered some very interesting information that we weren't aware of. According to Todman, Fabien claims that with this evidence he can deliver Moreland to me. That is why for the time being I am allowing this operation to continue.'

'So what has Fabien got on Moreland?' asked the senior official.

'I don't know at this time, sir. Fabien is keeping things very close to his chest. Quite frankly I don't blame him. If I was in his shoes I'd do the same. But we'll get that information and knowing Fabien as I do I'm confident we'll get Moreland.'

'Michael Fabien. He's a bit of a maverick isn't he?' said Jackson. 'You don't seem to run a very tight ship do you Henderson? Allowing one of your operatives to do this.'

'He gets results, even if his methods are sometimes unconventional,' replied Henderson.

'He's dangerous and as I stated earlier, he has gone too far this time. I think you understand what I'm saying.'

'Yes, and maybe the powers that be will be looking for me to do something about this, but at the moment Fabien is crucial to this operation and he stays in the field.'

'So what's the plan then? How long is this going to take? when will we get a result?' asked the third official.

'Soon, gentlemen, in fact I'm going to take a trip up to Ashbury Falls myself. Todman has asked for some reinforcements. This sounds serious so I'm sending in more agents.'

'So you're hoping that if you do manage to deliver Moreland, the State Department will turn a blind eye to this and it will all have been under the guise of getting Moreland. Nobody, including you, gets busted for this and the case is finally closed. Would that be a correct assumption?' added the senior official.

'If that's the way you see it, sir, that's your prerogative.'

'But how do we know that information hasn't spread?'

'We can't be sure of that of course, but I don't believe Fabien would be stupid enough to reveal anything damming. Whatever he may have said to Hank Jebson would be enough for him to know,' replied Henderson.

'You obviously have confidence in your man, Henderson. So why have you been after Charles Moreland?'

'Our investigations lead us to believe that even when the project was closed down, Moreland was still pumping cash into Sterling Medical Research. I have been trying to find out why.'

'We were not aware of this line of investigation, why is that, Henderson?' asked Jackson.

'Orders.'

'This is irregular; our department should have been informed.'

'I agree, Peterson, but for some reason the powers that be decided to keep your department out of this.'

'How do we know Fabien is telling the truth? Maybe he's just stalling, realising that he is going to be busted when you bring him in. How are you going to guarantee he doesn't disappear? I recall that he has managed to stay one step ahead of us in the past.'

'Going on information from Todman, when Fabien downloaded the files from Sterling, he discovered something that neither the Bureau nor the State Department know of. Fortunately for him he has that information. It could be a scam of course, but I don't think so.'

'Your brief then, Henderson, is to use this information, bring Moreland in and deliver him to the State Department?'

'Yes, sir.'

'How can the State Department hang this mess on just one man?'

'I don't know that either, but I guess we will find out in due course.'

'So what will you do with Fabien when you bring him in?' asked Peterson.

'That's my decision, and I'll decide when the time comes.'

'Perhaps you can enlighten me on something.'

'Go ahead.'

'Connor Newman, he's suddenly gone missing. Can you shed any light on this?'

'I imagine, sir, that he's probably on his way to Ashbury Falls.'

'So this is becoming more complicated by the day.'

'It would appear so, sir.'

'Then I do hope for your sake that we get Moreland, nothing irregular comes to light from this operation, and once this case is closed, the words Ascension Project are never mentioned again. Have I made myself clear, Henderson?'

'I understand perfectly, sir.'

'I want results, Henderson. If that's all, gentlemen, I have work to do.'

'Good luck, Henderson,' said Peterson sarcastically, and then left the room along with Henderson's superior.

Thomas Jackson headed towards the open door and closed it when the others had left. He turned to Henderson.

'Well it seems you've got a bit of a mess to clear up.'

'There will always be messes to clear up. Who were you trying to impress?'

'Do you trust Fabien? Because I don't. He was assigned to me once on a case I was handling. I won't bore you with the details. I never liked the way he operated; it's got to be by the book I always say. What makes him tick, Henderson?'

'I don't know, he may bend the rules and I think he's bent them too far this time, but he's a good agent and if he gets a result on this one, well...'

'You should have been keeping closer tabs on him. Your career could suffer for this.'

'And you'll be waiting in the wings won't you, Jackson.'

'Maybe. Tell me, Henderson, what will you do with him once the case is through?'

'He's served the Bureau for twelve years since his graduation. Came in straight from college. He's still young and as far as I am concerned he still has his career ahead of him, so let's be clear on one thing, Jackson, while he's under me, his career is in my hands and I'll deal with him the way I see fit. So you have nothing to worry about, do you?'

'One more question,' said Jackson as he headed for the door. 'Why have you decided to involve myself and Peterson now?'

'Orders.'

'From whom?'

'It doesn't matter. Let me do my job. I'll bring in Moreland, after that he's all yours.'

28

The glow of the open fire flickered on Reuben's face as he sat in one of the tall-backed leather armchairs in the lounge of Charles Moreland's mansion. He was staring into the flames as his body rocked gently back and forth in its usual metronomic manner, the way it always did when he found himself in a state of contemplation over a serious matter. The faceless expression he wore made his whole demeanour frightening to anyone unfortunate enough to observe it. His former secretary Rita had on several occasions walked into his office and seen him in this trance-like state and he would never respond immediately to her arduous attempts to converse with him. This had always worried her and had contributed to her resignation.

Roberts was experiencing the same problem in drawing his attention. For well over an hour Reuben had been locked away in his own world playing out in his mind how he was going to fulfil his obligations to Charles Moreland and whether the two lives that would be in his hands that evening were worth more than the million dollars he had been promised.

His latest attempt at wooing Jamie Farrington had ended in humiliation. He had promised himself that one day she would pay for the way she had treated him and it seemed that tonight would be the hour of retribution. But somewhere deep within him he knew that he couldn't go through with it. His father would never have remotely considered such an abhorrent idea.

'Reuben!' said a voice.

He looked up and saw his father standing in front of the fire looking down at him with the same disappointed expression he had always used.

'I'm ashamed of you, Reuben. What have I told you about these development deals? You can't just dive in to make a quick buck; you've got to be shrewd, check out the facts. You're out of your depth, son. I never taught you that way! Now look at you; they've got you by the neck and feet. I never taught you that way.'

'I'm sorry, Father.'

'Too late for that, Reuben; you're a big disappointment to your mother and I. Didn't they teach you anything at the college that we sent you to? All that money that your mother and I put up for you to go there, did it pay dividends?'

'I'm sorry, Father,' he repeated just as he had been forced to do so many times as a child.

'MR STEIN!'

He was startled as he heard Roberts trying to get his attention for what was the third time now.

'Mr Moreland wants to see you now.'

Dazed, he stood up from the chair and walked out of the lounge and into the hallway. He began his ascent of the large stairwell to the landing feeling like the executioner who had been summoned to receive his orders. As he walked along the long corridor to Moreland's office he wiped his face dry as he nervously observed the portraits on the wall, the eyes of nameless people immortalised on canvas following him all the way to the end, silently cheering him on. He reached the door and stopped to take a deep breath before knocking on it.

'Come in.'

'You wanted to see me,' he said as he swung it open and walked in.

'Sit down.'

Reuben closed the door and did as he was requested. Moreland leaned back in his chair with his hands together, staring at Reuben with a condemnatory look as when a boss is about to fire an employee for underperformance.

'I am very disturbed. Michael Fabien is late; his deadline expired an hour ago.'

'He'll be here, I know he will,' replied Reuben.

'I hope you're right.'

Reuben became nervous, finding it hard to swallow. He was afraid of Moreland and regretted the day he had ever tried to take him on.

'So are you ready for your assignment, Mr Stein?'

'I can't do it,' he whimpered.

'I'm sorry?'

'I can't do it,' he repeated looking at the floor.

'Look at me!'

Reuben instantly raised his head.

'Now what was it you said?'

'I can't kill them, I just can't.'

'Oh but you must,' replied Moreland.

'Can't you get two of your men to do it, why me?' pleaded Reuben.

'You're not taking me seriously are you, Mr Stein? I think you'll change your mind when you see this.'

Moreland handed Reuben a letter.

'What is it?'

'Read it carefully, Reuben.'

He began to read. A sickly feeling came over him as he reached one of the central paragraphs. Then he looked up at Moreland and felt like he was going to vomit.

'How do you know about this?' stuttered Reuben.

'I did some digging around. I have many contacts and I managed to find out all about this little fraud that you were involved in last year.'

'But I didn't know anything about this!' pleaded Reuben. 'I thought it was all legitimate!'

'That's irrelevant. The bottom line is that you subscribed to the deal and your name is on the contract.'

Reuben quickly tore up the paper and threw it in the waste paper basket, shaking as the tiny pieces of paper floated gently into it. Moreland laughed as Reuben looked bug-eyed at him in shock. He grabbed Reuben's tie and pulled him over the desk.

'So, if you follow through on tonight's assignment, not only will you receive a cheque for a million dollars, but your name will mysteriously disappear off that contract. You had better calm yourself down and think straight. I don't like it when my employees are not focused on the job at hand.'

Moreland signalled to Baxter who had been standing in the corner of the room to remove Reuben. He looked up at Moreland with disgust as Baxter grabbed his arm and escorted him out of the office.

A car pulled up at the turning of the road that led up to Moreland's estate. The lights were turned off and the engine stopped. Inside were Todman and Willis with Mike sat in the back.

'From what I saw of the place it isn't that heavily guarded. I think it should just be a case of scaling the wall and staying unnoticed,' he said. 'I can't say whether there are any hidden alarm triggers in the grounds, but I know that he has a number of aids working for him who appear to come and go. Watch out for them.'

'I'll have seven of them posted in the grounds to make sure the girl is released, then we'll move in and arrest Moreland. Hopefully you'll still be alive when we do. There are two men posted at the Aurora Motel to pick her up as you requested.'

'I'd better go. Remember, Todman, you need me alive.'

'We haven't forgotten,' remarked Willis.

Mike got out of the car, picked up a briefcase from the back seat and walked up the dark tree-lined road towards the entrance of Moreland's estate. He had been in similar situations as this before, but never had he felt this nervous.

His life was in the hands of colleagues who didn't have much regard for him, and he would have felt a little easier if Jennings was there. Jamie weighed heavily on his mind. Nothing could go wrong. After nearly ten minutes he reached the gates and pressed the intercom. This time Moreland answered.

'You're late, Mr Fabien.'

'But I'm here,' he replied.

He heard a click and then the gates swung open. Mike walked slowly up the drive towards the house. As he approached the top, one of Moreland's aids approached him from behind and held a gun to his back. He escorted Mike through the entrance doors and into the hallway he had entered two days previously. Roberts and Baxter, whom he recognised, were there to meet them. Roberts was a tall slender man possibly ex-military, Baxter was big and cumbersome, intimidating nevertheless with his shaven head.

'Search him,' said Roberts.

'Nothing, no wires, no weapons, he's clean.'

The entourage led Mike towards the stairs – Moreland had decided to come down and greet him personally.

'Mr Fabien, glad you could make it.'

Mike remained silent. The less he needed to say to Moreland the better in his view.

'Hand me the briefcase.'

Moreland put it on the table in the hallway and opened it. Inside was a brown padded bag. He opened it and pulled out two CDs.

'Very good, Mr Fabien.'

'Now let Jamie go.'

'Reuben,' called Moreland.

Reuben entered the hallway with Jamie, holding a gun to her side.

'Mike!' she called and tried to run over to him.

Reuben pulled her back and put the gun to her head.

'I want your men to take her to the Aurora Motel on West-Kemper Road. You've got me, now let her go, she has nothing to do with any of this,' said Mike. His calmness had left him.

'I'm afraid there has been a change of plan,' said Moreland.

'We had a deal. I'm here; it's me you wanted.'

'How do I know that these are the only copies of the stolen data, Mr Fabien?'

'I haven't taken any copies.'

'Really?'

'You have my word.'

'Maybe you haven't, but I'm sure your colleagues must have had access to this data by now.'

'What are you talking about, Moreland?'

'It's a trick, Mike. Reuben told me that Moreland plans to kill us both,' cried Jamie.

'Careless, Mr Stein. Did you really think I would let her go Mr Fabien? Now please stop playing games with me. I know who you are and I know your colleagues will try to rescue you.'

'Mike, what's he talking about?' asked Jamie frantically.

'Don't you know, Miss Farrington? Agent Fabien and his colleagues in the FBI have some information that I didn't want leaked. But now I guess it's too late. Too late for all of us.'

Mike looked at Jamie and could see both shock and anger in her eyes. She stared at him coldly for a few moments until the sound of opening doors made everyone look around. In walked Ritchie Templeman.

'Just on time, Ritchie,' said Moreland.

'You?' said Fabien recognising the face.

Reuben looked straight at Moreland.

'Him! What's going on! You hired him! He humiliated me in front of all those people!'

216

Reuben thrust Jamie aside. She fell to the floor and was picked up by Baxter. Then he pointed his gun at Ritchie.

'Nobody does that to me!' he shouted.

Ritchie instantly put his hands up.

'Put the gun down, Reuben. We're all on the same side.'

Reuben lowered the gun, shaking as he did so, his eyes fixed on Templeman.

'I have to leave now,' said Moreland.

'What did you do with the antidote?' asked Mike.

'What antidote?' asked Reuben, nervously. 'What's he talking about?'

Moreland glanced at Reuben and then back at Mike. Mike's words had momentarily shaken him.

'I don't know what you're talking about,' he replied.

'Yes you do. But don't worry we'll find it.'

'You won't find anything, Mr Fabien. You'll be dead!'

'Reuben, Ritchie, you know what you have to do.'

The two men looked at each other, shocked.

'Bring the girl,' said Roberts to Baxter.

Jamie looked at Mike, pleading for him to do something, but right now, he had no options.

29

Four FBI agents that had been sent by Henderson to Ashbury Falls stood at the edge of the tall stone boundary wall of Charles Moreland's estate. They were dressed in black field suits, three men and one woman. In turn, they each pointed a gun at the metal railings at the top of the wall and fired. As each of the metal claws clamped themselves around the railings, the thin black threadlike ropes were pulled tight and they began their ascent of the wall. As they finished their descent on the other side they left the ropes dangling, split up and spread out until they each reached a vantage position in front of the trees at the edge of the lawn that gradually sloped up to the house. They waited until some visible activity would occur, expecting two men to lead Jamie Farrington out into one of the two cars parked by the entrance.

Five minutes had passed and nobody had surfaced from the house. One of them radioed to a colleague who was positioned to the rear of the house.

'Any sign of Moreland?' he asked.

'Negative,' was the reply.

'What do we do?' radioed his female colleague.

'We wait a little while longer and then we take a look,' he replied.

The wait wasn't long. Finally they saw Mike and Jamie being escorted out by two men, one in a suit, the other dressed casually. They opened the trunk of one of the cars and forced their two captives to get inside at gunpoint.

'Todman, this is Shapiro.'

'Go ahead.'

Fabien and the girl have just been bundled into the trunk of a car. It looks like a Ford Convertible. I don't think they're being taken to the Aurora Motel. You'd better have them followed.'

'Acknowledged. Any sign of Moreland?'

'Not yet.'

'Keep the house under surveillance,' said Todman, but he was then interrupted. 'Wait, I can see Moreland now, with two of his aids, they're leaving in a black Lincoln.'

'Check the house, I'll deal with Moreland.'

Todman's brow creased as he got off the radio.

'Something wrong?' asked Willis.

'Change of plan, they've got Fabien and the girl. They must be taking them somewhere else. Fabien didn't plan on this happening so something's gone wrong.'

Todman picked up his radio again and called one of the agents in another car that was parked nearby. 'Ellis? Follow Moreland's Lincoln when it reaches the main road, and then call the Sheriff's office. Get them to head him off. Whatever you do, do not let him escape!'

'Understood,' came the reply.

'There will be a Ford Convertible driving past us very soon with Fabien and Miss Farrington in it. We need to intercept it,' said Todman to Willis.

'I won't forget that incident at the town hall,' said Reuben to a worried Ritchie. He hadn't expected to be involved in something of this gravity. A quick kidnapping was enough for him. The payment had been generous and now he was wondering why he was getting himself into this.

'Where are we taking them?' he asked Reuben, ignoring his comments as he turned the wheel of his car and swerved out onto the main road.

Reuben calmed down. He needed to focus on the task at hand. One million was a lot of money to lose out on. Payback was for another day.

'I know somewhere quiet where nobody will find them,' said Reuben. 'Just keep driving along this road. We'll meet the river soon, and when we do, follow alongside it for a few miles and then we'll take a turning off which leads into the woods, I'll tell you when. Nobody ever goes there, they'll never be found.'

'How do you know?' asked Templeman.

'Because my father took me there once when I was boy,' replied Reuben in an angry tone.

'Why would he take you up to a place like that?'

'To teach me a lesson.'

'That figures,' said Ritchie quietly.

'Drive!' said Todman to Willis as he saw Ritchie's car race past the lay-by in which they were parked. Willis pulled out onto the road and accelerated after them, the back end of his car swerving slightly as it joined the road.

'Did we pass a road junction back there?' asked Ritchie as he saw a pair of headlights appear in his rear view mirror.

'No, why?' replied Reuben.

'Then we've got company!' exclaimed Ritchie looking at Reuben nervously.

Reuben turned around and saw a car gaining on them.

'Lose them!' he shouted.

Ritchie pushed down hard on the accelerator and the car took off, increasing the distance between them and their pursuers. Reuben got his gun out in readiness and then saw that the car behind them was starting to gain ground. He aimed the gun and fired a shot, his hand shaking as he squeezed the trigger. Reuben wasn't used to guns or the world that he had suddenly been dragged into. All he could think about was the money that Charles Moreland had promised him. But at that moment a painful reality hit him, in that he realised that now he would probably not see a dollar of it. The bullet hit the windshield of Todman's car, causing it to shatter as it passed through, leaving a clean hole where it had impacted. Todman managed to duck his head in time as it entered the car and embedded itself in the top of the rear seat. Willis swerved the car in automatic reaction to the shot and slowed down in the process, allowing the Ford Convertible to gain some distance.

'Are you OK?' he asked Todman.

'Yes, just keep driving.'

As the bullet had partially shattered the windshield Willis had to lean over towards the door to get a clear view of the road ahead of him. Todman put his arm out of the passenger door window and aimed his gun at the tyres of Ritchie's car. He fired but missed. They reached the section of the road that converged with the river. The road was a good twenty feet above and there was a crash barrier that separated the road from the steep bank that descended to it. Ritchie again put his foot down and accelerated as Willis desperately tried to keep up with him.

As Willis pressed his foot hard on the gas the road took a bend in the distance and Todman saw the Ford Convertible disappear around it.

'Keep up, Willis, don't lose them!

'I'm trying.'

As the two FBI agents turned the bend, the road straightened and they could see Ritchie's car again well in the distance. The road was straight as it followed directly parallel with the river. Willis kept his foot firmly down on the accelerator pedal almost feeling like he would breach the bulkhead if he pressed any harder. Gradually they got closer to the car in front, and Todman pulled his body partially out of the window to take another shot. Reuben opened fire, again missing the exposed Todman. Steadying himself, he aimed his gun at the back of Ritchie's car and took a shot. The bullet hit the metal bumper leaving a small dent in it.

'Damn!' shouted Todman.

As Ritchie tried to gain ground, he thought about the damage that was being caused to his Ford Convertible.

Reuben fired another shot that went hopelessly into the air. Todman returned fire and this time the shot was on target. The bullet from his gun hit the rear right tyre of Ritchie's car, causing a blowout which made the vehicle swerve into the middle of the road. Ritchie began to lose control as his car then headed back towards the crash barrier that ran alongside the road.

'Turn the wheel!' shouted Reuben.

'OK, OK, I've got it,' shouted Ritchie, trying to look as though he was in control. But whatever he did, the car would not straighten and the tyre began to shred under the weight of the wheel and the speed of the car. As Ritchie's car swerved out into the middle of the road again, another car was fast approaching his from the opposite direction.

'Oh no! This is it!' thought Ritchie as both vehicles headed towards each other. The driver of the other vehicle just managed to avoid the head-on collision as it raced past with the sound of its horn blowing at full blast.

Willis drew close to Ritchie's car, closing in fast, as Todman again pulled himself out of the window and aimed his gun down at the left tyre. As he was about to fire, Willis drove over a small crater in the road causing the shot to miss, hitting the lock of the trunk instead. As the trunk flung open, Mike and Jamie emerged shaken, being thrown about with the swerving motion of the car. Willis pulled back allowing a good distance between the cars.

'Good shot!' he cried.

'I was aiming for the tyre!' replied Todman.

'Jump!' cried Mike to Jamie, and before she could think, he grabbed her hand and leapt out of the trunk pulling her with him. The two of them landed hard on the tarmac of the road. Mike rolled over to the side of the road, stood up and then ran out to Jamie. Grabbing hold of her he dragged her to the side as Todman's car swerved into the middle of the road to avoid her. As they got to their feet they heard a loud crashing sound in the distance and then saw Todman's car come to a sudden halt, the tyres screeching on the road as Willis braked heavily.

The two men got out of their car and rushed to the side of the road as Mike and Jamie ran as fast as they could to join them. As they caught up with them they looked down into the river to see the rear end of Ritchie's Ford Convertible slowly disappear below the surface of the murky water, with no sign of him or Reuben. Jamie's face turned white as she stared into the rippling water.

'That could have been us, Mike!' she said as the culmination of the events of the past few days finally hit her and caused her eyes to swell with tears.

'Did they jump?' asked Mike.

'No,' said Willis. 'No time, the driver lost control, it happened so quickly.'

'Nearly lost you too,' remarked Todman with a grin on his face.

'You must be my guardian angel, Todman!' replied Mike.

At that moment Mike heard Jamie vomit as he turned around and saw her leaning over the crash barrier.

'Are you OK?' he asked, putting his arm around her. She was too upset to reply.

A muffled voice could be heard from Todman's radio in his car. He walked over and picked it up.

'Hold on a second. Willis, you'd better move this vehicle to the edge of the road. We don't want any more cars in the river.'

Mike was stood a few feet away still with his arm around Jamie. Her knee was badly cut and her leg heavily bloodstained. Willis moved the car to the side of the road.

'Todman. Go ahead.'

As he listened to the words of his colleague at the other end he brushed his hands hard through what little hair he had left. Mike had seen him do this before and knew it was bad news.

'You cannot be telling me this, Ellis!' he said and then paused to listen to the rest. 'OK, regroup and wait until I call you.'

'Moreland?' asked Mike.

'They lost him,' replied Todman in sheer dismay. 'Henderson will have my guts for this, make no mistake!'

'Relax, Todman,' said Fabien. 'We'll find him.'

'How can you be so sure?' asked Willis.

'He knows we are on to him now and I know exactly where he's gone. Henderson will have his man, I promise.'

Mike turned to Jamie. She looked completely drained and traumatised.

'We'd better get that knee looked at,' he said.

'I'll be fine,' she replied indifferently.

'OK, Fabien, what now?' asked Todman.

'Go back to your hotel and get some rest. I'll call you tomorrow morning.'

'But Moreland could be miles away by then,' said Willis.

'Trust me, he won't.'

'Trust you,' muttered Jamie, remembering Mike's words when they had had their first encounter with Todman and Willis back at the hotel.

'Henderson's on his way up here,' said Todman.

'Then we'll discuss this when he arrives. Right now Jamie could use a lift back into town, so I think we'd better get going soon. Can you call the Sheriff's office and tell them what's happened here, while I talk to her.'

'OK,' replied Todman.

Mike led Jamie up the road just past the point where Ritchie had driven his car into the river so that they were out of hearing distance of his two colleagues.

'We need to talk,' he said.

'There's nothing to say. I just want to go home,' she replied.

'I think there is.'

'You lied to me, Mike, about everything.'

'I didn't lie; I just couldn't tell you the truth then. If I had—'

'I don't care anymore,' she interrupted. 'Just go. I hope you get Moreland after what he put me through.'

'OK,' said Mike.

'And give him this from me!' she added slapping Mike hard in the face. As she walked away a single tear ran slowly down her cheek before dripping off her face and disappearing onto the surface of the darkened road. 'And one more thing, Mike,' she said turning to him. 'Please don't call me.'

30

The Ashbury Falls Sheriff's office was located on Cambridge Road about a quarter of a mile from the centre of town. It was an old building that had been built in the fifties, but had been refurbished back in 1984. Things had been a little busier than usual that morning. The events of the previous night had been the main agenda and there had also been a shooting incident reported just outside of town in the early hours of the morning. A local named Tom Wheeler had thought that he had seen an intruder snooping around his house and the neighbours had reported the trigger happy Tom firing three shots at around 4.00 am. There was no sign of the would-be intruder, but it needed to be checked out.

Sheriff William F. Conway was sat in his office with his feet on his desk, leaning back in his chair and peering through the blinds on the window. He saw Deputy Rolands getting out of his car and walking into the building. Conway was a tall well-built man in his mid-fifties, a year away from retirement. Things had been quiet in Ashbury Falls and the surrounding county in the last couple of years, and he had hoped that things would stay that way. A few break-ins, two homicides and a major traffic incident had been the highlights of police activity in the area and that was enough for him as he began to wind down towards that happy day when thirty-five years in the force would come to an end.

He would never forget however, the events of twenty years ago when he had been involved in the Ronnie Jebson case as a young deputy. The FBI had been around during that period and he had been instructed to keep a check on the reporters who had been snooping around. The Jebson boy's death had always remained in the back of his mind and he knew that something had been amiss with the case all the way through. Keen to impress his superiors at the time, he had followed a lead that had taken him close to discovering the truth about what may have happened that day twenty years ago. But at a crucial time in the proceedings he had been ordered to drop his line of investigation and was re-assigned to another case. This had troubled him for a long time, but as time passed he began to put it behind him and move on. When he was finally promoted to County Sheriff he became more aware of the politics of law enforcement than ever before.

It was 11.12 am when Deputy Rolands knocked on the door and entered his office.

'Hey, Rolands, got anything on the shooting at Brantford Road this morning?'

'Not yet, Sheriff, I'm still digging. Can you sign this report please?'

'Sure. Have there been any other reports of intruders?'

'No, Sheriff.'

'Did they get a good description?'

'Too dark.'

'Well keep on it, for the time being anyway.'

Conway signed the report and handed it back to his deputy who was staring out of the window.

'You're looking a little thin these days, Rolands. Is that pretty wife of yours looking after you?'

'She certainly is. Here comes trouble, Sheriff,' said Rolands.

'What are you talking about, son?'

Rolands pulled open the blinds and pointed to three men dressed in suits through Conway's internal office windows as they proceeded to make their way towards the door.

'FBI,' commented Conway despondently.

'I'd better get back to work, Sheriff.'

Rolands opened the door for the three men and then promptly left as they stepped inside.

'Sheriff Conway, I'm Lawrence Henderson and these are Agents Todman and Fabien.'

'Gentlemen,' said Conway as he shook their hands. 'We don't get the FBI around these parts too often so when two of my deputies got a call last night regarding the crash in the river and telling me that the FBI was in town it got the alarm bells ringing, believe me. It came as a surprise to me to know just how many of your people are up here. What's going on?'

'I need you to provide me with men to assist in an operation that Agent Fabien has been involved in for some months now,' replied Henderson.

'What sort of operation?' asked Conway.

'We need to arrest Charles Moreland on a matter that I am not at liberty to discuss.'

'Charles Moreland, he's that millionaire guy isn't he? Sounds serious, but then I guess you wouldn't be up here if it weren't.'

Henderson nodded.

'Do you know something? Every time I've dealt with you guys we've always been kept in the dark. How the hell am I going to arrest the guy if I don't know what the charges are?'

'You can bring him in for the kidnapping of Jamie Farrington,' said Mike.

'Isn't she the girl who runs the hotel just the other side of town?'

'Correct.'

'So where is he now, where do we pick him up, is the girl OK?' asked Conway.

'She's fine. Have your men ready, Sheriff. You'll get a call at 19.00. We'll tell you the location then,' said Henderson.

'Is that it?'

'Two State Trooper cars should do it. Make sure they're well armed, Sheriff, and have back-up available just in case,' said Mike.

Conway was a proud man. As far as he was concerned this was his county, his patch, and he didn't take too kindly to being ordered around by some FBI official and his men from Washington DC.

'If you want my co-operation, Mr Henderson, you'll have to give me more than that.'

'Sorry, orders from on high,' said Henderson.

Suddenly, Conway recalled hearing those words before as though having a sense of déjà vu. He experienced a flashback that triggered something in his memory that made him realize that he had met Henderson before, somewhere. His face was familiar and those words, he had heard them, somewhere. Then it came to him.

'You were here.'

'I'm sorry?' replied Henderson.

'You were here, when the Jebson boy was killed. You were investigating. FBI, you were one of the...'

'FBI agents all look the same!' joked Mike.

'Speak for yourself, Fabien,' remarked Todman.

'I think our business is concluded for the day, gentlemen,' said Henderson. 'I can count on your support on this can't I, Sheriff? We need Moreland. I'm sure you understand.'

Conway looked Henderson in the eye, making him feel a little uncomfortable. For an instant Henderson thought that he recognized Conway too.

'OK, 19.00 tonight. But I'm not happy about the lack of information. You men in the Bureau are all the same. You just think you can come in and give your orders...'

'We really appreciate your help in this matter, Sheriff,' said Henderson.

'We'll be there.'

'Wait for my call.'

Henderson and Todman walked out leaving the door open. Before he left, Fabien turned and gave Sheriff Conway a warm look as he shook his hand again.

'Thank you, Sheriff.'

As the three men went to their cars, Conway watched them through the window of his office.

'He recognized you didn't he, sir?' asked Mike.

'Call it a day, Fabien,' remarked Todman.

'Yes, Agent Fabien, I was here during the Jebson investigation. It's difficult following orders when you know things aren't right, but follow them I did. If I'd stepped out of line back then, I'd have been out of the Bureau – history.'

'What's the plan?' asked Todman.

'Agent Fabien?' said Henderson.

'I'll call you at 18:50, with the location,' replied Fabien.

'Don't let me down, Fabien,' replied Henderson. 'We need this guy or we'll all be history.'

Mike opened the door of his Nissan, got in, started the engine and drove off as quickly as he could. Henderson turned to Todman.

'Follow him. Call me if you suspect anything.'

31

Carla opened the front door to the house, hung up her coat and headed into the lounge. She had left work early so that she could cook something special for the family for dinner. Before she started she decided to check for any messages first. There were two. The first was from Jenna asking her to call her to catch up on things. The second was from someone she had been desperate to hear from for many days now.

'Carla, this is Mike Fabien. Sorry I haven't made contact, but it's vital that you and Jack meet me at Hank Jebson's house this afternoon at 4.30 pm. Please be there, I don't have much time.'

She quickly called Jack at the store, her tone urgent.

'Is everything OK, Carla?' he asked.

'Yes. Listen to me – close the store now and come home. We've had a message from Mike Fabien. We have to meet him at Hank's at 4.30.'

'What's it all about, Carla?'

'I don't know, Jack, but please we have to be there.'

'OK, I'll be home as soon as I can.'

'No, Jack, please leave now.'

Hank Jebson was cooking soup on the stove when there was a knock at his front door. He turned the stove off and walked out of his kitchen and through the lounge to his front door. He was surprised to see the face in front of him as he opened the door. A smartly dressed Mike Fabien greeted him.

'So you decided to return, I guess you had better come in then. Where have you been, son?'

'It's a long story and I'm not going to even begin to tell you, but I do need to speak to you. I promised you some information didn't I?'

'As I recall, yes.'

'I'm waiting for two others to come and then I'll tell you why I'm here.'

'Who?' asked Hank.

'Some friends of yours, Hank, they should be here any minute.'

'You look like you've got the weight of the world on your shoulder,' said Hank, observing Mike's nervous expression. Then there was another knock at the door.

'That should be them,' said Mike.

Hank opened the door; it was Jack and Carla.

'What's going on here?'

'Jack, Carla, it's good to see you,' said Mike placidly.

'I didn't think we would see you again,' replied Carla as Mike shook hands with Jack.

'So what's this all about?' asked a perplexed Hank.

'Please sit down all of you,' said Mike. He paused momentarily. 'I'm afraid I haven't been completely honest with you all. I'm not a writer but I think you knew that all along, didn't you, Hank?'

'Well, son, that doesn't come as a surprise. So you're a cop aren't you?'

'I'm an FBI agent.'

'Why didn't you tell us?' asked Carla.

'For some months now, I've been unofficially investigating something called the Ascension Project. Back in the 1970s the government sanctioned research into developing a way by which the immune system could be enhanced. They engaged the Sterling Medical Research Corporation in Boston, and with the help of some private investment, Sterling began to do tests and research into producing a drug that could do just that. Carla, Reuben Stein and Ronnie were amongst a small group of people in this area that were involved in Phase II of the experiment.'

'But, I don't recall that ever happening, Mike. What are you talking about?'

'You don't recall, Carla, because you were never meant to know. Sometime back in your late teens you were injected with the drug that Sterling had been developing. You, Reuben and Ronnie were all given it. Many local doctors were involved, institutions, colleges, it was all under cover, a secret, but they knew who the test subjects were, and you were monitored for some time afterwards. That drug caused your condition, Carla. You began to experience blackouts shortly afterwards because the drug had some unforeseen side affects which caused neurological disorders in the subjects. That's why you've still got them today. I don't know all the medical details, I'm not a doctor, but having done some research into this I can certainly tell you that this is the cause of your problems. Reuben experienced the same symptoms as you, Carla, but it was only when Hank told me about Ronnie that I managed to put all the pieces of the puzzle together.'

'My Ronnie was an experiment? Who the hell do they think they are?' said an angered Hank interjecting.

'I acquired some data on the project. They called it 'Ascension' because they based it on the biblical account of Adam and Eve. You know that many cultures describe the eating of the forbidden fruit as mankind's fall. Well the US government decided that they wanted to go some way to reversing that fall and hence they called it the Ascension Project. Taken to its ultimate conclusion they would have tried to develop a drug to eradicate most, if not all, illnesses. A Utopian dream, but it had small beginnings. Unfortunately they realised fairly early on that Phase II was failing. Reports came back of the neurological disorders that were being experienced by their subjects. So they decided to bring one of them in, subject 37. That, Hank, was your son Ronnie.'

'What do you mean, Mike?'

'They decided that they needed to take him away, so they faked his death, Hank.'

'But how, Mike, how?'

'Remember you told me how suspicious you were of the circumstances surrounding Ronnie's death, and that you told me how the case was covered up. You were never allowed to see the body they had found were you?'

'That's right, Mike, I always knew there was something wrong.'

'I had suspected this from early on, during my time doing the research. Ronnie had been down by the river on the jetty with his then friend Reuben. Reuben had apparently left Ronnie a little while before his so-called disappearance. He had been under surveillance. When they realised that he would frequently go down to the river they chose to take him from there. When Reuben left they drove a small dinghy along the river which they had launched from the slope that led up to Eastfeldt Road. He was abducted, Hank. They took him back up the river where a car would have been waiting in Eastfeldt to drive him off. A few days later, a body turned up which the local Sheriff's office identified as being Ronnie's, but, of course it wasn't. It was the body of a young man called Steven Tompkins who had drowned in the river about 30 miles north of Ashbury Falls. There were physical similarities to Ronnie and so they used his body as a means of proving that Ronnie had actually drowned. That's why you were never allowed to see the body, Hank. You would have known straight away that it wasn't Ronnie.'

'So what happened to him? Mike, please tell me what happened to him?'

'He was taken, debriefed and given a new identity, but they used him for further research.'

Hank put his head into his hands. Carla and Jack moved over to comfort him.

'We can't undo the past. Carla, you're going to have to live with your disorder for the rest of your life. But from my research I have at least discovered that things won't get any worse than they are. Your condition should stabilise as long as you don't overdo things. I know that is no consolation, but at least now you know why this has all been happening and you can move on with your life. Hank, there's still the future.'

'What future?'

Mike picked up his radio.

'Jennings, we're ready.'

The three of them looked up at Mike wondering what was going on. Mike got up from his chair and opened the front door. He stood there for just over a minute and then two men walked into the house.

'Carla, Jack, Hank, this is Agent Jennings, a colleague and a good friend of mine. He's been helping me with this investigation and this, Hank, is Connor Newman. Hank looked at the stranger who had just walked into his house and then his eyes widened with disbelief. He touched Connor's face.

'Ronnie?'

'Yes, Pa, it's me.'

'Ronnie is it really you?'

'It is, Pa.'

With that Hank looked at Mike, who nodded. Hank embraced Ronnie as tears rolled down his face. Slowly Ronnie put his arms around his father, and the two men stood there hugging each other. Carla began to cry.

'Why, why all this time, twenty years?' asked Hank.

'For many years I didn't even know who I was. They must have pumped me with all sorts of drugs and things. They relocated me, gave me a new identity. I got a new life. I even got married eventually. Her name's Pamela and we've got two great kids, Jake and Molly. We live in Washington State near Grays Harbour. When I finally realised who I was, they stopped me from making contact. It was only when Agent Jennings visited me, told me the truth, and told me what Agent Fabien was doing that I knew what had really happened to me. They told me we would be reunited but that I just had to wait for a while. But I'm here now, it feels so strange.'

It was then that Ronnie noticed the tree house in the garden. He stared at it for a few moments and suddenly the memories came back to him.

'The tree house, Pa, you kept it!'

Tears rolled down Hank's cheeks.

'Twenty years, Ronnie – it's such a long time,' said Hank.

'Looks like we've got twenty years of catching up, haven't we. Say, Carla, I don't remember much about you, but I know who you are. Agent Jennings told me.'

'It's good to see you again, Ronnie,' she replied.

'I have a question, Mike,' said Jack.

'Go ahead.'

'Why? You're an FBI agent. You've just uncovered something very dirty. Why have you gone to all this trouble?'

Before Mike could answer, there was a voice behind him at the front door.

'Yes, Agent Fabien, why?'

He turned around to see Henderson standing in the doorway. Henderson walked in with Todman slowly following him. Mike looked around at all the people in the room as though this was the moment of truth, time to account for his actions.

'Why? Agent Fabien, I'd like to know too,' repeated Henderson.

'How did you know I was here?' asked Mike.

'We followed you,' said Todman. 'And I think that was a good idea under the circumstances, don't you?'

'When are you going to cut me some slack, Todman?'

'We're not, at least not until this operation is concluded.'

'So,' continued Mike, 'You want to know why I have risked my career, opened up an investigation that the FBI and the State Department would rather have kept the lid on. I was born in Chicago and lived there for most of my childhood. Then when I was fourteen years old, my father moved to Ashbury Falls after the death of my mother. I went to school here. Ronnie was two grades above me.

'I can't remember you, Agent Fabien,' said Ronnie.

'No, Ronnie, there's lots of things you probably won't remember, but I was there at Ashbury High. You and Reuben were best friends, weren't you? Do you remember Reuben?'

'Yes, I remember him.'

'You liked to go down to the jetty by the river. I did too. One day in September, twenty years ago I was on the walkway that descended to the Jetty; the same one that's there today. I stopped. I heard two guys arguing. It sounded like they were having a bit of a bust-up over something. I could see you and Reuben through the trees. You pushed him over. When he got up I thought you were going to deck him. He came back up the walkway and I remember he looked at me on the way up but he didn't know me, I was just another kid from school. Then I looked down again and saw you standing alone on the jetty.

'I had walked back up to the parking lot after a minute or so and watched you from there. I sat on one of the benches at the top of the walkway thinking where I should go next. You must have been chucking stones in the river or something when I heard what I thought sounded like a motor dinghy on the river in the far distance. There was nobody else around, just you on the jetty and me in the parking lot. I can't recall a lot, Ronnie, but I do remember hearing that motor dinghy. Then I headed off into town to see if my friends were in the diner by the square. I had been walking for about five minutes and then I stopped, turned around, and headed back to the walkway. I thought I would go back down to the jetty and just ask if you wanted to come, get a soda or something.

I remembered that you were in that band in school and that you played a white Telecaster. I guess I just wanted to talk to you about the band or something. When I got down to the bottom of the walkway and to the jetty you were gone. All I could see was the ripples of the water and a handful of pebbles on the jetty.

'I remember the investigation by the Sheriff's office. You'd gone missing and they were asking for anyone who had seen you. I told them what I'd heard but then nothing came of it. Then I heard that you had drowned and the case was closed. I was the last one to see you alive. A few years later I left Ashbury Falls and went to college in Albany whilst my father returned to Chicago. I joined the FBI after I graduated. The memory of that day in September '77 has haunted me to this day. If only I'd gone down and risked getting decked too, you would still have been alive. So that's why I have been investigating this case for the last few months. I was involved too and I guess all this time I have been searching for an absolution. And now I've found it.'

'It must have been tough for you, son, carrying that with you all this time,' said Hank sympathetically.

'Yes, Hank, it has.'

Hank held out his hand to Mike.

'You're a good man, Mike,' he said, 'Thank you.'

'I'd like to thank you too, Mike,' said Carla as she looked at him affectionately. Jack nodded in agreement.

'Well, I guess my business is finished here,' said Mike.

'Not quite,' said Henderson.

'Let's go, Fabien, Jennings,' said Todman.

Jennings and Todman left the room and headed out to the cars that lined the sidewalk at the front of the house.

'You've all got a future now. Live it,' said Mike as he followed his colleagues.

Henderson stood on the lawn for a few moments. Memories of the case that he had been involved in twenty years previously when he was a young FBI agent came flooding back. He looked respectfully at Hank and then nodded as he turned to go, his heart weighing heavily within him.

32

Under the veil of darkness a car pulled up outside a pair of iron gates, with three men inside. Two of them got out of the car, one of them with a pair of chain cutters in his hands. The other grabbed hold of the chain that was wrapped around the gates, pulled it as tight as he could whilst his colleague quickly snapped it in two with one hard wrench of the cutters. The man holding the chain quickly unravelled it, pulled it from the gates and pushed them wide open so that the car could enter. The two men got back in the car and one of them proceeded to drive it up the dark track. As they approached a cluster of trees, the spots of water on the windshield turned into splashes as the rain became heavier. The driver switched on the windscreen wipers and continued driving until he reached the shore of a large lake.

Following the first car was another vehicle that was towing a small motorboat. Eventually it caught up with the car and parked alongside it by the lake. Two men got out and detached the trailer from the back whilst the other two from the car helped them to pull it down to the gravelled shoreline of the lake. From there they launched it into the water and two of them waded out, pushing the boat to a safe deep distance before getting in. Once the boat was in position on the lake, the engine was lowered into the water and they started it up.

The third man got out of the car and stood on the shore of the lake as another of the men in frogman's gear entered the water and waded over to the boat.

'You know the location.'

'Yes, I've gone over the map and checked your co-ordinates. I know where to dive,' replied the frogman.

'Good. Make sure you have all that you need to retrieve that box. We don't have a lot of time.'

'We're ready,' replied one of the men in the boat.

'Then get to it and flash me when you've located it. The lake is probably around ten metres deep. At the location you will find a red metal box about a foot cubed. You will probably have to uncover it from weeds and mud on the bed. There should be something on the box to hook the chain to, so that you can pull it to the surface. Be careful when you lift it onto the boat.'

The men slowly drove the boat out to the centre of the lake. After a few minutes the boat stopped at the instructed location. The frogman dived into the water with a large chain in his hand and swam down towards the bed of the lake. His two colleagues watched eagerly when they saw the underwater flashlight dim as the frogman went deeper. The frogman reached the bed and searched around him for the metal box. He searched a radius of some ten metres from where the boat had stopped, but could see nothing but bits of debris and weeds on the muddy bed. He returned to the surface and pulled himself back onto the boat. He pulled off his mask and instructed the men to take him about twenty metres further out onto the lake.

On the shore of the lake, his boss watched nervously. He could just see the boat disappearing further into the distance. They hadn't found it. Then he saw the boat come to a stop and some activity as he again saw the frogman's searchlight disappear into the water.

The frogman submerged again and surveyed another area, but this time a greater radius to see if he could locate the object. He moved his searchlight around the bed but was still unable to locate the box, so he turned ninety degrees and headed about fifteen metres in the opposite direction, moving his flashlight left to right slowly until his eye caught something cube-like in the distance. He swam over and there bedded in the mud he saw what looked like a metal box.

Brushing off some of the mud, and underwater weeds, he saw a red metal box with the words 'Sterling Medical Research Corporation' printed on the side. This was what he had been sent to find and so he wrapped his chain round the U-shaped hook at the top of the box. He had to tug fiercely to free it from the bed but finally it became dislodged as clouds of mud moved up through the water. He pulled the box up from the bed of the lake and dragged it up towards the surface. The two men in the boat watched as the flashlight became brighter and the frogman returned to the surface. As the frogman re-emerged he signalled a thumbs up indicating that he had found what they had been looking for. He pulled the box to the edge of the boat and handed the chain to one of his colleagues. The two men lifted it carefully out of the water as the frogman guided it in.

'We've got it.' said one of the men as the other helped pull the frogman back into the boat. His colleague turned the boat round and headed back to the shore.

The frogman picked up his flashlight and flashed it three times so that his boss on the shore could see that he had found the box. The rain became more persistent as the weather began to deteriorate but that didn't dampen the delight of a jubilant Charles Moreland. As the boat came back to the edge of the lake, the frogman jumped out and waded to the shore. The men in the boat stopped the engine, lifted it out of the water and then dragged the boat in. The three men lifted the box out of the boat and carried it across the edge of the grass where Charles Moreland was standing. The frogman held his flashlight to the box as Moreland took out his gun and fired it at the lock with a silencer attached. The lock broke open instantly and Moreland quickly opened the lid of the box. Inside were a large number of thin metal canisters.

'Well done, all of you,' said Moreland as he gleefully looked at the contents.

'This box and its contents could have caused me grievous trouble. Quickly get it into the trunk of the car, we need to take it somewhere where nobody will find it.'

At that moment four spotlights were turned on, blinding Moreland and his men.

'Those antidote canisters are going nowhere, Moreland.'

'What the hell!' exclaimed Moreland.'

Suddenly Mike Fabien, along with Henderson, Todman, Willis and Jennings appeared. Henderson picked up his radio.

'OK, Sheriff Conway, bring your men in now.'

As Moreland's aids tried to pull out their guns, another four FBI agents arrived with much larger armour.

'Well, Moreland,' said Fabien, 'what a location to dump the antidote, the bottom of Chakowah Lake.'

'How did you know?' asked Moreland calmly.

'When I discovered that Chakowah Park has never been an ancient Indian burial ground and that all this was just a scam to halt the Logan development, I asked myself, who stands to lose most if it went ahead? I knew from the information that I had obtained from Sterling that the antidote that had been developed to counteract the affects of Phase II of the Ascension project in the early '80s had gone missing. So I figured that the man who funded the research must have taken it. What better place to hide it than the bottom of the lake where no one would find it, until that is a luxury housing development would be built around it.'

'So what are the charges, Fabien? All we have here is just a metal box with canisters of antidote.'

'True, but if the US government knew what substances were used in its production and where they came from, if they were to sample the contents of those canisters, I suspect that not only yourself and your fellow investors, but also Sterling would have some explaining to do, wouldn't they?'

'I'm saying nothing,' replied Moreland.

'I wonder whether the antidote would really have worked. Or was it just a pretence to make you all look like you actually cared about the people whose lives you helped to ruin.'

At that moment three cars turned up with US State Troopers inside.

'I've waited a long time for this moment, Moreland,' said Henderson. 'Take them away, Sheriff, but leave Moreland, he's mine.'

Moreland looked at Fabien and Henderson indignantly.

'You know nothing,' said Moreland. 'Even with all the information you've got on this case, you haven't even scratched the surface on Ascension. Do you know what it's like to watch someone you've loved, gradually deteriorate with no hope of being cured? Slowly having the force of life drained from her in front of your very eyes.'

'I know more than you think, Moreland,' said Fabien.

'Whatever you think of me, the investors, Sterling or even the damned State Department, that project was ethically sound, but someone in authority who thinks they're standing on high moral ground decides to pull the plug. It will continue. Somewhere and somehow there will be money and there will be organisations that will do this all over again. Neither you or the State Department can ever stop that.'

'Todman, Willis, get him out of here,' said Henderson angrily. 'Ellis, we're taking that box back to Washington, don't lose it.'

'OK, let's go,' replied Agent Ellis as he and two others picked up the antidote and carried it away.

Moreland gave Henderson a piercing look as he was taken away. Henderson watched for a while as Todman and Willis escorted Moreland to one of the FBI security vehicles. Then he signalled for his agents to disperse, and for the police to leave Chakowah Park.

'Old scores have been settled tonight, am I right, sir?' asked Fabien.

'Maybe,' replied Henderson as he stared across the lake with his back to him.

'If you'll excuse me, sir,' said Fabien, as he walked over to Jennings.

'Wait,' said Henderson. There was a momentary silence. All that could be heard was the distant sound of activity behind them and the falling of rain as the downpour continued and pummelled the lake's surface. 'We still have some unfinished business. I'll see you both tomorrow morning at the Sheriff's office. Don't be late.'

33

The alarm clock sounded by the side of Mike's bed in his motel room. It was 9.00 am. He searched with his hands to find it and eventually his fingers touched the buttons. Pushing each one he could find he finally managed to switch it off. His eyes opened slowly until he could see the time. It had been a very successful night's work. He had got his man and the reinforcements would by now be on their way back to Washington DC with the box of antidote canisters that they had retrieved.

Climbing out of bed he walked over to the chair and put his dressing gown on before walking over to the coffee machine and heating up the half-full jug. As he opened the curtains he was bathed in sunlight. The storm clouds of the previous night had disappeared and not just in a literal way. His work in Ashbury Falls was done and soon he would be returning to Falls Church, Virginia, where he had been living in recent years. All that remained was his meeting with Henderson that morning at Sheriff Conway's office. He quickly went into the bathroom and turned on the shower while the coffee warmed up. Badly in need of a shave he opened the bathroom cabinet to take out his razor. It was the one that Jamie had given him; perhaps it would bring him luck, something he needed now.

When he had finished showering, he got dressed and quickly drank a cup of coffee before making his way downstairs to the motel lobby. He helped himself to a Danish for breakfast and then asked the receptionist to call Jennings in his room. As he sat in the lobby waiting for Jennings, Todman and Willis arrived to check out.

'Heading back?' he asked Todman.

'Yes, we're going straight away, we're done here. I'll tell you something, Fabien, I'd love to be a fly on the wall in Sheriff Conway's office this morning when you and Jennings meet with Henderson.'

'See you around, Todman,' replied Fabien.

Todman laughed.

'Maybe.'

The two men checked out, left the motel, got in their car and drove off. Shortly thereafter, Jennings arrived in reception.

'I'm checking out too. Once we've met with Henderson I'm heading back to DC.'

Minutes later the two men were on their way in their respective cars to the Sheriff's office on Cambridge Road.

'Do you have an interview room free, Sheriff?' asked Henderson.

'Sure, follow me.'

Sheriff Conway led Henderson down the corridor to one of the interview rooms. It was small, dingy, but adequate.

'Can I get you some coffee?'

'No thank you, but I'd be grateful if you could get one of your staff to send Agents Fabien and Jennings down here when they arrive. I'm expecting them at around 10.00 am.'

'Sure,' replied Conway. 'I guess you've finished your business here then, Mr Henderson what with you getting Charles Moreland last night.'

'This business is far from over but at least we got our man. Thanks for your help. It was a clean operation last night. If I need any further information I'll call you from Washington.'

'OK,' replied Conway and then he left Henderson alone in the interview room.

As he returned to his office he passed Deputy Rolands.

'Nice work last night, Rolands, say have you got any leads yet on that intruder at Brantford Road?'

'Not yet, Sheriff.'

'Well maybe it was just an isolated incident. I don't want you to spend much more time on it.'

At 10.00 am precisely, Fabien and Jennings entered the Sheriff's office. Conway was waiting for them.

'Mr Henderson's down the end of the corridor in interview room 2.'

The two agents walked down the corridor and as they reached the interview room Fabien knocked on the door.

'Come in, gentlemen,' said Henderson. 'Sit down.'

Jennings closed the door and then sat down alongside his colleague. Henderson looked at them both for a few moments before speaking.

'So, Agent Fabien,' he continued, 'we got our man, we even got the evidence. I'm sure the labs will find some very interesting substances in those canisters. Don't you agree?'

'Yes, sir,' replied Fabien.

'Good work, gentlemen. Very resourceful of you, Fabien, you delivered just as you said you would, I'm very pleased. We'll discuss you in a moment, but first I would like to know what Agent Jennings' involvement in this illegal operation has been. Agent Jennings, perhaps you could shed some light on this.'

'There's nothing much to say, sir,' interrupted Fabien. 'He checked a few things out for me, got some information that I didn't have access to at the time.'

'Is that correct, Jennings?' replied Henderson.

'Yes, sir, just as Agent Fabien said.'

'That would make you an accomplice then.'

'With respect, sir, he didn't know the full details of my operation,' added Fabien.

'I see. But you did deliver Connor Newman to Agent Fabien, so you went against clear orders. Connor Newman was to stay under. You could have caused a lot of trouble. On reflection I guess there's nothing more they can do with him now. I'll tell my superiors that subject 37 is no longer needed. OK, Jennings you can go, but I'll be entering a formal reprimand in your records.'

'Yes, sir,' replied Jennings. He touched Fabien's shoulder to give him reassurance as he walked out of the door, closing it behind him.

'Well, Agent Fabien, what am I to do with you? You broke protocol, you disobeyed orders, and you potentially caused our senior colleagues and the State Department a great deal of embarrassment. You knew Ascension was closed and yet you deliberately persisted in re-opening it, just so that you could put right something that you were involved with twenty years ago. Very noble, Agent Fabien, but also very stupid. I must admit I was a little touched myself by that family reunion at the Jebson's house yesterday. I've no doubt that you had your reasons for doing this, but you've put me in a difficult position. There will be some in the Bureau that will want your scalp. There will equally be some that will be very grateful that you have delivered Charles Moreland to them. You've been a good agent for me over the years. I don't necessarily agree with your methods and there have been times when I have wanted to pull the plug on you. But for what it's worth, Fabien, I'd like to see you remain in the Bureau and dare I say it, in my team. I'm prepared to speak for you on the condition that you tow the line right now. You've damaged your career but hopefully not ended it. It's time you stopped being a maverick, Fabien. Personally I think you've crossed the line on this one, but all things considered I'll see what I can do for you. No promises, but I do have friends in high places who will listen to me and who respect my judgement. There will be a hearing four weeks from today in Washington. Until then, Agent Fabien, you are suspended from duties. I suggest that you do a lot of thinking about your future over the next few weeks. I have to return to DC now. I'll see you in four weeks. That will be all.'

'Sir.'

Mike left interview room 2. Jennings was waiting for him at the end of the corridor and as they passed through the main office on their way to the exit, Deputy Rolands was speaking with one of his colleagues.

'We'll try a few more people in the Brantford Road area to see if they saw anyone.'

'The intruder may have been from out of town. For all we know he could be miles away by now,' replied his colleague.

'You're probably right, but we'll give it another shot, try some of the folks that weren't in last time. If nothing comes up, we'll leave it.'

Henderson picked up his briefcase and walked out of the room. He headed back up the corridor and briefly called in to see Sheriff Conway.

'Thanks again for your help, Sheriff, we're finished here.'

'Well, Mr Henderson, don't be offended if I say I hope we don't see you again, at least not until I've retired!'

Henderson smiled, shook Conway's hand and then proceeded to leave the building. As he left he saw Fabien and Jennings conversing over the other side of the parking lot. He glanced at them, and then got into his car, drove out onto Cambridge Road and headed off towards the freeway.

'Well, Fabien,' said Jennings 'At least things don't look so bad. Henderson's a good man, I'm sure he will help you.'

'We'll see,' replied Fabien.

'This has certainly been an experience for me to say the least. I'd better go now, I'm due back at DC. What are your plans?'

'I'll probably stick around here for another day or so and then I'll head home. Thanks, Jennings, you're a good friend. Take it easy now.'

The two men shook hands and then Jennings left. Fabien unfastened his collar, took his tie off and threw it into the car before getting in and driving back to his motel room.

34

Jamie came out of the office with a number of letters in her hand. Stella was standing at the desk and had just finished the paperwork she had been studiously going over.

'Can you drop these in the mailbox on your way home?' asked Jamie.

'Sure. Well that's my stint for today over. Are you sure you're going to be OK?' she replied.

'I'll be fine thanks,' replied Jamie.

'You can stay at my place for a few days if you want. You've been through a dreadful ordeal, Jamie. I do hope the police have caught those men.'

'Go on, Stella, get yourself home now and thanks again for looking after things. You can take the week off if you want to, you deserve at least that. I'll manage here; the work will take my mind off things.'

'That's very kind of you, Jamie, but I think you need all the support you can get at the moment. I'll see you tomorrow.'

'Thanks, Stella, you're a good friend.'

Stella put on her coat and walked towards the hotel entrance.

'Bye for now, take care,' she said as she opened the door and left the hotel.

Jamie waved and then returned to the office to finish up what she had been doing. Stella had really looked after things well which gave her even more of an incentive to move to Boston. She could keep the hotel and let Stella run it for her. Then if things didn't work out, she would always have a business to come back to.

She sat there alone for a few minutes staring at a photograph on the wall of her parents standing on the lawn at the front of the hotel, back in the seventies, and she wondered what they would have thought about her moving to Boston.

'What should I do?' she asked them.

She opened the drawer of the desk and pulled out an opened packet of cigarettes. She was about to take one out but then she threw them into the waste bin and covered her face with her hands. She was tired, confused and had still not got over the shock of her ordeal.

'I'll finish this tomorrow,' she thought and decided to retire to her room.

She turned the light out in the office and walked out into the reception area. As she was about to walk down the corridor that led to her apartment, she heard a noise. Cautiously, she walked down towards the kitchen. The window was open and blowing the curtains into the room. She quickly shut it and opened the door out to the courtyard at the rear of the hotel. As she stepped outside, the memory of the events at the old mill house came rushing back to her and she shuddered. She noticed that one of the trash bins had been knocked over and as she went to pick it up, her neighbour's ginger cat sprang out from inside it making her jump out of her skin. Her fear quickly turned to relief as it darted off into the rear parking lot.

She sighed and then went back into the kitchen, closing the door and locking it. She poured herself a cup of tea, carried it through into her lounge and left it on the coffee table in the centre of the room before entering the bedroom to take off her jewellery and slip into something more relaxing. She thought she heard another sound and looked back quickly into the lounge.

'You're getting paranoid,' she thought and took a deep breath.

She had been feeling jumpy for the last couple of days and was becoming concerned that the anxiety she had been experiencing might not subside for a long while. Nothing like this had ever remotely happened to her before and it had caused disturbing ripples in what had otherwise been an ordinary, quiet life. She looked around the bedroom and out of the window just to make sure. Nothing. Sitting on her bed she took off her boots and then walked over to her dressing table to sit down and remove her earrings. The mirror in front of her was facing upwards. She pulled it down to adjust it so that she could see herself. As her face came into full view she saw the figure of a man standing behind her by the door. As she screamed, he slammed the door shut. She turned around in terror to see Reuben Stein standing there, back from the dead, staring at her with the eyes of Medusa.

She was unable to scream; her throat had become tight. 'Nobody in the hotel will hear me down here,' she thought as fear paralysed her.

Reuben grabbed her and pulled her to the bed.

He began to tear her shirt open as he pressed down hard on her body. She was helpless. Tears rolled down her cheeks as she resigned herself to the inevitable. As his other hand reached between her legs, an evil grin appeared on his face and he then pressed his other hand hard across her mouth. With a menacing smile he started to unbutton the fly of her jeans, but his ecstasy suddenly turned cold as he felt a gun pointed at his head and two of the Sheriff's men seize him by the arms to pull him off her.

Mike took the gun away as Rolands and another deputy carried Reuben off. He caught hold of Jamie and held her tightly as she wept bitterly on his shoulder.

'Is everything OK?' said a voice from behind them.

Mike looked around to see Sheriff Conway standing in the doorway.

'She'll be OK, Sheriff.'

'OK, son, call me if you need anything.'

'It's over, Jamie; no one's going to hurt you now.'

She managed to compose herself and let go of Mike. She looked at him, still with tears in her eyes.

'How did you know he'd be here?' she asked.

'I overheard Deputy Rolands talking about an intruder lurking around the Brantford Road area to the north of town. That's not far from where Ritchie Templeman drove his car into the river. I called in later and spoke to Rolands. He told me he'd finally got a description of the intruder from someone they'd missed first time around. The description was similar to that of Reuben, so if he had survived the crash I figured that he'd be back for you.'

'What will happen to him?'

'He'll be sent down for this, for how long I can't say, but he's out of your life, Jamie, he won't be back.'

'I never thought he would ever go this far,' she said still sobbing.

'I'd better stay for a while. Do you want me to call somebody for you?' asked Mike.

'Please, call Stella, her number's in my book over there.'

'OK.'

Jamie went into the kitchen, poured herself a fresh tea and quickly lit up a cigarette from a new packet on the shelf. She took a few deep drags before stubbing it out in the ashtray. Her make-up had run down her cheeks and as Mike came out of the lounge he could see that she looked completely shattered.

'Stella's on her way, I'll stay until she arrives.'

'It's OK, Mike, you can go, I'll be OK.'

'I don't expect you to forgive me for what's happened to you.'

'It's OK, Mike, really, I'm sorry for what I said, but I really need to be on my own right now.'

'Are you sure?'

'Yes, I'll be fine.'

'I'd better go then.'

'Mike.'

'Yes.'

'Thanks.'

'You're welcome. Look after yourself now. I'll see you around.'

As he walked out the door, tears came to her eyes again as she stood alone in her apartment waiting for Stella to arrive.

35

Mike opened the doors of the wardrobe in his motel room and began placing his clothes into his suitcase. During the past two days he had spent the time sightseeing in and around Ashbury Falls, reflecting on the events of the past month. The weather had been warm and sunny and Mike had allowed himself to relax and unwind. His future in the Bureau was out of his hands now and there was no point thinking too deeply about it. Now it was time to leave Ashbury Falls and return home to Falls Church, Virginia. With his future uncertain he was, to his relief, finally at peace with himself. He had confronted his demons and like Carla and Hank, he could move on with his life too.

As he packed his toiletries into his bag, he held the gold-plated razor that Jamie had given him. It glistened in his eyes as he rotated it in his fingers. He stood staring at it for a while, thinking of Jamie, then smiling he gently placed it in his suitcase before adding the remainder of the contents. The last thing to come out of the wardrobe was the bag that contained his laptop. Agent Willis had removed all the data that he had acquired on the Ascension Project from his hard disk and the copies he had made to CD. All of them except the one he had carefully concealed in a hidden pocket of his briefcase. The things that he had discovered were indelibly written in his memory, things that disturbed him, things he had not even divulged to Carla or Hank. Hard as it would be, the time had now come to put the Ascension Project behind him too. It was coming up to 11.00 am, the time he needed to check out. He picked up his bags, looked around the room one last time, opened the door and left. The girl behind the desk in the motel lobby smiled as he came down the stairs.

'Checking out, sir?' she asked him.

'Yes, I'm afraid so, I will miss this place. Have you lived here long?' he asked.

'All my life, sir,' she replied.

She was young, probably in her early twenties and part of a new generation that would not have been party to the things that occurred back in the mid 1970s. She swiped his credit card and then gave him the ticket to sign.

'Thank you, sir,' she said 'Have a nice day and a safe journey home.'

'I will,' he replied.

As he put his wallet in the inside pocket of his jacket, he smiled at her and then opened the lobby doors to walk out to his car. After packing his bags into the trunk he got in and started the engine. As the car idled he opened the glove box and took out the map of Ashbury Falls that he had had with him since his arrival. He couldn't quite remember the way back so he checked his route out to the main highway and then drove off. As he got to the end of the road he was about to turn right, but then he stopped. There was one last place to visit and so he turned the wheel in the opposite direction and drove back towards town.

Jenna Kirshaw was busy serving up brunch at the Pied Piper. The diner was quite full that day, but luckily she had called one of her casual employees to help her. Sat at the counter drinking hot chocolate with cream smothered on top was Carla Dempster.

'So you and Jack are really going to take off then?' asked Jenna.

'Yes we are, but we're going to miss this place.'

'I'm going to miss you. You'll have to make sure that you write, OK?'

'Of course I will.'

'I'm glad for you, Honey,' said Jenna. 'And it's good to see you looking so happy. You and Jack deserve that, considering what you have been through.'

'We'll be heading to North Carolina, to the coast.'

'I went there once,' said Jenna. 'You'll love it.'

Carla smiled. At that moment another customer entered the diner and as Jenna and Carla looked around, Mike approached the counter.

'Hello, stranger,' said Jenna. 'Nice of you to call in, I was beginning to think you'd gone off my coffee.'

'No chance of that,' said Mike.

'So where have you been all this time?'

'It's a long story, Jenna, maybe Carla will tell you one day,' replied Mike as he smiled at her.

Carla smiled back.

'Mike, it's good to see you again.'

'How does it feel to know the truth?'

'I feel like a new woman, Mike. Knowing what happened in the past has helped me come to terms with my future. I have you to thank for that and I will always be indebted to you.'

'This sounds serious,' said Jenna. 'What are you talking about?' looking at them both with a puzzled expression.

'Maybe I'll tell you one day,' said Carla as she smiled at Mike.

'Decaf?' asked Jenna, looking at Mike.

'Decaf would be great.'

'On the house,' she said. 'Anyone who can make my best friend happy deserves a free cup of coffee.'

'Thanks.'

Jenna moved around the front of the counter with a plate in each hand and walked over to the corner of the diner to give it to one of her customers.

'So, Mike, what will you do now?' asked Carla.

'I'm heading back to Virginia today,' he replied. 'There's going to be a hearing in four weeks time back in Washington where I will have to explain myself to my superiors.'

'You're a good man, Mike. You risked your career to help us. I've never seen Hank so happy. You did a wonderful thing for him, Mike.'

'I'm sure he's got a lot of catching up to do, hasn't he.'

'He certainly has.'

'Well it's never too late to rebuild relationships is it?'

'No Mike, it's not. Jack and I have decided to leave Ashbury Falls, we're going to North Carolina, to the coast. We might open a little café. I've learnt lots of hints and tips from Jenna over the years, but I doubt if I'll ever be able to cook as well as she does.'

'She's certainly a hard act to follow,' agreed Mike. 'What about Jack, what does he want to do?'

'He wants to buy a boat and take tourists off for trips around the coast. He's always loved the sea so now he's got the chance to live his dreams.'

'Few in life will ever live their dreams,' said Mike, 'but I hope you and Jack live yours.'

Jenna returned to the counter.

'Mike's leaving today,' said Carla.

'So you've got enough material for your next book then?' asked Jenna.

Mike looked at Carla and smiled.

'Yes, I think maybe I have,' he said.

'I want a signed copy sent through,' said Jenna.

Mike laughed.

'Anyway, Mike, how's Jamie Farrington?' asked Jenna.

'I think Jamie's going to be fine,' replied Mike.

'So did you enjoy your stay at the hotel?' she asked further.

'I was very comfortable,' replied Mike.

'You know what I'm talking about,' she replied.

'Jamie is a fine woman,' said Mike. 'I got to know her quite well during my visit. If anyone deserves happiness she does.'

'And how is she going to find it?' asked Carla.

'I don't know,' said Mike.

'I think you do,' replied Carla.

'What do you mean?' he asked.

'She came in here,' said Jenna.

'When?'

'It was when you were out of town,' replied Carla.

'She came in here asking if we'd seen you,' added Jenna.

'She looked lost, Mike. She had that look in her eyes. A look of a person missing someone,' said Carla.

'I'd say that you must have got to her, Mike,' added Jenna.

'Things have changed,' said Mike.

'Have they?' said Carla. 'It's like you just said, there's always time to renew relationships. Go to her.'

Mike didn't reply, instead he drank his coffee.

'Go to her,' said Carla again, softly touching Mike's hand.

Mike tried to look away but she persisted in looking for a reaction.

'What?' exclaimed Mike as he glanced back round at her. 'It wouldn't work, Carla. Anyway I think she's planning to move back to Boston where she went to college. Relationships are difficult in my line of work, ask my ex-wife.'

'I'd better be getting back,' said Carla. 'Jack could use some help at the store, we're going to put it up for sale very soon, so we've got a lot of work to do before we leave. Better get to it.'

'I'll see you again, Honey,' said Jenna.

'OK, see you soon,' said Carla. 'Well I guess this is goodbye,' she said turning to Mike.

'I guess so,' he replied.

'I hope everything works out for you.'

'Things always do,' replied Mike. 'It's been good to meet you, Carla, you and Jack. You are fine people.'

'It's funny, Mike. I never remembered you from high school but you must have been there somewhere amongst the mass of souls.'

'I guess there are lots of people in our lives that we just don't notice and we never know when they'll cross our paths,' said Mike philosophically. 'I really wish you and Jack all the best for the future.'

'Thank you, Mike, and thanks again for everything. Have a safe trip now.'

Carla kissed him tenderly on the cheek and then headed for the exit. As she opened the door she turned round and smiled back at him. He returned the smile as she made her way out of the diner.

'What is it with you two?' asked Jenna from behind the counter.

'I guess it's time we said goodbye too, Jenna.'

'Leaving so soon?, why don't you stick around a bit longer, we don't get writers around here very often.'

'I wish I could, Jenna. It's been a pleasure. Maybe one day I'll see a whole string of Pied Piper restaurants across the USA. You could do it, Jenna, you know how to run a good diner.'

'Well maybe,' she said grinning.

'You take care now,' he said as he gave her one last smile.

'And you too, Mike Fabien. See you around.'

With that Mike turned, headed for the door and left the diner.

As Mike drove off towards the highway, he suddenly felt lost within himself. He felt as though he had reached a crossroads in his life and never expected to feel the way that he did. He was going to miss Ashbury Falls in some ways and not in others. The town had changed since he had left to go to college and was not quite as he had remembered it. Upon

261

arrival he had had expectations of what he would find there, only to find disappointment. Perhaps he had been away too long he thought or maybe things weren't actually as he remembered them after all.

He would usually put on a Bruce Springsteen tape for a long journey, but this time he just wanted to be alone with his thoughts. As he got near to the junction that would take him back to the freeway and southbound to Virginia, he stopped the car and got out to take one last look back down the road that led to Ashbury Falls. He stood there for a few minutes until a car pulled up beside him.

'Are you lost, Mister?' asked the driver.

'Yes,' replied Mike 'Maybe I am.'

'So where you heading?'

'I don't know, I guess I'll find out when I get there.'

The driver of the car looked at him with a weird expression.

'Hey man, I've got to go,' and then he sped off down the road.

Mike got back into his car, put it into drive and continued towards the junction of the freeway. As he turned onto it, he saw the sign for Ashbury Falls in his rear view mirror. He accelerated away and began the long journey back to Falls Church.

About five miles down the freeway, he decided that he would put a tape into the cassette player in the car. It was the one that he had been playing when he had made his narrow escape from the Sterling Medical Research Corporation. The last song on the first side of the tape began to play. He listened carefully to his favourite artist singing the words to the song 'I'm on fire', and as the song progressed, it was as though the lyrics seemed to be telling him something. He continued down the lonely highway with his eyes focused on the long road ahead, but his mind was focused on someone he had left behind in Ashbury Falls.

36

The last group of tourists left the Farrington Hotel as the coach turned out onto the main road leaving for Manchester. The hotel would be quiet for a few weeks and then the busy fall season would begin. Stella had been on hand and with Jamie now in a better frame of mind and resting in her apartment she knew that she would now have the time to try to get over her ordeal. As she entered Jamie was sat on her sofa drinking a cup of coffee with the telephone beside her.

'Good morning,' said Stella. 'You're looking better.'

'Thanks.'

'Can I get you anything?' asked Stella.

'No thanks, I think you'd better get yourself off home now.'

'Are you sure?'

'I'll be fine, honest. It's over now and I just need to try to put this all behind me and get on with my life.'

'It'll take you a while to get over this, Jamie – you need to give yourself time.'

'I really appreciate all that you've done, but it's not fair to ask you to keep working like this. You should go home and get some rest. As things are going to be quiet here over the next couple of weeks I did promise you a week off didn't I? I think you should take it.'

'If you're sure that's OK.'

'I'm sure. I've been making some enquiries about flights to Boston. I'm going back for a few weeks to catch up with some old friends from college. It's time I had a vacation.'

'Good,' replied Stella. 'Maybe that's the right thing to do. You should get away; forget all about Ashbury Falls for a while. I'll manage the hotel if you like, but I'll need to employ some temporary staff.'

'Do what you have to.'

'You make sure you call me if you need me,' replied Stella.

'I will.'

Stella walked out of Jamie's apartment and back into the reception area to pick up her coat. Jamie picked up the notepaper that was beside the phone. She had jotted down a number of flights that might be suitable for her to travel to Boston in a couple of weeks. She knew she would have to dig out her old address book and phone to see if she could track down any of her old college friends. She dialled one of the numbers that was scribbled on the note pad and after a short while someone from American Airlines reservations answered and asked if he could help.

'Yes, I'd like to book a flight to Boston please.'

The time was approaching 2.00 pm and Jamie was feeling restless. Nobody had rung the bell on the desk at reception. She had a buzzer in her apartment that was connected to the bell at the desk so she knew that the hotel was quiet as expected. She decided to go into reception and see if there was anything to do and then she would go into town to get some fresh air and do a spot of shopping. Before that she had another call to make. She picked up the telephone and called her friend Heather Johnson. There was no reply, so her voice mail kicked in.

'Hi, Heather, it's Jamie, can you call me please. I was hoping you'd be free tonight and we could go out someplace, maybe Rendezvous 9. Try the hotel, if not my mobile. Thanks, bye.'

She put the phone down and decided to look in the office, expecting to find some work to do but discovered that Stella had finished all the paperwork for the last two days and it was neatly filed in various places. She would have to get a computer system soon; that had been long overdue.

Suddenly her thoughts were on Boston as she wandered into the dining room. She remembered her friends, the parties, and a time when they had spent a glorious spring day on Boston Common just hanging out together. Whilst there, she planned to put out some feelers for jobs, maybe look at some apartments. She was going to ask Stella to manage the hotel. The bank balance was looking very healthy so she knew that she could afford to get Stella to take on extra part-time employees.

As she looked up at the shelves on the wall in the corner, she noticed a paperback book resting there. It was the one that Mike had given her. She had started to read it, but when the FBI had arrived she had put it down and forgotten all about it. She picked it up, sat down and opened it to the page where he had signed it. She read the words again and pondered for a moment. Then she noticed that the bookmark was still left at Chapter 8. Opening the book to that page, she rested her head on her arm and began to read.

She had only got into the book for about ten minutes when she heard the bell ring in reception. Inserting the bookmark she closed it, put it down and walked out to see who was there. As she approached the desk she saw a man with his back to her. She recognised him immediately.

Mike turned around and the two of them stood looking at each other, saying nothing. Eventually Mike broke the silence.

'Hi,' replied Jamie in a neutral tone.

'I was wondering if room 3 was still available,' he asked.

'It's already taken. I'm only letting out rooms to people who are planning to stick around. I thought you'd gone back to Virginia. Room 7 is free. It overlooks the parking lot to the rear.'

'I didn't come here to rent a room.'

'Then why are you here?' she asked.

'I wanted to see how you were and to say goodbye properly.'

'I'm fine.'

From her tone of voice she clearly wasn't. He waited for her to continue.

'Actually I'm not. I'm just carrying on. Stella tells me this will hit me in a couple of weeks. Life goes on doesn't it, Mike?'

'So what are your plans?' he asked.

'I'm going to Boston in two weeks to look up some old friends, have a vacation, and maybe see about a job.'

'Is that what you really want?'

'I don't know, Mike, but I guess I've just got to go and find out, haven't I? Stella will run this place for a while, so I will be leaving the business in good hands.'

'That's good,' replied Mike.

'I've started reading your book, that is, if it really is yours. It's good, but I'd like to know who the real author is.'

'I am,' he replied.

'Come on, do you really expect me to believe that? It's obvious isn't it? You work for the FBI. If you can make devices to crack encrypted computer passwords, you can surely fake a book. It worked very well didn't it?' Now she was becoming agitated. 'It certainly fooled people into believing you were a writer. It fooled me. Did that message at the front mean anything, Mike?'

'Yes and I really did write that book. It's my first; maybe it won't be the last. It took me three years to write – you don't get that much time for things like that in my job. A friend of a friend works for a publisher and they liked it. It's my book, Jamie, no FBI scam. Keep reading; I hope you enjoy it.'

Mike turned to go.

'Wait! I'm sorry. Maybe I will finish it,' she said, her voice softening. 'Do you want some coffee or something?'

He paused as she was looking at him in a pleading manner.

'OK,' he replied and so he followed her back into the dining room.

'Go and sit over there,' she said pointing to the table in the corner by the window, the one he had sat in the first time they had met.

Mike looked out of the window. Across the lawn he could see the bench where he and Jamie had sat watching the stars the night before everything had happened. He took off his jacket and slung it over the seat behind him and then sat there in anticipation of Jamie's return. A few minutes later she arrived with a pot of coffee and two mugs. She poured them both a drink.

'Didn't we do this once before?' asked Mike.

'It seems a long time ago,' replied Jamie.

'I apologise for what you've been through.'

'Damn right you should,' she replied. 'Anyway, I forgive you, but that doesn't mean that I'm not hurting inside.'

'I understand,' replied Mike.

'I don't think you do,' said Jamie. 'But despite all I've been through, you were there when I really needed you. I'd hate to think what Reuben would have done to me if you hadn't come back,' she said and then held his hand tightly.

'It wasn't in the line of duty. I came back because I didn't want to lose you. When I put the gun to his head, for just a split second I actually felt like pulling the trigger.'

'I'm confused, Mike. You're not the same person that I fell in love with. It's different now. You're an FBI agent; you've got to go back to your life of catching bad guys like Charles Moreland. I wanted Mike Fabien the writer, but I can't have him because he doesn't exist.'

'I wanted to tell you. Anyway, as it is I'm a writer and an FBI agent – one in the same. This is who I am, Jamie. I was ten miles down the freeway heading back to Virginia, but I got off and turned back. I came back for *you*.'

'We can't do this, Mike. I can't deal with my feelings right now,' she said touching his face tenderly. 'I have to go to Boston. I need to think things out, do you understand?'

'And I have to be in Washington in less than four weeks,' replied Mike. 'My career is hanging in the balance. Maybe I will be the writer after all.'

'Will you be OK?' she asked.

'I guess so. Go to Boston, Jamie, and when you return call me. Here's my number,' he replied handing her a white card.

'And what if I don't come back?' she asked.

'Call me from Boston.'

She paused for a while, considering her reply.

'I will, I promise,' she said.

'I'd better go now,' said Mike giving her one last kiss on the forehead before getting up and walking back into reception.

Jamie followed and as she got to the front door her eyes swelled with tears.

'Don't leave it too long,' he said getting into his car.

'I won't.'

He looked at her one last time as he started to pull away. From the hotel entrance she watched his gold Nissan Primera as it disappeared down the sloped driveway and onto the road. She stood at the entrance, gazing at the empty parking lot before her and holding on tightly to the card that he had given her. A cold breeze suddenly blew across her face signalling that maybe fall was now on its way. For the first time she noticed that a few of the leaves on the trees that bordered the hotel had begun to turn red.

'Changes,' she thought and then she walked back into the hotel, closing the door behind her.